Searching for Peace

A COASTAL HOPE NOVEL

JESSICA ASHLEY

B.A.D.
PUBLISHING

Searching for Peace

A woman with a harrowing past. The wounded veteran who never breaks a promise.

After the sudden death of her grandmother, Andie Montgomery finally returns home. It's the last place she wants to be, especially when she discovers her grandmother has left her house not just to Andie–but to a handsome, yet grumpy former Army Ranger.

Dealing with him is the last thing she wants to do, but when someone tries to kill her, he risks his life to save hers.

After making a deathbed promise, former Army Ranger Elijah Breeth is pulled into danger alongside the cold, unfeeling woman he swore to protect.

And the only clue they have as to who is after Andie, is a box of letters left beneath her grandmother's bed.

As Elijah digs deeper into Andie's past, he begins to realize that the dark-haired beauty is more than what she seems...and her secrets might just be enough to bury them both.

B.A.D.
PUBLISHING

Coastal Hope, book 2
By Jessica Ashley
Copyright © 2024. All rights reserved.

Edited by HEA Author Services
Proofread by Dawn Y
Cover Design by Covers by Christian
Photographer: Wander Aguiar
Model: Manuel

To anyone who has never felt good enough.
You ARE.
To anyone who has never felt loved.
You ARE.
To anyone who has ever felt like your sins are too great to find peace.
They're NOT.

———

1 John 1:5-9

A Note From The Author

The world really is a battlefield.

If you're like me, you may not even have realized it at first. I spent *years* running from my faith. Hiding from God and everyone else because I was too ashamed of the mistakes I'd made.

Choices that ripped me away from Him because I'd been focused only on the day-to-day rather than an eternity that awaits once this life is over.

I've done so many things I regret, so many things that– if I let them–still haunt me.

Spiritual warfare is something every single one of us has experienced and will experience for the rest of our lives. Those voices that slip in, telling us we're not good enough. That we're not loved enough. That we're unworthy of forgiveness. That we were a mistake. That we're broken. That there is something fundamentally wrong with us.

But you know what?

Jesus knew us. And He died for us, anyway.

He died to give us new life.

To give us the chance at an eternity of peace rather than suffering.

But it's up to us to make the choice to follow Him. To fight against the sinful nature of this world and stand up against the enemy.

There are lots of people out there who consider Christians to be pacifists. They look at us like we're weak, when in reality it's the exact opposite.

We are warriors.

Fighters.

And we follow the one and only King who has already won the war.

Ephesians 6:10-18 says:

"10 Finally, be strong in the Lord and in his mighty power. 11 Put on the full armor of God, so that you can take your stand against the devil's schemes. 12 For our struggle is not against flesh and blood, but against the rulers, against the authorities, against the powers of this dark world and against the spiritual forces of evil in the heavenly realms. 13 Therefore put on the full armor of God, so that when the day of evil comes, you may be able to stand your ground, and after you have done everything, to stand. 14 Stand firm then, with the belt of truth buckled around your waist, with the breastplate of righteousness

in place, 15 and with your feet fitted with the readiness that comes from the gospel of peace. 16 In addition to all this, take up the shield of faith, with which you can extinguish all the flaming arrows of the evil one. 17 Take the helmet of salvation and the sword of the Spirit, which is the word of God.

18 And pray in the Spirit on all occasions with all kinds of prayers and requests. With this in mind, be alert and always keep on praying for all the Lord's people."

This is my absolute favorite verse, and one I remind myself of anytime I face off with another attack.

When my past tries to weigh me down I remember that I am loved.

I am forgiven.

And while I am not worthy of His sacrifice, I can continue to fight so that one day I can thank Him face-to-face.

I hope that after you have finished reading this book, you are called to pick up your Bible and read some of the verses sprinkled throughout Elijah and Andie's story. I hope you will remember that even though we fail, even though we fall, He is always there to pick us back up.

Happy reading,

-Jessica

CHAPTER 1

Elijah

I hate funerals.

As an Army Ranger, I've unfortunately attended my fair share, and if I can go the rest of my life without seeing another flag-draped coffin, I'd be more than happy.

Then again, the dark wooden box before me is adorned with flowers rather than red, white, and blue. Still, it doesn't make it any easier. In a lot of ways, this might be even harder. After all, Edna wasn't a soldier on the battle-field. She was an elderly woman—a grandmother who'd been in her home.

The lump in my throat grows.

An aged woman smiles back at me from a large, framed photograph, her silver hair pulled up in a bun, her green eyes bright with joy. She looks so happy, so completely thrilled to be staring back at whoever took that photograph.

All I feel is pain.

Grief.

We may not have been family by blood, and I may not have known her more than a few years, but Edna Montgomery was as good a woman as they come. After the first time I helped her carry groceries into her house, she'd practically adopted me as a surrogate grandson. I'd been surly when we first met, jaded by the horrors I'd seen on deployment, and she'd refused to let me continue to be bitter.

I spent three Easters, Thanksgivings, and Christmas afternoons with her. We'd sipped lemonade on her porch on lazy Sunday afternoons when I didn't have to work, and I'd listened to her stories about her late husband and the joy he'd brought into her life before being stolen far too soon.

Now she's gone. Heaven has gained an angel, but I lost mine.

"Mrs. Montgomery was a staple in this town," Pastor Redding says sadly as he grips each side of the podium, his own eyes misty. His wife, one of Edna's close friends, sniffles in a front pew. "She was a shining light, the kindest woman any of us have ever met. She'd never met a stranger and welcomed everyone as though they'd been a part of her life for as long as anyone can remember."

All around me, people cry. Mrs. McGinley—the town's librarian and Edna's best friend—sniffs beside me. Reaching out, I cover her wrinkled hand with mine. She sets her other one over it and leans against my shoulder.

"Edna never had a negative thing to say about anyone,

and I think we can all agree that her s'more cookies were the best ones around."

"Best in the world!" Michael, my co-worker and brother in everything but blood, calls out.

People mutter in agreement. A few laugh softly. One woman lets out a choked sob.

"I know we're all hurting," the pastor says, "but take solace in knowing this is not the last time we will see our sister. For, one day, we will walk alongside her in heaven." He bows his head. "Let us pray. Dear God, thank You for the time we were blessed to know Edna here on Earth. Thank You for blessing us with every moment spent. Every laugh shared. Please, God, be with her family and close friends as they mourn, and comfort us all in our pain by reminding us that she is with You. Amen."

"Amen," I murmur alongside everyone else in the pews.

The pastor smiles softly as his gaze travels over the congregation. "There will be another service at the gravesite, and we hope to see you there. Thank you all for coming." He steps down, and everyone stands, lining up on the side of the church to greet the dark-haired beauty standing near the coffin.

Andie Montgomery—Edna's granddaughter. She grew up here, living with Edna after her parents got divorced. Her father left town, and her mother dropped her at Edna's then never came back.

According to what Edna said over the years, Andie was a quiet girl. Kind. But ended up leaving town with a man almost two times her age. It was a scandal though, in true Hope Springs fashion, no one will openly talk about it.

I do know that Edna gave her every penny in her savings account so Andie could start her own business. Which is exactly what she did as soon as she graduated from design school. The fashion company she started in New York has grown substantially in the last couple of years. It would be impressive if I weren't so disgusted by her refusal to come visit the woman who'd raised her.

While I've never met Andie, Edna spoke about her nonstop. Raving about her brilliant granddaughter. Frankly, I don't care much for a woman who couldn't even be bothered to visit her grandmother on Christmas.

As far as I know, Andie Montgomery has not stepped foot in Hope Springs since the day she shook the dust off her fancy heels.

Even when Edna had been lying in the hospital bed, so weak she could hardly keep her eyes open, she'd begged me to watch over Andie. Urged me to reach out and make friends. Despite the fact that the woman never answered the dozen phone calls I made to her when I'd arrived at the hospital and discovered Edna would likely never leave her bed.

I should go up and introduce myself now, but the memory of Edna's tear-stained cheek as she drew her last breath makes me think better of it. Better that I am not in the same room with Miss Montgomery longer than necessary.

My temper is already something I struggle with. And I've got more than a few unkind things to say to the woman.

"How are you doing?" Eliza Knight asks as she steps into my path, Lance—her husband and my boss—right beside her. Her blond hair is wavy and falls to her shoulders, and her eyes are red and swollen. She'd loved Edna too. We all did.

"Fine," I reply. It's far from the truth, but I'll get there. It's not like death is a stranger to me. First, my parents. Then, my grandmother. Over a dozen of my comrades. Now Edna. Nope, death and I are practically old friends, aren't we?

"Edna was an amazing woman," Eliza says as she brushes her hair behind her ear. "She sat front row at the library when Mrs. McGinley brought me in for a signing after my book released." Her eyes mist. "I'll never forget how she'd smiled at me when I'd been so nervous."

Lance wraps an arm around her shoulders, and she leans into him.

"She was great," I reply with a smile then turn to Lance. "I'm going to head home and check on a few things, then I'm headed to the office. You going to be in today?"

"Later," he replies. "We're going to head to the cemetery then the wake. You're not coming?" His brows draw together, likely in surprise.

"Nope. No need to. I said my goodbyes when she was in the hospital." Edna had a heart attack and had fallen in the shower. The paramedics called me first since I was her emergency contact, so I was with her right before she died. I was the one who called Andie over a dozen times to let her know she needed to fly out. And I was the one she hung up on when I'd finally gotten ahold of her and offered to help plan the service.

So, no. Spending any time with Andie Montgomery in any capacity is something I am just not interested in. Not now. Not ever.

"Are you sure?" Eliza questions. "You can ride with us."

Because I can see that she's worried about me, I plaster on a smile then lean in and kiss her noisily on the cheek. "I'm fine, I promise. See you both at the diner later?"

"Absolutely." Lance waves, and he and Eliza head toward the line while I slip outside.

Early June rain drizzles down on me, but I pay it little notice as I head to the parking lot. The moment I turn the corner though, I stop, practically freezing in place. Andie is leaning against a black sedan parked directly next to my truck, eyes closed, face tilted up toward the sky.

Great. Fantastic.

Hoping she doesn't notice as I slip by, I slide the key into my truck door and pull it open. The aged door groans in protest, and I cringe, silently scolding myself for not oiling the hinges this morning when I'd remembered I should. I'd nearly driven my car over instead, but Edna loved this truck.

It had been her husband's, and I've been in the never-ending process of restoring it ever since she'd insisted I take it out of her garage.

"You're Elijah Breeth."

Here we go. Taking a deep breath, I turn. "Yes."

"We spoke on the phone." Very cut and dried, matter of fact.

"We did."

"My grandmother adored you."

"I felt the same for her."

"She talked about you all the time." Her gaze flicks to the truck. "Told me about how you were restoring my grandfather's old truck."

I cross my arms, unease prickling my spine. If she's planning on taking this truck from me, she'll have a fight. I have the title, a bill of sale, and enough money to take even her to court.

"Is there something you need?"

She narrows her gaze on me, piercing green eyes that might as well be emeralds for the color and lack of emotion. "You don't like me." Once again, it's a statement rather than a question.

"I don't know you," I reply. "Difficult to not like someone when you don't know anything about them."

"According to my gran, you knew everything about everyone." Her tone leaves no room for a rebuttal. "She said you made it your job."

She wants to play ball? Fine. "Miss Andie Montgomery. Twenty-seven. Fashion icon out of New York. Never been married. No long-term relationships to speak of. Couldn't be bothered to visit her grandmother once in the few years that I knew the woman. How am I doing?"

Most people will look at least mildly uncomfortable when you spout out facts about their lives. But this woman doesn't even flinch.

"Congratulations on being a fantastic cyber stalker, Mr. Breeth. My grandmother undersold you." Her tone drips with sarcasm. "As for not visiting, I've been busy building a business. My gran knew that. And our visitation schedule is none of your business."

Her cool tone infuriates me. "You're right. My mistake. Though it seems as though the woman who raised you dying alone in a hospital bed is the right time to set your business on hold."

If looks could kill, I'd be joining Edna right about now. "My gran knew I loved her."

"Sure she did." I climb into the truck, but before I can close the door, Andie wraps slender fingers around the side of the door. Nails tipped with black, they're nearly a perfect match for the dark hair cut to her shoulders.

"Are you going to the cemetery?"

"No," I reply.

"Now who's not making time?" she asks, releasing the door. "Have a good day, Mr. Breeth."

Before I can say something I'll need to seek repentance for later, I slam the door and pull out of the parking lot.

Fury burns in my veins, and I know going home to check emails is just not going to do the trick.

I need the gym.

First home to change. Then straight to the gym to work off some steam.

Everything about Andie is in contrast to her grandmother.

She's cold. Unfeeling.

Edna was the warmest, most loving woman I've ever known.

And as much as it pains me to admit it, I hope to never, ever have to cross paths with her granddaughter again. Edna's final request echoes in my mind.

"Please watch over her, Elijah. She's not as tough as she seems. She needs someone to watch out for her. You will, won't you?"

I'd promised. How could I not? Edna had died a few heartbeats later, a smile on her face because I'd agreed to always watch over Andie.

Taking a deep breath, I whip into the parking lot of the lighthouse that now serves as our office building and my apartment.

Sorry, Edna, I think this might just be the one promise I have to break.

CHAPTER 2

Andie

I t's been nearly a decade since I was last in Hope Springs, Maine. Truthfully, I'd never meant to stay away from my gran this long. Even though coming back to this place felt like an unattainable task.

The house I grew up in still looks the same. A simple white cottage with bright green shutters and a door the color of the ocean. Sea glass wind chimes my gran made hang on nearly every eve of the wraparound porch. Fresh paint adorns the handrails, and I know that it was Elijah who painted them.

Elijah. My gran told me he was attractive, that he had kind eyes that reminded her of my grandfather. But now that I've met him, I can admit she undersold the looks department. Even if she did oversell his personality. He's strong, built like a fighter, sharp jaw coated with stubble, hazel eyes that shine even in the overcast afternoon.

Every time we'd spoken, and we talked quite a lot, my gran spent more time talking about him than she had about what was going on in her life. Maybe, if she'd focused on herself rather than him, she would have remembered to tell me about the heart problems she'd been having. I could have gotten her to New York, found her good doctors, gotten her on some sort of medication.

I close my eyes and take a deep breath, urging the tears to disappear. I do not cry. It's my rule. Tears do nothing but make things worse.

"Keep it together, Andrea," my mother would have sneered. *"Tears are for the weak, girl. Are you weak?"*

No. I'm not.

"Get it together, Andie," I whisper to myself as I start up the cobblestone walkway, my suitcase in hand. I have one month to get everything in order here before I need to go home and prep for the spring show. One month, and I'll leave this town behind and never look back.

After all, there's nothing left for me here anymore. Just bad memories and heartache.

I push open the door and am hit with the delicate floral aroma of freshly cut flowers. It's like a knife to the gut when I move into the living room and see two vases of wildflowers. Who put them there? Given that they look fresh, it wasn't Gran who chose them. It wasn't her who carefully picked every bloom from her garden.

A soft meow fills my ears, and I turn as the largest black and white cat I've ever seen steps out of her bedroom and pads down the hall. After carefully setting my bag on the floor, I lean toward him and hold my hand out.

"Hey. You must be Aggie," I say as the cat touches its cool nose to my fingers then arches up under my hand. "Gran told me all about you." Hesitantly, I pick the cat up. He rubs against me some more, and I smile.

I've never been much of an animal person, but my gran always had a cat. And now, I suppose, I do too.

"I hope you'll be okay with New York," I say as I carry him into the living room and set him on the cat tower. Large picture windows make up the back wall of the house, and outside, Gran's garden is in full bloom. Flowers, rows of lettuce, green beans, and what looks like carrots sticking up from wooden garden beds that have been completely re-done since the last time I saw them.

Elijah again, no doubt.

He apparently made it his personal mission over the last three years to make sure my gran had everything she needed. While the town would pitch in here and there when they could, he'd gone through and polished off her entire to-do list in a matter of months, then meticulously main-tained the yard, bushes, and even helped her upgrade a few things throughout the house.

The master bathroom remodeled.

The carpet replaced.

When she'd first told me about him, I'd thought it was sweet. Kind gestures from a kind man. Until she'd told me she'd given him my grandfather's truck. That was the first time I'd realized that there was probably more to his intentions than simply helping an elderly woman.

A wave of anger rushes through me at the image of him sitting in the front seat. Even if he had looked good behind the wheel.

The moment she told me she'd deeded it to him, I'd realized just what kind of man he was. I've seen plenty of them during my time in New York. Elijah Breeth is the type of man who uses older women, offering them kindness and a shoulder until he drains them of everything they have.

What else did he take from her?

With that in mind, and knowing he has a key, I head straight for her bedroom. Seeing her bed carefully made, her slippers waiting for her feet the moment they touch the floor, is a stab to the heart, but I have a reason for being here, so I focus.

Turning, I reach for the free-standing jewelry cabinet my grandfather made for their fifteenth wedding anniversary. It was the last one they'd shared before the accident, and my gran treasured it. I open it, mentally prepared to see it completely cleaned out.

But when I see the glittering diamonds of her wedding ring sitting beside diamond stud earrings, pearls, and other pieces of expensive jewelry, I breathe a sigh of relief. Had he not taken these because they'd be so obvious? Because I would have noticed right away?

Someone knocks on the door, so I shut the cabinet and turn toward the living room, pausing by a mirror to make sure I look relatively put together. My dark hair could use some time with a straightener, thanks to the humidity, but other than that I look relatively put together.

So I reach for the door and pull it open.

Lilly, one of my oldest friends. stands on the other side, still wearing the black dress she'd been in for the funeral. Her hair, nearly the same color as her outfit, is up in a tight bun, and her bright blue eyes are rimmed with red from tears shed for a woman who was practically a second grandmother to her.

"Hey," I greet, plastering a smile on my face. "Come in."

"Thanks." She smiles tightly and steps into the house. "How are you doing?" Lilly asks as she sets her purse on the floral-printed couch.

"I'm okay. It's just weird being back here."

"I can imagine." She looks around the room. "It's been a long time."

Nine years, seven months, and three days. But who's counting? "It has."

"I remember being so shocked that the town still looked exactly the same as I'd left it." Like me, Lilly had bailed on Hope Springs the second she could. Of course, her reasons had been quite different than mine. While I was following a man who I had no business following, she was running from one. Her high school sweetheart and fiancé, Alex, had joined the military. Without any warning, he'd broken things off and left town.

We'd caught up a few times when she'd been in New York or I'd been traveling for work, but three years ago, Gran told me that she'd returned and gotten back together with her Alex, who is now the owner of our small town's diner.

They got married a few years ago and had a daughter.

Sarah, I think, is her name.

"Can I get you something to drink?" I ask as Lilly takes a seat on my gran's couch.

"No, I'm okay." Her gaze drifts to the garden, and I wonder if she's thinking of all the times we'd played tea party when we'd been kids. Sitting out amidst the floral blooms, speaking in fake accents, all while Gran delivered us tiny peanut butter and jelly sandwiches cut into various shapes. "I can't believe she's gone."

"It seems surreal," I agree.

Lilly smiles sadly, tears in her eyes, and I fight to control my own.

I do not cry, I remind myself.

"Do you remember when I'd tried to pierce my nose and it—of course—went *horribly* wrong?" She laughs, reaching up to touch the side she'd shoved a needle through when we'd been sixteen. She'd been furious with her mother for something—I don't even recall what now—and she'd jammed that needle through her nose, then came running here before her mother or stepdad had been able to see it.

"Gran gave you a washcloth and told you to make

better life choices." I snort, recalling the way she'd tried to hide her own laughter.

"She did." Lilly shakes her head, a smile still on her face. "And Felix hadn't even been mad," she recalls. "He'd told my mother—who had been furious—that sometimes we have to do dumb stuff in order to avoid doing dumber stuff when we get older."

"That's absolutely Felix," I muse. Lilly and her mom had come to Hope Springs after her mother met and fell in love with Felix during the town's children's toy drive. Held every Christmas, a group of volunteers takes presents to the shelters in Boston. She and her mother had been living in one of those shelters, and according to Lilly, it had been love at first sight for the hardware store owner and her mom.

Love.

I'd once believed in such things. Honestly, it was their love story that put stars in my eyes in the first place.

That and the romance novels I'd snuck out of Gran's home library as a teen.

Now I know better.

"How are things? How's your daughter?" I ask, trying my best to change the subject.

"Sarah is good. Getting big. She just turned two." She shakes her head. "They say terrible twos will start any day now, but I'm not seeing it yet."

I smile. "Then you're lucky. My assistant a few years back had a toddler. He was a menace."

Lilly scrunches her nose. "Yikes."

I shrug. "I thought he was cute, but I didn't have to deal with the meltdowns." She'd quit shortly after she'd found out she was pregnant with number two. As far as I know, she's now on four, and they're happily living in New Jersey. Occasionally, I still beg her to come back in some capacity since everyone I've hired since hasn't lasted more than two months.

Except this last girl. Mia has potential, thankfully.

"How about you? Any prospects where you're at?"

It takes me a minute to realize she's talking about men. "Hardly." I snort. "I have zero interest in relationships."

Her expression turns serious. "Have you heard from him since—"

"You mean since he took off with one of his students and left me a sticky note on the refrigerator of the four-thousand-dollar-a-month apartment he saddled me with? No." Honestly, some would say it was bound to happen, given the history between the two of us. But I hadn't seen it coming. I'd been young and naïve.

"Yikes." She visibly winces. "I still can't believe—" She stops talking, and I know what she would have said.

Because I am the girl who ran off with her history teacher. An eighteen-year-old who'd left everything she'd ever known behind to follow the divorced thirty-seven-year-old she'd been too stupid to realize had been grooming her from the moment they met.

The entire town knew it even if they didn't talk about it.

While secrets spread like wildfire in most small towns, gossip is not tolerated in Hope Springs. If it's good, they'll share. If it's bad, it gets buried.

And a troubled teen chasing her high school history teacher is pretty bad.

He'd left me a year later. Saddled me with an apartment I couldn't afford and a credit card I'd been unable to pay down. My credit took a hit, and I'd been homeless for the better part of a year, sleeping on the couches of my college friends and an occasional park bench. Doing whatever I had to in order to survive. Gran never knew that though.

When I told her I was leaving, she'd voiced her concerns, her disgust, then let me make my own choice. If I'd told her how much trouble I'd been in, she would have sent me more money. But I hadn't had the heart to tell her I'd blown every penny of her savings not wrapped up in my tuition on the apartment and a car for George.

There are so many things I wish I could take back. It's too bad you can't bury your past in a pine box, six feet down.

I clear my throat. "How is Alex?"

"Great," she says, her cheeks turning pink. "He's playing softball this season with the guys from Knight Security. Pastor Redding is on the team too."

"Knight Security?"

She cocks her head to the side. "I was sure your gran would have told you about Elijah. He was with her all the time."

"She told me about him," I say. "Just not Knight Security."

"He works there. They're a private firm, run out of the old lighthouse. Well, they were above the bakery before it got blown up."

"I'm sorry, *what?* The bakery got blown up?"

Lilly throws her head back and laughs. "We have so much to catch up on."

"Apparently." Though I desperately want to know what would have led to Pastor Redding's wife's bakery being blown up, there's one person on my mind. As he has been since I saw him in that parking lot. "Tell me about Elijah."

"He's nice. Helpful. Keeps to himself most of the time, aside from when he was with your gran."

"How long have you known him?"

"Since I got back into town. They'd just opened the firm, and he came into the diner with Lance Knight and Michael Anderson."

"Anderson? Wasn't he with—"

"Reyna Acker," she finishes.

"Gotcha. He's a few years older than us."

She nods.

"I don't know a Lance though."

"Lance moved his security company here. Both he and Elijah served with Michael."

"He's military." Which makes complete sense now that I've seen the man. He looks every bit a soldier.

"Your gran didn't tell you that? I'm surprised. They were close."

"She didn't mention that he'd served. She told me that he helped her. That he fixed things around the house and sat with her on Sundays. She'd tell me about things he said, conversations they had, but that was it."

"And you didn't ask the backstory of the man hanging with your gran?" She doesn't mean it as a jab, and I don't take it as one. Lilly has always been blunt. To the point, no sugar coating. Which is something I really appreciate about her.

"I was busy." But it's a weak excuse, and we both know it. "Our phone calls were brief. Often, but brief." And how much am I regretting that now that she's gone?

"Gotcha. Well, he was an Army Ranger, and while I don't know the details, I do know that all three were involved in some incident that nearly got them killed when they'd been overseas. He's single though. As far as I know." She wiggles her eyebrows.

"Hard pass," I reply. "The two minutes I spent with him in the parking lot of the church were long enough."

"Not a good impression, huh?"

"You could say that." I push to my feet and cross into the kitchen. In pure Gran fashion, the large glass jar on her counter is full of cookies. Reaching in, I pull one out. "I need to get started going through her things. The will reading is tomorrow, and I only have a month to get this place cleaned out and sold."

"You're not staying?" Lilly stands.

"No. My life is in New York," I reply.

"You're not even going to keep the house?" When I don't respond, she holds up both hands. "Sorry, not my business."

"No problem. Thanks for coming by."

"Of course." Lilly grabs her purse and stops just short of opening the front door. "Come by the diner, okay? We'll make you some dinner. Best coffee around."

I smile. "Will do."

CHAPTER 3

Elijah

C offee in hand, I step out onto the balcony of the lighthouse that now doubles as Knight Security's office space. The apartment upstairs is small, just a bedroom and bathroom, but it's quiet. And I like the quiet.

Another sleepless night under my belt, I practically inhale the steaming liquid. One of these nights, I won't have nightmares. One of these nights, I won't dream of blood, carnage, and death.

But not last night.

And probably not tonight.

"Yo! Elijah, you in?" Michael's voice carries upstairs, so I shut the balcony doors and head through my bedroom. As I walk down the stairs, I mentally go through my checklist for the day.

Check on the Petersons' security update.

Install a new panel in the Mastersons' home.

Background check for Felix's new hire at the hardware store.

Will reading.

That last one feels an awful lot like me being cut off at the knees. Especially since it wasn't just my friends I watched die in the desert last night, but the granddaughter I'd promised to protect also lay there, dying in the sand.

Why she's making an appearance in my routine nightmare, I've no clue. It's not like I spent a lot of time with her. Though I did promise Edna I would protect her.

Did Edna believe Andie was in danger? Or was it simply the dying wish of an old woman that her only grandchild remain safe?

Michael is making a cup of coffee in the kitchen, so I polish off what's in mine. The lighthouse's living room isn't overly spacious, but after some creative rearranging of the room by Lance's childhood buddy, Everett, we managed to fit two decent-sized office spaces and a waiting area. Given that most of our clients are a few hours away in Boston or small-town residents, we rarely use it, but it's there.

Michael looks up at me with the same darkness in his eyes that clouds mine.

"No sleep for you, either?" I ask.

"When do we ever sleep?" he quips then reaches for my mug. I hand it over, and he pours me another cup. "Same one for you?"

"Almost," I reply.

Since Michael and I served—and nearly died— together, our nightmares are just twisted versions of the same horrific event. Watching those you consider brothers screaming in agony as they slowly die isn't something you can walk away from unscathed. There's a part of me that honestly wishes I'd died that day in the desert. Just so I didn't have to suffer through the event over and over again.

Truthfully, I battle with the fact that it wasn't me nearly every single day.

"Almost? Anything you want to talk about?"

"Not particularly." I take a seat behind my desk and pull up my emails.

"Phillip said you were at the gym until nearly midnight. What's going on?"

Michael's way of dealing with PTSD included opening a gym so he could return to his boxing roots. He'd been a local champion growing up and managed to gain a bit of a reputation when we'd been overseas too. His place is where I work off my steam and has become a staple in my life, just as it is in his.

"You keeping tabs on me?"

"I did last night. Losing Edna was hard, brother. More so on you than anyone."

"I'm sure her granddaughter will argue that."

He scoffs and takes a seat in the leather-backed chair across from me. "She doesn't seem like the caring type. Likely just here for whatever inheritance Edna left."

It's a crude statement, but not one I haven't thought of. "Did you know her? Growing up."

"She was quite a few years behind me," he says. "But my mom filled me in on all the gossip when she left town with her high school history teacher."

"What?" *How did I miss that?*

"It wasn't on the internet," Michael says with a laugh. "Learning that would require you to actually talk to people. And since you don't like to do that—"

"Edna never mentioned it."

"Not surprising. She never had a negative thing to say about anyone, least of all her granddaughter."

"So she chased after a history teacher?"

"She did. Not entirely sure what happened after that."

I open a browser on my computer. "You got a name?"

He chuckles. "George Johnson."

After typing it into my search bar, I put feelers out for information on him with all of my contacts in law enforcement. The wheels in my head are already turning. If Andie and Edna had a falling out over this guy, it would explain why Andie took off and never came back. And if she's just here for her inheritance, as Michael suggested, it would also explain why she'd been so angry with me at the funeral for driving her grandfather's truck. What if she and this guy are after everything Edna owned?

"I know that look," Michael says. "You're on the hunt for trouble."

"Not trouble. I'm preparing," I say.

"For what?"

"I won't let her take everything Edna owned and scatter it in the wind."

"You still have the will reading, right?"

"Yeah." My email dings, and I open it.

You caught me right before a meeting. Good timing. Guy is a douchebag. Not sure what you're looking into him for, but I hope it's to put him behind bars.

-Jaxson

"Jaxson sent me something on the guy," I tell Michael. The LAPD homicide detective has helped us out on more than one case. A former Marine, Jaxson is one of the few men I'd trust with my life.

Interest clearly piqued, Michael comes around and leans against the wall behind me as I open up the arrest record.

"Forty-six. Married once. Been arrested for public indecency and solicitation of a minor." Michael shakes his head. "Fitting for a guy who would run off with his student."

"Yeah." I keep scanning, then open my browser again and type in the guy's name. An engagement announcement in a Boston newspaper pops up with a photograph.

The man staring back at me looks like a relatively clean-cut citizen, his blond hair styled well, smile wide. The woman next to him is far younger and, based on the announcement, twenty-five years his junior.

I nod at the photo. "Looks like he's planning to get married."

"So he's not involved with Andie."

"It would seem that way." I close it out. "I want to keep an eye out though. If this guy is back in town, we need to be sure he doesn't leave with any other young girls."

"He's got an older brother. Keeps to himself. Never liked him. I'm headed to the hardware store later, so I'll see if Felix has any info for us too."

"Great. Thanks."

Michael moves back around my desk and takes his seat in the chair. "What's on your task list for today?"

"I have to check in with the Petersons about their system update then install a new panel at Danielle Masterson's place. Their four-year-old got ahold of one of Zeke's golf balls. Apparently, he's got an arm on him. The screen was shattered."

Michael laughs. "Future baseball player right there."

"Danielle is less than happy about it," I reply with a laugh as I recall the fury in her voice when she'd called.

"Let me handle the new install. You take the update since I've got the tech knowledge of a gorilla."

"That's an insult to all gorillas," I say.

"Fair enough." Michael chuckles and gets to his feet. "What time is the will reading?"

I check my watch. "Three hours from now."

"You need me to go with you?"

If I asked him to go, he would without hesitation. He'd sit beside me, silent, a brother there to support me.

A part of me would like for him to go. Hearing the final will of a woman I'd considered family isn't going to be easy. But it's also personal. And something I want to do alone. Or rather, as alone as I can be given Andie will be there.

"Nah, I'm good. Go handle the install. Are you headed to Boston tomorrow?"

Michael shakes his head. "Lance is going to do the rounds out there this month since he and Eliza are going to see his parents this weekend."

"They're back in town?" Mr. and Mrs. Knight travel nearly year-round. They've been all over the world, staying in some places for a month or so before moving on. It's rare for them to be in Boston, and I honestly wish I could head out there so I could swing by and say hello. No one cooks like Lance's mom.

Her stir fry is legendary.

"They are. We're all invited to dinner on Friday."

I chuckle, my mouth already watering. "Count me in."

Michael pulls his phone out of his pocket and answers a call. "What's up?" His expression morphs from joy to full-on annoyance. "Seriously? Fine. I'll be right there. Love you too. Bye." He ends the call. "Install is going to have to wait an hour or so."

"Everything okay?"

"It's fine. My nephew has decided that playing racquet-ball against the sheriff's car is his new favorite pastime."

"Yikes."

"This kid." He looks about ready to explode but reins his temper back in. "My sister needs me to go pick him up. She can't get away."

"Go. Let me know if you need me to cover the install."

"Should be fine. I'll make him come with me and do some actual work." Michael heads out as I finish my coffee. His sister runs the only B&B in town, and ever since her husband took off on her a few months ago, Michael's been playing babysitter off and on as his nephew works out all his frustration over his deadbeat dad on his mother and this town.

It's sad. He's a good kid, just thirteen and not thinking clearly.

I push to my feet and cross over to the coffeemaker to fix cup number three. I try to cut myself off at two, but with the will reading today, three seems like it might even be falling short. Especially when I have to face off with Andie Montgomery again. Who will likely not be thrilled that I'm attending in the first place.

CHAPTER 4

Andie

With fresh cookies on a platter and coffee freshly brewed, I wait for Gran's lawyer. Normally, I wouldn't have bothered for something that probably won't take more than fifteen minutes. But since Gran would serve refreshments to anyone who walked through her door, it seemed an insult to her memory not to do the same.

I haven't seen her attorney since I was seventeen, but I remember him being a kind man.

Because there's time to spare, I cross over to the back windows and stare out over Gran's garden. I spent over an hour watering everything late last night. Even if I don't plan on keeping the place, watching everything she grew wither and die isn't something I can do.

Whoever buys the place will be able to decide what

they want to do with it, but until then, I'll be treating it like Gran would. And then I will imagine that it is flourishing.

The doorbell dings, so I run my hands down the front of my black blazer before heading to the door. When I open it, instant recognition leads to a broad smile.

"Mrs. McGinley. It is so good to see you again."

"You too, honey," she says as she pulls me in for a quick hug. I shut the door behind her and lead her into the living room. "I was surprised to get the call from Otto. I told Edna not to put me in her will."

"She loved you like a sister," I tell her.

"She was basically mine too. Sisters in everything but blood," Mrs. McGinley says as she sniffs delicately. "I still can't believe she's gone."

"Same." My throat tightens with the threat of tears, but I swallow them down. No crying today. No crying ever.

"So, how have you been? Edna couldn't talk about you enough." She beams up at me. "You have to know she was so proud of you."

"I've been good. Business is picking up, and I'm getting more and more boutiques to carry my designs, so that's been great."

"I'm so glad." She pats me on the hand. "After everything you've been through, it's nice to see how happy you are."

"Happy? I'm definitely happy." It's fairly far from the truth though. Am I unhappy? Not really. But the work I've been doing hasn't brought me much of the joy it once did.

Honestly, I've been contemplating a change. I'm just not sure what I want to do. And with Gran gone, I don't know that I should even make one.

Aside from her, my work has been the only constant in my world. If I change that now, then I know no part of my life will ever look the same.

The doorbell dings again. I cross over to open it, expecting to see Otto. So when it's not an elderly man but a dark-haired woman on the other side, I all but freeze in place. Wearing a black hat and a black dress that hugs every single curve, Rebecca Montgomery sniffles on the front porch of my Gran's house, her green eyes red and swollen.

What do I say to the woman I haven't seen since she abandoned me at the age of seven? I've kept tabs on her, ensuring I know where she is and who she's married to, but we haven't been any contact in well over a decade.

"Are you planning on moving aside or should I just walk through you?" she demands, glaring at me.

How can she not recognize her own daughter? Then again, why am I not surprised?

"Mother," I say, my tone sharp as I regain my ability to think. "I didn't expect to see you here."

Her eyes widen in shock. Which I suppose shouldn't come as one to me. Even before she'd left me, Rebecca had been more wrapped up in her own life than mine. "Andrea? Look at you!" she exclaims then grips me in a hug.

I cringe at the mention of my birth name, and the

contact makes me uncomfortable, so I back away as quickly as possible.

"I can't believe she's gone," she sobs, strangled sounds that are more a production than anything. As far as I know, she and Gran hadn't spoken in years. "How are you handling it? I'm just a mess! An absolute mess!"

"I'm sorry to hear that. Come in."

She breezes past me without another look. I'm about to close the door when none other than Elijah Breeth parks at the curb.

Of course he would show up.

Of course he would be here.

Vultures come in all shapes and sizes after all.

Even ridiculously handsome, handy, former Army Rangers.

He steps out of the sedan and heads up the drive wearing dark jeans and a black jacket, a white t-shirt underneath. I hate that he's ridiculously attractive. Even more so knowing that, based on the tabs I keep on her, my mother is in between significant others and will likely try to dig her claws into him the second he comes into the room.

I've yet to see a man deny her and don't expect Elijah to be any different.

"Andie," he greets.

"Mr. Breeth. I hadn't been expecting you."

"I was invited." He stands on the porch, and the tension between us grows. His strong jaw is set in frustration, but he gives nothing else away. Is he even sad that my gran is gone? Or curious about what she left behind?

"Come in. Otto should be here any minute."

"Here, now!" a man calls out.

Elijah turns, granting me the sight of the older lawyer rushing down the sidewalk. When he sees us, he smiles and slows.

"You're going to hurt yourself, Otto," Elijah jokes.

"I may not be as young as I used to be," he says, "but I can still take you on in the ring." He carries a briefcase in one hand and balls up the other into a fist to lightly tap Elijah's arm.

Elijah chuckles. "I'll take that bet."

The easy banter between them makes me nervous. Did Elijah work his way into the lives of everyone in Gran's inner circle?

Otto walks into the room, and I step aside so Elijah can come in as well. The moment he enters the space, his presence fills it. The man is tall, sure—muscled, absolutely. But it's more than that.

It's the way his gaze travels over the room. The way I know he misses nothing as he heads into the living room and steps into a corner. He stands stiffly, clearly bothered by being here, and the way he focuses on Gran's garden out the back windows is the first real show of an emotion other than irritation that I've seen from him.

Shoving thoughts of him aside, I move into the living

room. Rebecca is chatting Mrs. McGinley's ear off about how she's been living in Rome for the past few years but just discovered her fiancé was cheating on her.

She tells her how heartbroken she is.

How he was *the* one.

Mrs. McGinley looks about ready to strangle her with the pearls she wears, so I step in front of the group and clear my throat. "Thank you all for coming. I have some cookies and coffee ready if anyone is interested."

"I couldn't possibly," Rebecca says, her tone breaking. "I haven't eaten since I heard the news of my dear mother's passing."

"We missed you at the funeral, Rebecca," Elijah says. His tone is annoyed, but the fact that he calls her by name is personable. It leads me to wonder just how they know each other.

Rebecca's gaze narrows on him. "Why are you here? I didn't realize my mother needed her lap dog even in death."

"Easy, easy," Otto says as he pulls out a manila envelope.

I steal a glance at Elijah, who is watching Rebecca angrily. Honestly, knowing he can't stand her raises my opinion of him just slightly. Not much, but it's higher than it was when he first walked through the door.

"Everyone is here because Edna loved you all very much. She was a kind, generous woman who always put others above herself."

Elijah straightens and crosses his arms.

"Now, if you all are ready, I will begin the reading. Her will was updated just six months ago."

"Yes. Yes. Please, let us hear what my mother wanted," Rebecca says as she dabs her eyes with a handkerchief.

One stolen look at Elijah rolling his eyes nearly has me smiling. Did I read him wrong?

"To my best friend, my sister in Christ and in heart, Carmen McGinley, I leave my collection of books. May you find yourself a Scottish Highlander to run off with one day."

Mrs. McGinley chokes on a sob, and I reach over to grip her shoulder. She pats my hand in return.

"I leave the belongings in my house to my lovely granddaughter Andie, as well as the contents of my collective accounts. I hope you use the money to continue doing great things, my dearest. And be sure to check under the bed. There's a wooden box containing letters I would like for you to read. In order, child. No skipping to the end." Otto meets my gaze. "She made sure I promised to read that part."

Tears burn in my throat, but I shove them down. *No. Tears.*

"To Elijah, I leave my late husband's collection of tools and records. Use them, and the truck I already gave you, to impress a wife one day, Elijah. You need all the help you can get. There's no getting by on those looks alone."

Otto's cheeks redden as he reads the letter, and Elijah laughs.

"Yes, ma'am," he mutters.

Another notch for him. Even if I still can't understand just why my gran came to care for him enough to leave him anything. Could just be my guarded heart, and I admit that.

"To my daughter, Rebecca, I leave my collection of dinner plates. That way, she may host all the dinners she pleases."

Elijah chokes on his coffee.

I look at Rebecca, a smile playing at the corners of my lips. Gran hated her dinner plates. They broke constantly and chipped too easily. Based on the confused look on my mother's face, she's expecting more, so when Otto continues, I'm only half paying attention.

"As for the house itself, I leave its future up to Elijah Breeth and my granddaughter, Andie Montgomery, to decide on together. They will be co-owners until they both decide what to do with it."

"I'm sorry, what?" I ask, my head whipping toward Otto so quickly it nearly gives me whiplash. "Can you repeat that?"

"As for the house itself, I leave its future up to Elijah Breeth and my granddaughter, Andie Montgomery, to decide on together. They will be co-owners until they both decide what to do with it," he says.

I whirl on Elijah. "Did you know about this?"

"Do I look like I knew about it?" he growls. "Surely you're mistaken," he says to Otto.

"I assure you, I am not. We had a very detailed conversation about it when she asked that it be added to the will. The house belongs to the both of you. So whatever happens to it must be agreed upon."

I don't even have time to fully process the news before my mother's temper tantrum starts.

"She left me *dinner plates?*" Rebecca snaps as she shoves to her feet. "What else? You're mistaken. My mother left me money. She knew I needed it, and she left it for me."

Otto shakes his head. "She did not."

"Dinner plates?" she screeches then whirls on me. I barely have enough time to get to my feet before she's in my face, fury in her eyes. "You traitorous little brat. I always knew you were going to be a blight! How dare you take what is mine! How dare you!"

"I didn't take anything. Gran—"

"*My mother* would never have left me nothing! She knew how much I needed help! You stole all of this! Didn't you? You little—"

"Rebecca." Elijah's stern tone leaves absolutely no room for her to continue. He steps up to my side, so close I can smell his woody aftershave. I hate that the nearness of his body calms me just enough to be noticeable. "Get out of Andie's face. Now."

"Or what?" she sneers. "My mother isn't here to pat

your head, so what, you're moving on to my daughter instead?" She looks at me, gaze murderous. "He's probably a bit too young for your tastes, isn't he, darling? And unmarried. I heard you like them attached." Lifting her hand, she uses her thumb to brush over the inside of her ring finger.

My cheeks heat, and I choke on my words. Pain burns in my chest, and bile rises in my throat. *How dare she.*

"Your mother left you nothing because she knew what a parasite you are. Something she made very clear eight months ago when you showed up here, begging for money," Elijah replies before I can get my head together.

Rebecca's cheeks turn bright red. "You have no right—"

"To what? Keep you from attacking the only family you have left?" he asks, sliding between us. His muscled back momentarily shields me from Rebecca. Which gives me just enough time to get my bearings.

"She stole from me! You little brat! You are still ruining my life! First, you turned your father against me, and now this!"

The harshness of her tone shoves me back into my adolescent years, a young girl who just wanted her mother to love her. "I didn't steal anything," I whisper.

"Your grandmother was so furious when she found out I was pregnant. Did you know that? I chose to keep you! Even when your father wanted nothing to do with you. And this is how you repay me?"

Closer to tears than I have been in years, I struggle to keep my composure. "Leave," I tell my mother. "The will reading is over, and you need to get out of my house."

She looks from me to Elijah then back to me again. "It's not just your house. She didn't trust you to keep an eye on it alone."

"Then get out of *our* house," Elijah says. "Or I'll call the sheriff and have you forcibly removed."

Rebecca mutters something under her breath then grabs her purse. "Keep the dinner plates. I don't need her charity." She marches out the door and slams it behind her.

Adrenaline spiking, my vision wavers. When was the last time I ate? I start to fall, but a hand on my arm steadies me on my feet.

"Are you okay?"

I look up at Elijah, momentarily surprised to see him standing so close. Until I realize it's his hand on my arm. I yank it away and place a hand on the back of the couch for support.

"Fine." I turn to Otto. "Is that all?"

"It is. I'm sorry, Andie. I didn't realize how bitter she would be."

"It's not your fault."

"Honey, are you sure you're okay? You look pale." Mrs. McGinley reaches up and gently pushes some hair behind my ear.

The tenderness makes me squirm. "I'm fine."

"If you need me, call," Otto says as he reaches into the

folder and pulls out a slip of paper with *Deed and Title* written across the top. There, in black and white, are the names Andrea Montgomery and Elijah Breeth.

Seeing them there makes it all the more real. Why in the world would my grandmother leave her house to both of us? And what am I going to do about it?

CHAPTER 5

Elijah

"I didn't need your help," Andie states as soon as we're alone. Both Mrs. McGinley and Otto fled the moment he'd handed over the deed to Edna's house, probably because the tension between us is unbearable.

Even for me.

"Sure you didn't." I head into the kitchen and pour myself a cup of coffee while Andie follows me, the deed still clutched in her manicured hand.

"You had no right to step in like that," she continues.

"Actually, I had every right because, while you were living your best life out in New York, I was here, dealing with your mother trying to get her gold-digging fingers on everything your gran owned. I was the one who threatened to call the cops on her after I showed up and found that she'd physically assaulted Edna."

Anger burns hot in my veins, and I slam the mug down on the counter a bit harder than I should have. Andie jumps, but I don't let up. "And it was me who helped Edna bandage the cut on her head, left behind by the fact that your mother threw a dinner plate at her head." Which honestly makes the fact that Edna chose those to leave even more amusing.

The color drains from Andie's face. "She did *what?*" Crimson returns, painting her cheeks a deep shade of red. Why does it make her even more attractive?

"Oh yes, Andie," I continue. "Your gran has been dealing with assaults from your mother for the last eighteen months."

"I didn't know."

"How could you have known? You were never here. Tell me, did you even bother to check in on your gran? Did you even think of asking her about what was going on in her life? Or was it all about the glamour of your own?"

Andie's glare turns even more murderous. "As I told you, *Mr. Breeth,* my relationship with my gran is none of your business. And as far as my mother goes, I haven't seen or talked to Rebecca in a decade. I didn't know she was harassing my gran, or I would have handled it."

"How would you have handled it?" I demand.

"It's none of your business."

"It is my business," I reply. "Because you and I both know we haven't seen the last of her."

"That's not your concern."

"It is since my name is on the deed for this house." I take a step closer. "I will never let Rebecca get her hands on this place."

Andie takes a step closer and tilts her head up to glare at me. "Then it seems we finally agree on something, Mr. Breeth. Because I won't let my mother get a single thing my gran owned aside from the dinner plates she was left in the will."

I stare down at Andie, noting the shades of gold in her emerald eyes. Had I seen those before? Her lips are painted a deep red, her strong jaw stubbornly set. Something between us shifts, and I force myself to take a step back as the image of me slamming my mouth onto hers assaults me.

No.

Hard no.

Absolutely not.

"Good. Then we're in agreement."

"Fine." Andie moves away from me and pours herself a cup of coffee. "Now, on to the reason my gran thought it necessary to add you to the deed. I can have Otto draw up a power of attorney so you don't have to deal with the sale. I will, of course, give you fifty percent of the profits."

"Excuse me?" Still captivated by the sight of her, I'm only half listening. "What did you just say?"

She turns to face me and leans back against the counter. "I will handle the sale of the house. It's one of the reasons I'm still here."

"You want to sell it?" Knowing what I do about her, why does it surprise me that she doesn't want to keep the house?

She narrows her eyes. "Why wouldn't I? My life is in New York. It doesn't make sense to hang onto a house here when any reason I ever had for returning is gone."

"You cannot sell this house."

Andie sets her cup aside and crosses her arms. "Yes, I can."

"No. I own half of it, and I'm not going to allow it."

"Mr. Breeth—"

"I'll buy you out of it then. We can have it appraised, and I'll pay you half of the value."

She stares at me for a few moments, likely contemplating my offer. "There's no way you have that kind of money."

Now, it's my turn to be annoyed. "Why is that?" I question. "Because I was in the military? Because I don't drive a ridiculously expensive car or wear thousand-dollar suits? Tell me, Miss Montgomery…why is it that you think I can't afford this place?"

"I won't go down on the price," she says. "Whatever it's appraised at, that's the value we go with."

"Fine." I reach into my pocket and pull out a business card then slam it on the counter. "Call me when you've ordered the appraisal. I'll pay for half of that too." Without looking back, I march toward the door and slam it behind me.

*W*ITH *A* BRAND-NEW, ALBEIT EMPTY, VASE IN ONE HAND, *I knock on Edna's door. Since she refuses store-bought flowers, this is the only thing she'll allow me to get her on Valentine's Day. I even tried chocolate last year, and she'd told me that I didn't need to fuss over an old woman.*

I'd laughed and insisted that even grumpy old ladies needed something on Valentine's Day. That's when she'd conceded and agreed that she could always use more vases for flowers. So, here I stand, crystal vase in hand, a green ribbon tied around it.

Edna pulls the door open and smiles widely at me. Her silver hair is braided over her shoulder, and she's wearing a bright blue dress, a black shawl around her shoulders. "You clean up nice," she says with a laugh as I offer her the vase. Her eyes light up, her expression complete delight over the gift.

Finally. A winner.

"You look beautiful," I say, leaning in to kiss her wrinkled cheek.

"I still don't know why you insisted we get all dressed up," she says as she carries the vase into her kitchen. Stooped over just slightly, her movements are getting slower, and it worries me. Is she eating like she's supposed to?

"Because everyone deserves to get dressed up," I tell her as I step into the kitchen. "This looks delicious." I

survey the pot roast covered in gravy, sitting on a bed of potatoes and carrots, as well as the fresh rolls and platter of cookies.

"Well, it's not every day an old woman gets a date on Valentine's Day."

I laugh.

"Now, you really should be out on a date. You're not getting any younger."

"I'm in my prime," I argue as I pluck a carrot from the pan and stick it into my mouth. "Besides, I'm waiting for the right one."

She laughs. "I can appreciate that. You know, my Charlie was the best thing that ever happened to me." As they always do when she speaks of her late husband, her eyes mist. It hurts me to know she still grieves, but it's also refreshing. Gives me hope that maybe one day—when I'm ready—I'll find someone who will love me as much as she loved her Charlie.

"You've told me that a time or two," I say then wink. "So. What can I do to help?"

"Nothing. You go sit."

"No. You go sit. You cooked." I take her by the arm and guide her to the table. After pulling her chair out, I help her sit and scoot her toward the table. "I will serve."

"Only because I'm tired," she says with a smile that doesn't reach her eyes.

I swallow hard, trying to decide how much to press. The last thing I want to do is ruin her Valentine's Day, but I know she needs help. She's just too stubborn to admit it. I pull down two dinner plates then pile food on them before carrying them to the table.

After they're served, I put the basket of rolls in the center then retrieve the bottle of cold, sparkling juice from the fridge. As soon as I've filled our glasses, I take a seat across from her and reach out to take both of her hands.

They're so slender in mine, her skin so pale.

"Thank You, God, for the food on our table. Please forgive us our transgressions and bless this meal we are about to eat. In Your name we pray, amen."

"Amen," Edna says and plucks a roll from the basket.

"Did you not get enough sleep?" I ask as I smear some butter on my roll. I take a bite, the delicate flavor of Edna's rolls far surpassing anything I could have picked up from a restaurant on the way here. Which is what I offered to do and nearly got smacked for my efforts.

"Late-night phone call," she replies.

Which I know means early morning. Likely sometime around two or three. "Rebecca?"

She sighs. "That girl just doesn't understand what it takes to survive on your own. I don't understand how I failed so badly in raising her."

"You didn't," I reply.

"I had to have failed somehow. Charlie and I were good to her. We gave her everything she'd ever wanted."

I don't have the heart to tell her that is likely what led to Rebecca's spoiled attitude. *"All you have to do is say the word. I can handle it for you."*

Edna chuckles softly. *"No, it will be fine. She's harmless. Just lonely."*

Lonely only because her latest fiancé left her for greener pastures after she'd cheated on him. It's all self-inflicted, which means I have no pity. Lance would tell me that prickly people need grace too, but sometimes you have to avoid them to escape getting skewered by the thorns.

He's a better man than me, that's for sure.

"All you have to do is ask," I tell Edna. *"And I will make sure she doesn't bother you ever again."*

Edna doesn't respond, just takes a small bite of her roast. *"Did I tell you that Andie called me earlier?"*

"No, you didn't," I say as I take another bite. Andie is Edna's pride and joy. The granddaughter who left Hope Springs for the bright, shiny lights of New York. While Edna does nothing but speak highly of Andie, I align her with her mother. Both women abandoned Edna as soon as they'd drained everything they wanted out of her. And to me, that does not deserve such high praise.

"She told me that she got a small boutique in New Jersey to pick up her line of clothes! Isn't that wonderful! She's been working so hard. I wish that girl would slow down now and then. But she's always been a worker. When she was sixteen, she had two jobs. One at the hardware store—Felix always treated her good—and the other at the pharmacy. I hardly saw her. She'd been so focused on

saving money so she could see the world. I'm glad she's seen more of it than this tiny town." But as she says it, her tone softens, betraying the sadness I know she feels without actual family around.

I can be here. I can spend time with her. But at the end of the day, I'm not blood. She didn't watch me grow up.

Reaching over, I touch her hand. "If you want, we can drive out to New York and visit her."

Edna's face lights up. "Really?" But as excited as she is, it fades within a few seconds. "No, I can't bother her. She has so much going on."

"Edna, she's your granddaughter. She can take time to see you. Especially if you're driving out there."

She smiles softly and shakes her head. "No, it's okay. How is your roast?"

With the subject change, I know she's done talking about this. But even as I smile and engage in light conversation, my mind is still on the fact that Andie Montgomery has managed to make her gran feel so unwelcome that she doesn't even feel like she can drive out and visit her.

What type of person treats their family that way?

———

THAT WAS THE LAST VALENTINE'S DAY I SPENT WITH Edna.

We never got the chance to drive to New York, and the more I think about it, the more grateful I am. After meeting

Andie, I can't imagine she would have made her gran feel overly welcome, and it would have led to an argument because I wouldn't have been able to keep my mouth shut.

I take a drink of water then pluck another fry from my plate.

"You doing okay?" Lilly asks as she offers me a refill.

"Yeah. It's been a day."

"The will reading," she says softly then slides into the booth across from me. Since it's past lunch but not quite dinner, the place is slow. It's honestly my favorite time to be here. Talking to people I don't know is not a favorite pastime of mine.

I'm better around a computer.

Machines, I understand. People? Not so much.

"How did it go?" she asks.

"It could have gone better," I reply, thinking of Rebecca's outburst.

"How is Andie handling things?"

Lilly simply saying the name brings that image of Andie staring up at me back to mind. I shove it back down. Uninterested. That's what I am. The woman is toxic. "Fine. I think. From what I understand, they didn't have an overly close relationship."

Lilly snorts. "Seriously? Andie and her gran were inseparable her entire childhood. Even before her mother abandoned her. I'm honestly surprised that Andie hasn't broken down. I don't think I've seen her cry at all."

"Broken down?" Now it's my turn to snort. "Andie

doesn't strike me as the type of person who feels very deeply."

As usual, Lilly is unoffended. She simply smiles and shakes her head. "Elijah Breeth, don't you think it's possible that computer of yours can't tell you everything there is to know about a person?"

The bell dings overhead, so I glance up just in time to see Rebecca stroll in on a pair of heels that might as well be stilts. She's changed out of what I would call a funeral dress, swapping it for tight jeans and a black t-shirt, and has ditched the hat for a long braid.

"You have got to be kidding me," Lilly mutters then pushes out of the booth and crosses the diner. "Mrs. Montgomery, nice to see you."

"You're the hardware store owner's stepdaughter," she says, tone disinterested. "You ran around with Andrea."

"Yes. Felix is my father." Lilly's tone is friendly, but her expression is ice. Cold enough that, even though I'm a significant distance away, I can see it. "Would you like a table?"

"Yes, I—" She scans the diner, her greedy gaze finding me. "Never mind, I think I'll join my mother's friend. After all, we're both suffering a loss and could likely use some company." Without waiting for an invitation, she crosses over on her stilts and slides in across from me.

Behind her, Lilly mouths "*Sorry!*" then heads for the kitchen, likely to tell her husband that a gold-digging hurricane just blew into town.

"I didn't invite you to sit here," I tell her.

She leans in, the front of her shirt dipping to show off cleavage that's won her more divorce settlements than should be legally allowed. "We got off on the wrong foot."

"Which time?" I ask.

Rebecca pouts and sits back. "You don't like me."

I'm thrown back to the parking lot of the church when Andie said that same thing. This time, I can't even claim that I don't know her. "You're perceptive."

"So, what can I get you to drink, Rebecca?" Lilly asks. Alex stands behind the bar now, having slipped from the kitchen to watch the show. His expression is one of anger, and he watches the woman across from me like a hawk.

"Whatever he's having," she says, gesturing to my cup.

"You mean water?" I ask.

She scrunches her nose. "Water? I thought it was vodka."

"I don't drink," I reply cooly.

"Fine. Whatever. Water." She waves Lilly off like she doesn't matter.

I take another bite of my burger but lose my appetite the second she plucks a fry from my plate. "What do you want, Rebecca?"

"You seem like a practical man. Strong. Caring." She bites the fry in half then sticks the uneaten side on my plate. "Why is it you took such an interest in my mother?"

"I don't see how that's any of your business."

"It is when you took off with my inheritance."

"Your inheritance?" I laugh. "If it were up to me, Edna wouldn't even have left you the dinner plates."

She leans in once again, her gaze darkening. "You should think better of toying with me, boy. I eat men like you for breakfast."

"I'm sure you've had your fill," I tell her as I slide out of the booth. "But I can guarantee you have never met a man like me. Have the evening you deserve, Rebecca. I truly hope to never see you again."

"Leaving so soon?" Lilly asks as she meets me by the door.

Reaching into my pocket, I pull out enough cash to cover my food and a generous tip then offer it to her. She doesn't bother counting it, just shoves it in her apron.

"Does Andie know she's in town?" Lilly asks.

"Since Rebecca attended the will reading, I'd say so."

Lilly shakes her head. "That woman is a stain on this town. And I don't say that lightly. I know we're supposed to love our enemies, but—"

"People like her make it hard. You going to be okay?"

"I'll be fine. It's not my first run-in with Rebecca, and I'm sure it won't be my last."

"Great. See you tomorrow." I slip out onto the street and head for my car. I'd nearly driven the truck here, but since Rebecca would have spotted that a million miles away, I'm grateful I didn't. Then again, a lot of good it did me as she found me anyway.

As I turn toward the office, my phone rings. "What's up?"

"I need you down at the library," Lance says through the car speakers.

"Everything okay?"

"There was a break-in."

CHAPTER 6

Andie

Before Gran's funeral, I hadn't been to a church for years. Shame kept me from walking through those doors, despite the understanding that God forgives. I just don't understand how He could forgive the things I've done.

So many mistakes. Like a snowball rolling downhill, steadily gathering more weight. One mistake led to ten more, and before I knew it, I was living a life I didn't even recognize. Not that I'd wanted to even if I could.

It was easier to hide from the woman in the mirror than it was to face her head-on.

In a lot of ways, it still is.

The church in front of me is where I spent every single Sunday growing up. Even when my parents were still together and I was living with them, Gran made sure she picked me up every week and brought me here. I know the pews like the back of my hand. So why can't I take the next step?

Why am I still standing out front, staring at it as though it's going to devour me whole?

"Sometimes, we just need a little push, huh?"

I glance behind me at the pretty blonde standing a few yards away. She's dressed in a sundress with yellow flowers, a denim jacket covering her arms.

"Something like that," I reply then face the front again.

The woman moves up to stand beside me. "I'm Eliza Knight," she says.

"Andie. Knight. Your husband owns the security company in town. The one Elijah works at."

"He does. I recognize you from the funeral," she says softly. "Your grandmother was a great woman."

"The best," I agree, still staring at the church.

"Would you like to go in together? I need to talk to Pastor Redding about something, so I'm going in anyway. And sometimes, it's easier to go in with a friend."

"I practically grew up in this church."

"Sometimes, that makes it harder."

I turn to her, offering the woman a friendly smile. "True."

Facing off with the church again, I take a step. Then another, until I'm walking through the large wooden doors and standing at the end of the aisle.

"I hope to see you around, Andie," Eliza says with a

wave as she heads off to the right, down a hall where the church office sits.

"You too," I call out then force myself to walk all the way to the front. The large crucifix over the altar is the same one that has been there every day since the church opened. So why does it seem so much larger now?

Okay, God. I'm here. The burning desire to come to church this morning was not something I could ignore. Gran would have wanted me to come by and see everyone before I left, so this seemed like a good chance to do just that while avoiding the Sunday morning crowds.

And after spending all morning packing up gran's things, I'd needed a break. Even if I made more headway than I thought I would. Since Elijah plans to buy me out of the house, I won't have to put it up for sale, which means my time here can be cut far shorter than it would have been originally.

Why does that make me a bit sad?

"Andie Montgomery."

I jump then turn to see the pastor standing beside me, a wide smile on his face. "Hello, Pastor." Standing, I return his hug then take a seat on the pew. He sits beside me, and we stare straight ahead for a few moments.

"How are you holding up?"

"I'm doing okay."

"It's okay to not be, you know," he says softly.

Forcing a smile, I nod. "I know, but I'm okay."

"Well, I'm glad to hear that."

"Gran loved coming here on Sundays."

He chuckles. "Every other day too. Your Gran was in here almost every morning."

"Really?"

He nods. "She would come in and pray, then have coffee with Kyra, before heading home."

"How long had she been doing that?"

"Since you left," he replies.

My heart aches. I knew I broke hers when I left, I'd just been too young and immature to realize that I should have come straight back home. "How is your wife doing? I haven't seen Kyra around."

"You should swing by the bakery. She would love to see you. And she's doing well. Kassandra just got married not too long ago. They have a baby on the way."

"That's wonderful." I may not have known her well since I kept to myself, but Kassandra was always such a bundle of energy.

After a deep breath, I admit, "I have so many regrets... with Gran. And life in general."

"You shouldn't carry them," he tells me. "Seek repentance, and let them go."

"I wish it were that easy."

"It certainly sounds like it would be, doesn't it?" he asks with a chuckle. "Even as we know that our mistakes are forgiven when we pursue a life with Christ, asking seems an impossible feat sometimes."

"I don't suppose you take confessions, do you?" I ask, half-joking.

He laughs. "You don't need to confess to me, Andie. I'm a sinner just like you. God is the only one who can help you work through that pain." He faces forward. "However, if you need someone to talk to, my door is always open."

———

THE WOODEN BOX IN MY HANDS FEELS FAR HEAVIER THAN IT should as I sit on the edge of Gran's bed. Aggie purrs beside me, curled up in a ball on top of the throw blanket at the end of the bed. I glance over at him, honestly jealous. What I wouldn't give for some good sleep right about now.

My phone rings, and the cat raises his head, staring at me with annoyance. "Sorry, I forgot the ringer was on." I tap the screen and press it to my ear. "Hello?"

"Miss Montgomery, it's Mia."

"Hi, Mia, is everything all right?" My latest assistant almost never calls me. She's spooky good at handling anything and everything thrown her way, even without my direct intervention.

"It is. How are you?"

"I'm okay."

"The funeral?"

"It was a funeral," I say. "What can I do for you?"

"You'd emailed and asked about a storage unit for your grandmother's things?"

"You found one?"

"I did. It's a bit of a drive from your apartment, but it's the only climate-controlled one that is available in the area."

"Then that will have to do."

"Great, I'll get it reserved for you." The line falls silent for a moment. "You know, I lost my father when I was young. I know how you must be feeling."

"Thank you. I'm sorry for your loss."

"It was a long time ago. I can drive up, help out, then take a load back in my car if you'd like."

I consider telling her no, but then I peek out the door at the mountain of boxes. Truthfully, some help organizing would be nice, and there's no one better at it than Mia Harper. "That would be great, actually. You're sure you don't mind?"

"Not at all. I'll leave first thing in the morning." The call ends, and I set the phone down beside me.

I glance over at Aggie, who has already fallen back to sleep. "Must be nice," I tell him then run my hands over the carved flowers in the top of the wooden box. "All right, Gran, let's see what you've got for me." I open the lid and stare down at a row of envelopes lined up neatly inside.

"In order, I heard you."

Plucking the first message out, I set the box to the side and run my finger over the *One* written on the front. Seeing my gran's writing brings a fresh wave of grief over me, and

I nearly set the letter aside. However, doing so feels an awful lot like shutting the door on her.

And I did that enough when she'd been alive.

So, heart aching, I open the letter.

Dearest Andie,

You've been gone almost a week now, and the house still feels so empty. I haven't wanted to reach out because the last thing I want to do is drive you away when you're already gone. Pastor Redding suggested I start writing you letters. Then, if I get brave enough, I can send them to you. If not, it will at least help me to feel connected.

I hope you know that I am praying for you. I miss you something terrible, my Andie.

Come home soon.

Gran

I close the letter and shove it back into the envelope. Tears burn my eyes, emotion clawing its way to the surface. I beat it back down and drink a glass of water, hoping it will soothe the pain in my throat.

Did she detail everything that happened while I was gone?

How could I have left her like that? Why did it take her death for me to come home?

"Get it together, Andie," I tell myself as I set the glass down and straighten. As I turn to head back into the room, glass shatters.

Something hits my side, knocking me into the edge of the couch.

Pain shoots through my hip, and I hiss, falling to the side as glass sprinkles the carpet.

"What the—" I struggle to my feet just as car tires screech against pavement.

A white sedan races down the street.

Adrenaline pumping, I pull my phone out and dial 9-1-1. After giving my address to the operator, I shove the phone back into my pocket and study the damage left behind by the brick thrown through Gran's front window.

Rebecca. The name burns like a hot poker in my gut.

It had to be her.

She's furious that I got the house, and now she's going to do everything she can to make my life miserable, but what she just did gives me a picture window-sized reason to finally press charges.

CHAPTER 7

Elijah

The damage to the library is substantial.

Shelves are pushed over, leaving books scattered everywhere. Mrs. McGinley's employee lounge was ransacked as well, dumping her trash can upside down and scattering the garbage all over the place. Someone threw her coffee machine on the floor, shattering it to pieces.

The older woman is visibly shaken and beyond furious. Especially since whoever did this dumped what water bottles she had in storage all over some of the books, destroying them. "I just can't understand why someone would do such a thing!" she exclaims.

My mind immediately goes to Rebecca. What kind of coincidence is it that this happens right after Edna leaves all of her books to her oldest friend?

"Easy, Carmen," Juniper Kline says as she wraps an

arm around Mrs. McGinley's shoulders. The two women have been best friends since grade school. And given they are both in their eighties now, it makes that type of friendship quite a feat. They, along with Edna, have been inseparable as long as I've known them.

My heart aches just thinking about her.

"Do you know if anything is missing?" Lance questions. The former Ranger was my commander back when we'd served. He's one man I would follow straight into combat and not think twice about it, so coming to work for him only made sense.

"How could I tell?" Mrs. McGinley asks.

"Looks like some teens just got in here and took out their frustration." Michael crosses his arms as he surveys the damage.

"No. This was intentional," I say as I kneel in front of the door.

"That's my thought as well," Lance replies.

"But why?" Mrs. McGinley asks. "It's a library. No one would have come in to steal anything because anything they could have taken, they could have done for free by simply checking it out!"

"Clearly, they wanted whatever they took to be a secret, Carmen. We've seen *Murder She Wrote*. We know how they cover things up." Juniper offers me a nod in agreement with my suspicions.

I bite back a half-smile.

"If the alarm was triggered and there was no damage, what would you have done?" Michael asks.

"A catalog check to see what was taken," Mrs. McGinley replies.

"Which is why they destroyed the place." Lance crosses his arms. "Could be they were covering what they took. How long will it take you to sort through this?" he asks her.

"This mess?" she exclaims. "Weeks. A month even. Unless I can get Johnny to help." Her grandson is a good kid. And one who will come running the second his grandmother asks for help. "Then it will probably be about a week of sorting." She bends down and lifts a damaged book from the floor. "My poor books."

The sadness in her voice deepens the ache in my chest. "Can you get me a list of all of the books you have?"

"Yes, of course. Eliza helped me go digital last month, so I can email it over to you." She sets the book on a partially toppled shelf, taking great care despite the fact that its water-logged pages will likely never be read again.

"Great. I can narrow it down to what they may have taken with that. Then we can double-check it against what you find."

"Grandma?"

"Over here!" Mrs. McGinley calls out. She quickly wipes her eyes as Johnny comes around the corner. His hazel eyes are a near-perfect match to his grandmother's and father's, and they survey the damage with shock and anger.

"Who did this?" he demands. A high-school senior, he's mere months away from leaving for college out in Texas. He'd had a temper the size of the Lone Star state until his father had pushed him into football. Now the kid is a star quarterback and will be joining the Texas A&M football team next year.

"We're trying to figure it out," Lance says.

"Can you help her get things cleaned up?" Michael asks. "We need to know if anything is missing."

"Of course." Johnny wraps his arm around his grandmother's shoulders, and she leans into him. "Anything you need, Grandma. I'll let Felix know that I'll need some time off."

"I'm going to head out. Need to go pick up Rachel from school," Mrs. Kline says as she smiles at Johnny. "Let me know what you need. I'll be by tomorrow morning after drop-off to help get started on the cleanup."

"Thank you, Juni," Mrs. McGinley says.

Mrs. Kline carefully makes her way out of the library, and Johnny guides his grandmother over to a chair.

"You have that look," Lance says as he and Michael close in on me.

"What look?"

"The one that says you have a theory," Michael replies.

"I think it was Rebecca."

"Edna's daughter?" Lance asks.

"Yes. She was at the will reading and was furious that she'd only gotten dinner plates. This could be revenge."

"From what you said though, she was angrier with you and Andie. Why not start there?"

"She cornered me at the diner," I say. "And we have no way of knowing—"

Sirens screech outside, cutting me off as the sheriff's car, a fire truck, and an ambulance rush past the library. Adrenaline shoots through me, and I rush for the door, treating the fallen books like rubble in a war zone.

They make a right and disappear down a side street. Toward Edna's house.

I cannot explain the feeling that takes over, but I know —without a doubt—Andie is in trouble. Without looking back, I sprint up the street, making a run for the three-block distance between her house and the library.

As I come around the corner, body slick with sweat, thanks to the humid heat, I survey the scene before me. Andie stands on the lawn with the sheriff and one of his deputies. The house's massive picture window is shattered, glass shards likely covering the living room.

Gunshot? Did someone try to kill her?

Was it an accident and someone else called the cops?

Before I can speculate further, Michael's motorcycle rumbles past me, and he parks it right in front of the house. Lance's truck follows, and I suddenly feel like a fool for running here when I could have just jumped into my car.

By the time I reach the scene, Andie has just finished giving her statement.

She looks more angry than scared, and when that

emerald gaze lands on me, her anger deepens. "What are you doing here?" she asks.

"I heard the sirens," I reply. "What happened?"

"As I told your coworker here, it's none of your concern. I'm not in need of private security." She gestures to Michael, who looks beside himself amused.

"And if you remember, *Andie,* this is my house too. Therefore, it makes it my concern."

She would kill me if she could. I can see it in her eyes.

"Someone threw a brick through the window then drove off," Sheriff Vick says.

"Not someone. Rebecca," Andie corrects.

The library. Now this? It fits.

"You saw her?" I ask, already prepared to arrest her myself.

"Well. No. Not exactly. But who else would have done it?" She directs her question at the sheriff, who jots something down on his notepad.

"As I told you, Miss Montgomery, we will do a thorough investigation, and if Rebecca is responsible, she will be held accountable."

"If she is responsible?" Andie scoffs. "You've known me my entire life. Which means you know her. Do you seriously think I don't know my mother's handiwork when I see it? She's angry because I got the house."

"We got the house," I correct.

Andie glares.

Michael chuckles.

Even Lance appears to be amused.

"Fine. *We* got the house. When she's mad, she throws tantrums." Andie gestures to the window. "This is a temper tantrum."

"The library could have been a temper tantrum, too," I say.

"The library? What happened at the library?"

"It was trashed," I reply. "Have you collected the brick for evidence?" I ask Sheriff Vick.

"Not yet. We're leaving everything where it is until I can get some pictures."

"May I?" I gesture toward the house.

"Go for it," he replies.

"You're seriously going to let him walk into an active crime scene?"

"He knows what he's doing," he says.

"Debatable," Andie snaps but doesn't argue further.

I move carefully into the house, surveying the damage. Glass covers nearly every square inch of the living room, and the brick landed over halfway inside. Which means that whoever threw it has an impressive arm on them.

"That's way too far for Rebecca to have thrown it," Michael comments. "I even have my doubts she could have leveled the library the way someone did."

"My thoughts exactly." But if it wasn't Rebecca, who could have done it?

"Which way were they driving?" Lance calls out.

"West," the sheriff replies.

Lance surveys the damage again.

"What are you thinking?" Michael asks.

"Let's pretend for a minute that we didn't think Rebecca could have trashed the library. It's still entirely possible that whoever caused that damage could be the one behind this too."

"That seems a bit farfetched," Michael says, brow furrowed. "If not for Rebecca, what would both scenes have in common?"

"Possibly nothing," Lance replies. "Could very well be they picked a random house and threw it, hoping to overwhelm the small-town police force."

"Eh, still seems a little farfetched," I say. "But not impossible. Have you pulled anything off the library break-in yet?" I call out. They'd been there when we arrived, just finishing up their preliminary on the scene.

"Not yet. Haven't even had time to look." Sheriff Vick takes off his hat and runs a hand over his hair. "We'd just gotten back to the station when we got the call on this."

"Which could have bought whoever did it just enough time to disappear and put some distance between them and this town." Lance turns and leaves the house.

A soft meow comes from the bedroom, so I cross over to lift Aggie as he peeks around the corner. Glass crunches beneath my boots, making me glad the cat didn't try to run out here. Poor guy would have sliced his paws up.

"You scared, bud? You'll be all right." I carry him into

the bedroom and put him on the bed, noting an open wooden box full of letters.

Without perusing them, I close the door, leaving the cat safely inside for the time being.

"The library was destroyed?" Andie looks genuinely troubled by the news. Which makes sense, I suppose, given that Mrs. McGinley and Edna have been best friends since before she was born. She likely knows the woman nearly as well as she knew her grandmother.

"It was," the sheriff confirms.

"And you think it was Rebecca who did it?" she asks Lance.

"Possibly. But I don't think it was her who threw the brick through your window."

She mutters something under her breath. "I know what I saw."

"What you saw was a nondescript sedan driving by your house. You didn't see Rebecca throw it," the sheriff says.

"Given the distance the brick made it inside, I doubt it was her, too," I add, hoping to pull some of Andie's fury from the good sheriff." My bet is on a man. One who probably played baseball or football."

"A sportsman? That's who you've narrowed it down to? Wow. Your investigative skills are top-notch, Mr. Breeth. Seriously." She shifts her glare to the sheriff. "Find my mother. Otherwise, she's going to slip town before you can pin this on her. If she's even still here to begin with."

His cell goes off before he can respond, so he pulls it out. "Sheriff Vick. Okay. Thanks, Alex." He ends the call and slips it back into his pocket. "I called in your suspicion, and Deputy Lake just spotted your mother at the diner. Alex called to let me know she's been there all morning. Ever since you left," he points to Elijah.

Andie whirls on me. "You were with my mother at the diner?"

"I was eating at the diner and your mother sat at my booth."

She scoffs. "No wonder you pushed for her innocence. I guess congratulations are in order seeing as how you'll likely be husband number seven. Here's hoping this one sticks." She crosses her fingers and rolls her eyes as she pushes past me and into the house.

"She hates you."

I turn toward Lance. "Thanks for the update. I hadn't realized."

Sheriff Vick chuckles. "Get some pictures of the inside; then bag that brick," he tells his deputy. "You boys think it could be Rebecca Montgomery who trashed the library?"

"That or someone was looking for something," Lance says.

"I hadn't considered Rebecca. But the theory that someone was looking for something is one that crossed my mind too. Far too much damage to be vandalism in this town." He sighs. "I'll get working on prints and speak to Rebecca. Although I'm fairly certain it wasn't her."

"She could have hired someone. Then stayed at the diner as her own alibi," Michael says.

"This is true." He lifts his hat to run a hand through his hair again. "See you boys later. Call if you find anything."

"Will do."

As soon as he's out of earshot, Lance and Michael turn to me. Neither of them says a word, though their expressions reflect exactly what they're thinking.

"Yeah, yeah. I get it. In over my head. See you both later." I head up the walk and into the house. As I step inside, I silently pray, *Dear God. Please help me. This woman hates me, and I can't stand her. Please grant me the grace I need to deal with her. Amen.*

CHAPTER 8

Andie

The man just won't quit.

Here he is. Cleaning up glass shards, looking even more furious than I am. I guess it's a good thing he can't stand me either. A mutual distaste for each other is far better than him trying to make friends when it will never happen.

As I'm picking up the larger glass shards and sticking them into a bucket, a truck pulls up in front of the house, *Felix's Hardware* on the side in bold lettering. I can't help my smile. Felix was always a surrogate father to me. Even before Lilly and her mother came to town.

Dressed in jeans, work boots, and a green plaid button-down, Felix steps out of the truck and heads up the steps to the porch. I pull open the door with a grin.

"Look at what the cat drug in," I say.

He chuckles and pulls me in for a big hug. "I am trying not to be upset that you haven't come by to see me."

"I'm sorry. I've been a bit busy." Releasing him, I gesture to the mess.

He surveys it, anger on his aging face. Until he sees the man who just keeps turning up like a bad penny. "Elijah," he greets.

"Felix. Good to see you."

"You too. This is—" He removes his baseball cap and runs a hand through his graying hair. "I am so sorry this happened."

"Thanks. I'm sure the sheriff will get to the bottom of it." Since the evidence doesn't fit Rebecca as the one behind it, I've let it go...for now. She could have still hired someone, and even if they can't figure it out, I'm already planning what I'll say to my mother the next time I see her.

Especially since Gran's house and the library being targeted on the same day would have been one massive coincidence if Rebecca wasn't involved.

"Well, we'll get you fixed up in the meantime," Felix says. "Alex is headed over. He's got two sheets of plywood in the back of the truck. Once we get it measured for a new window, I'll get you boarded up. It will be dark in here but safe."

"You should stay at the B&B," Elijah says as he dumps a dustpan of glass into a bucket.

"I'm not leaving," I reply, not even bothering to look at him.

"It's clearly not safe here."

I turn toward him. "You do not get to dictate my life, Mr. Breeth. This was my gran's house, and I will be staying here until the day I sign the papers and transfer it to you."

He doesn't argue, just holds up his hands in surrender.

"I sense some tension." Felix laughs. "Funny since your gran always figured the two of you would hit it off if you ever met."

"I'm sorry, what?" How could she have thought we'd hit it off?

"Your gran used to joke about how the two of you would be perfect for each other. Both stubborn. Both extremely smart. Strong." He shakes his head. "Judging by this little exchange, she was either right on the money or far off."

"The latter," Elijah and I say at the same time.

"Right." Felix turns as a truck pulls into the drive. "There's Alex. I'll go get my measuring tape." He leaves quickly, practically going out through the wall like the Kool-Aid Man.

I turn toward Elijah. "You can leave now. I will deal with the rest."

He doesn't stop sweeping.

"Mr. Breeth—"

He throws the broom down, and I jump when it cracks against some of the glass still on the floor. "My name is Elijah."

"Excuse me?"

"Elijah. That's my name. *Not* Mr. Breeth."

"I don't see the need for us to be on a first-name basis." I cross my arms, pride digging its spiky heels right into my side.

"Well, I do. Because even though I can't understand how a woman as great as Edna managed to have a selfish granddaughter like you, the best thing we can do to honor her memory is call a cease-fire and at least *try* to get along until you've kicked the dust of this town off of your ridiculously fancy heels."

I look down at the basic tennis shoes I'm wearing. "No heels here."

His cheeks turn red, and I find myself enjoying the fact that I seem to be able to press his buttons. "You know what I mean."

"Sure I do. Fine. *Elijah.* Then tell me this. Why would a man like you take an interest in my gran?"

"Excuse me?" He appears to be genuinely taken aback by my question rather than offended.

"Why would a young, handsome man like you be interested in an eighty-seven-year-old woman?"

"Is that your way of telling me that you think I'm handsome?"

Now it's my turn to glare at him.

"Your gran reminded me of my own grandmother," he says. "She raised me after my parents died in a boating accident when I was a kid."

My negative feelings toward him soften just enough that I feel a pang of pity for his loss. "I'm sorry to hear that."

"She was a great person. And when I offered to help your gran carry her groceries one rainy afternoon, I decided that she probably needed help around here. She thought I could use a friend."

"So you were friends. That's it."

If he looked angry before, now he's downright furious. "Just what are you accusing me of, Andie?" he demands, moving in closer.

"I didn't think I was hiding it." Might as well dig my heels in. "Seducing an old woman to get an inheritance was a fairly obvious accusation."

Elijah steps even closer, cheeks red, eyes practically spitting fire. "I was in no way, shape, or form trying to seduce your grandmother. Sometimes people do things because they genuinely care for others. Not because they're hoping to get something out of it. Though I can understand how that is such a difficult concept for you to grasp."

His insult rolls right off me because, for the first time since we met, I no longer doubt his intentions. Do I like him? No. Obviously not. But Elijah Breeth is not the man I thought he was.

And he very clearly cared for my gran as much as she cared for him.

So, instead of arguing further, I take a step back and

offer him my hand. "Then here's to not wanting to smother you with a pillow every time we're around each other."

"A pillow is the best you got?" he asks, taking my hand and shaking it. I try to ignore the way my skin tingles at his touch.

"For now. But I'm creative. I can come up with something else if need be."

Elijah's anger dissipates, and he grins, a crooked smile that makes me feel things I'd rather not admit—not even to myself.

"Is it safe to come in?" Felix calls out.

Pulling my hand away, I call out, "Yes, you coward. We've officially called a cease-fire."

———

Dearest Andie,

It's been a month since you left, and I am still trying so hard to keep it together. The things being said about you around town are upsetting, but not nearly as infuriating as the knowledge that you were groomed by that man and I didn't even notice.

How did I not see it?

Were there signs I missed?

I am praying for you, child. Every single

day. Multiple times a day. We all are. No matter what happens, Hope Springs will always welcome you back.

In happier news, Carmen and I went to a flea market in Boston this past weekend and ended up with fourteen boxes of books for the library! Fourteen! Can you believe it? They barely fit in the back of her van!

She was so excited as she opened them. Like a kid on Christmas morning as she cataloged and shelved them. It makes me happy to see her happy.

Johnny is growing like a weed, and seeing him makes me long for the days when you were that little. So sweet and happy.

You loved to sing then.

Are you still singing?

Come home soon,

Gran

TEARS IN MY EYES, I SET THE LETTER ASIDE AND WIPE THEM away. I've been through thirty others so far. Thirty letters where my gran bares her heart to me on the page in a way I'm not sure I ever could. What did I do to deserve such love?

And why did it take her dying for me to realize it?

"I'm so sorry, Gran," I whisper and cradle my head in my hands. When the tears threaten to spill over, I push to my feet, scaring the cat, who was sleeping at the foot of the bed. "Sorry, Aggie. But I need food."

He settles down, so I start to slide the letters back under the bed, but the thought of leaving them here bothers me. Why? I'm not sure, but I know that I can't bring myself to leave these pieces of my gran behind. Even if I'm only going to be gone an hour or so.

With that in mind, I carry them outside and stick them in the back seat of my car before heading downtown.

Hope Diner hasn't changed even a little since the day I left. Well, aside from the owner. The elderly couple who'd opened and owned it sold it to Lilly's husband, Alex, when he got out of the service and came home looking for a life outside of the military.

But he didn't change a single thing about the décor, and for that, I'm grateful. It's like stepping back in time as I cross the threshold.

"Hey, Andie," Alex greets as I slide onto one of the red leather barstools at the counter.

"Hey. I don't suppose you make a good cheeseburger, do you?"

"I make a great cheeseburger," he replies. "Coke to go with it?"

"Tea, please."

"Coming on up." He taps the counter then heads into the kitchen.

A moment later, someone slides onto the barstool right next to mine.

"If it isn't Andie Montgomery."

Unease slips up my spine as I turn to face off with George's brother, Stanley. "Hi, Stanley."

He grins at me, the same charming smile his younger brother used to entice me in high school. "I didn't think I'd ever see you back here." The way he looks me up and down makes me feel slimy.

"My gran lives here."

"Lived, from what I understand."

I swallow hard, doing my best to ignore the anger creeping up my spine. *Jesus, help me, please.* "What do you want, Stanley?"

"I want to know why you thought you'd be welcome in this town after what you did to my brother."

"I didn't do anything to your brother."

"You seduced him, ruined his marriage, and sent him running from his home." His tone is low, and I glance around to see if anyone else is watching our exchange. Unfortunately, Alex is in the kitchen, and there's no one else in the diner.

The hairs on the back of my neck stand on end as he wraps a large hand around my upper arm. I try to move away, but he squeezes, and I'm instantly thrown back to being eighteen and sneaking over to his house where George had been staying.

There'd been one night in particular, when I'd been staying over and was half asleep on the pull-out couch. Someone climbed onto it with me, and I curled in closer, thinking it was George. Needless to say, it wasn't.

All rational thought leaves my head, and I'm struck near motionless.

"Maybe we should go have a conversation in private," Stanley says.

The bell dings overhead, but I barely hear it, thanks to the pounding in my ears.

"You're going to want to let her go if you want to keep breathing." The deep voice is not one I'd be particularly grateful to hear under any other circumstances.

"This isn't a conversation for you, Breeth. Andie and I are old friends. Aren't we?" That hand tightens.

Elijah. Safety. The idea hits me so fast that I don't even have time to argue with myself.

I shoot up off the stool, and Stanley falls backward. My arm is still in his grasp, and he starts to pull me down with him. But, thanks to Elijah's quick thinking, he's able to keep me upright as Stanley releases me the moment he hits the floor.

"That was assault!" he bellows. He gets up almost instantly and balls his hands into fists.

Alex rushes out of the kitchen, surveying the scene. His

cheeks redden, and he strides around the counter. "Get out of my diner, Stanley," he says.

"Me? I didn't do anything!" he yells. "She attacked me."

"You and I both know that's not true," Elijah all but growls. "But if you want to pin assault on someone, stick around. I'll take a few swings." He takes a step forward, but Alex holds up a hand.

"Get out, Stanley. I mean it."

"You're taking the side of the town home-wrecker and the new guy over me?"

"I am. Now get out before I call the sheriff."

"I'll be seeing you around, Andie." And with that, he storms out of the diner.

"Are you all right?" Elijah asks.

"I'm sorry, Andie. I didn't see him come in," Alex says.

"It's fine. I'm fine." But as the adrenaline wanes, I begin to shake. "I'm so hungry," I say with a half laugh that's meant to diffuse the tension but only seems to worry both men.

"Come on." Elijah guides me toward a booth at the back then sits me down in a seat before taking the side across from me. "Are you okay?"

"I'm—" I close my eyes and take a deep, steadying breath.

I am not eighteen.

I am not eighteen.

I am a grown woman with a successful business and

years of self-defense training. So how did Stanley manage to put me so far on edge that I'd forgotten all of that?

"I'm fine."

"He called you a home-wrecker."

"I don't want to talk about it."

"Okay." Elijah lets it go then pulls out his phone and fires off a quick text.

"You're not going to push?"

"Why would I? If you don't want to talk about it, you don't want to talk about it."

But I do, don't I? Is that what this heaviness is in my chest? This weight and desire to actually vocalize what nearly happened all those years ago. Gran trusted Elijah. Can I?

Safety.

That word pops back into my mind, and I get the overwhelming feeling that Elijah Breeth is a man to trust. Even if I don't particularly care for him. "I was involved with Stanley's brother, George. He was my history teacher, and after he left his wife, we—"

"How much older was he?"

"Twenty years."

Elijah shakes his head angrily, but he doesn't look surprised. "He groomed you."

"You already knew all of this."

"Is it that obvious?"

"Yes." Embarrassment heats my cheeks.

"Sorry. I found out after you got into town. But since he

was divorced before you ran off with him, I hadn't realized you might be blamed for ending the marriage."

"It was three months after the divorce was final, but people love to talk."

"Stanley blames you too?"

"Stanley is something else entirely." I close my eyes and take a deep, steadying breath. "When George and I started seeing each other, he was living on Stanley's pull-out couch. One night, I'd snuck out and was staying over. George had gotten up to go get a shower, and a few minutes later, Stanley got under the covers. I'd been half asleep, or I would have known right away. He made some moves on me, but George caught him, and he tried to play it off like it was a joke. But we both knew it wasn't."

I shake my head, trying to kick the memory out of my brain.

I don't even want to think about what would have happened if George hadn't returned. At that age, being around two older men like that, I wouldn't have had the courage to say no. And that thought terrifies me.

"So he's a pervert too. Good to know." Elijah growls the words, clearly furious. He glances towards the door, and I get the impression he's considering going after Stanley.

"I was there, and I was eighteen."

"You were still a child," he retorts.

"Not in the eyes of the law."

"In the eyes of a forty-one-year-old man and his

brother, you should have been." Frustration laces his tone. It's not judgment though, and for that, I'm grateful.

"Anyway. He caught me off guard, that's all. I'll be prepared next time."

Elijah doesn't respond, just nods.

"Here you go." Alex sets a glass of tea in front of me and then a coffee in front of Elijah. "Your burger is almost ready. Food, Elijah?"

"No, thanks. Eliza made some meatloaf last night, and I stole the leftovers from Lance's house. I need to eat the evidence before he shows up for work tomorrow."

Alex laughs, and I catch myself smiling.

"Is that a smile?" Elijah asks. "For me?"

"You can be funny when you're not being incredibly agitating."

He laughs. "Good to know."

I take a sip of my tea. "It's late for coffee, isn't it?"

"Not for me. I'm on monitor duty tonight, so I won't be sleeping."

"But you didn't sleep today."

"I grabbed an hour."

"That hardly seems like enough," I counter.

He shrugs. "It's the nature of the job."

I take another drink. "What exactly does Knight Security do all the way out here? I can't imagine you have a lot of systems installed here in Hope Springs."

"We don't," he replies. "We monitor some of the businesses and a few residentials. But most of our work is in

Boston. We have a few clients on an as-needed basis out of New York."

"What happens if an alarm goes off out there?"

"We contact the police. Depending on how bad it is, one or all of us will show up as soon as we can."

"So you're a private security firm in the small town of Hope Springs."

He nods. "We operate as bodyguards occasionally, though that's more Michael's wheelhouse."

"Not you?"

"I've handled a few clients, but since I'm better with a computer than people, I do best behind the scenes. Plus, bad hearing in one ear." He taps the side of his head.

"You seem to be pretty good with people. My gran liked you."

"That's because I brought her flower vases on Valentine's."

"Flower vases?"

"She liked to pick her own flowers and said she could bake anything better than what I could bring her dessert-wise. So, I always brought a vase."

My throat burns with emotion, so I take a drink. "She never told me that. What else did my gran like?"

"She enjoyed watching *Murder She Wrote* and *Bones* re-runs."

"She always liked to read too."

"Her eyesight was suffering more lately, so I'd read to her some nights."

I sit up in my seat. "Her eyesight was bad?"

"Not entirely gone," he replies. "But it was bad enough that reading anything would give her a bad migraine. She'd switched to audiobooks recently."

Guilt crashes down on my head like an anvil. My gran was nearly blind, and I didn't know? How did my best friend growing up—the woman who raised me—become such a stranger?

"Did she go to the doctor for her heart problems?"

"*That* I don't know. She didn't tell me she was having problems. It wasn't until I got the call that she'd…" He looks away and takes a drink of coffee. His grief is a match for mine, bringing another wave of guilt down on top of me for ever believing this man was out to take advantage of my gran.

Even my mother, expert actress that she is, isn't this good.

Elijah loved Gran. Just as she loved him. And I've treated him like crap from the moment we met. All because I was jealous of the relationship they had.

"Anyway. That was the first I'd heard of any heart problems."

Alex returns and slides the burger in front of me. My mouth waters as I take in the crisp fries and juicy patty. "This looks delicious."

"I told you. I make a great cheeseburger." With a smile, he heads back for the kitchen as a group of teens strolls into the diner.

"Can I ask you a question?" Elijah says. "A genuine, no judgment question."

"Sure." I take a bite off of a fry and nearly groan. So. Incredible.

"Why didn't you come back and visit? Why stay away for as long as you did?"

My stomach churns as I ponder his question. It's an easy answer but not a flattering one. "Fear. I made a mistake. A big one. And it cost my gran all of her savings account."

"But you started your business. That's why she gave it to you."

"I lost all of her money," I confess. I've never spoken those words out loud. Not to anyone. So why do I feel so comfortable talking about it now? "I bought George a car. Sent him on a few big vacations, all while he covered the rent on our apartment. Then, the moment he met someone younger than I was, he left, saddling me with a mountain of credit card debt he took out in my name. I lost the apartment, and since I couldn't afford another, I was homeless for a year."

"What?"

"Glamorous, right?"

"Andie—"

"I brought it upon myself." I want him to understand that I'm not trying to play the blame game, nor am I looking for sympathy. What are those infamous words? It is what it is. It happened. I moved on.

"I made a mistake, and because I wasn't sure how to tell my gran that I'd lost everything, I wanted to wait until I'd built something. So, I worked practically nonstop as I finished school, did whatever I needed to in order to find a safe place to sleep, and then, before I knew it, so much time had passed that I didn't have the guts to come back here. What would it look like? Hope Springs' biggest stain returning with her tail tucked between her legs?"

"I could never picture you returning anywhere with your tail tucked between your legs."

I laugh. "Believe me, Elijah, it was a thought."

"She would have understood."

"It wasn't just the money though." I push the burger back and rest my hands on the table. "I spent years running from this town. From Gran. From God. Years trying to hide because the stain of my mistakes was like acid against my skin."

"But you are forgiven for your mistakes," he tells me. "By God and by your gran."

"Sometimes, I'm not so sure."

His phone rings, so he pulls it out of his pocket and presses it to his ear. The volume is low enough that I can't make out the voice on the other side though, from Elijah's expression, whatever is happening is not good.

"Be right there." He hangs up.

"Everything okay?"

"That was Felix. He was driving over to drop off some

tools for tomorrow and noticed the front door of your gran's house kicked in."

I can all but feel the blood drain from my face. "Her house was broken into?"

"Yes."

Of all the things that could have been stolen, there's only one that worries me. "Aggie."

CHAPTER 9

Elijah

Every surface in Edna's once pristine house has been turned upside down. The table I've eaten countless meals at is flipped over, the legs of her chairs splintered. Her dresser drawers were removed, their contents thrown around the bedroom.

Clothes from the closet were yanked from their hangers, fabric torn, and every single dish in the kitchen was shattered. Including the vases I'd brought her every year since we met.

Even the picture windows overlooking her beautiful garden have been shattered. And the damage doesn't stop inside the house.

The plants she'd once tenderly cared for have been ripped from the ground, every single one of them uprooted.

The cat managed to hide somewhere, only coming out once he heard Andie's panicked calls. And as she cradles the fluffy cat against her chest, every belief I'd ever had about her vanishes. She's nothing like who I thought she was.

The walls are there, shielding her from feeling. But the woman behind them is as kind as Edna described. As caring. Though she tries really, really hard to hide it.

Tears shimmer in her eyes, but they do not fall as she surveys the damage.

Sheriff Vick moves through the house, carefully documenting every inch of the place. "They didn't miss a single item," he says as he shoves the camera into his pocket. "It's all been destroyed. Pictures on the walls, broken, mirrors shattered." He looks around, expression furious. "This feels personal."

"Are you liking Rebecca for it now?" Andie demands. "How could it get more personal than your mother giving half of her house to your daughter and the other half to a man she only met a few years ago? No offense," she adds to me.

"None taken." But even as I also recognize that Rebecca is most likely the culprit of this temper tantrum, it's a lot of damage to have been carried out by one person in the short amount of time Andie was gone. "Whoever did this was watching the house." I bend down and lift a small porcelain unicorn from the floor then set it carefully on the counter. It might just be the lone survivor from her collection. "They knew when you left. Probably came in as soon as you were out of sight."

She pales. "What if I'd doubled back?"

The mere thought of what could have happened to her puts a ton of gravel in my gut. "It's good you didn't." Could she truly have been gone that quickly? If she'd walked in on whoever did this, would they have killed her?

"Maybe not. I could have scared off whoever did this." Andie shakes her head. "All of her stuff. Every treasured possession…" She looks toward the front door.

"What is it?"

"I just. I had this feeling that I needed to take the box of letters she left me out of the house." She swallows hard and holds the cat closer. "I guess it's a good thing I listened."

"Sounds to me like God was giving you a heads-up," Sheriff Vick says as he withdraws his notepad and jots down a few things. "We dusted for prints, but I'd be willing to bet the ones we find belong to those closest to Edna. My guess is whoever did this likely used gloves."

"I'm going to install a camera," I tell him. "Link it to our server so I can watch who comes and goes. If that's okay with you," I add, looking at Andie.

She nods.

"You'll send over any footage?" the sheriff asks.

"Of course." Even though we're not law enforcement, the sheriff and Knight Security have a mutual respect. A working relationship that benefits the both of us. Especially when the tech we possess outperforms that of the local law enforcement.

"And I'll keep you updated if I have any hits on prints

that don't match the list you gave me," he says, slipping the notepad back into his pocket. "We'll catch who did this—you have my word."

"Thank you," Andie says, her tone clipped. She's angry that they won't just arrest Rebecca. And to be honest, while the rational side of me understands that there's a process, the other part of me wants that woman behind bars if only for Andie's safety.

"Do you need a place to stay?" the sheriff asks.

She looks at him like he grew a second head. "Excuse me?"

"You can't stay here," I tell her.

"Why not?"

"It was broken into. Ransacked. There are no windows."

"Felix is already coming out to board up the newly broken ones."

"Andie—"

"I won't be chased out of my gran's house," she all but growls. "This is my home. I grew up here."

"I know that." I move in a bit closer, softening my tone. I can't be annoyed with her because, if I were in her position, I'd probably feel the exact same way she does. "And once the windows are replaced, we will install a security system. But right now, it's not secure. Whoever is doing this—"

"Rebecca *is* doing this," she interrupts.

"Fine. But until we have proof that it's her, we need to play it safe. You can stay at the lighthouse."

"Excuse me?" Her brow furrows. "The lighthouse?"

"It's Knight Security's headquarters, but there's an apartment upstairs. Was recently renovated." I leave out the fact that it's also where I'm living because, right now, that doesn't matter. I'll pack a bag and move downstairs. Or, if she's not comfortable with that, I'll stay in Lance's guest room.

Right now, priority one is getting Andie somewhere safe.

"All right. But only if I can bring Aggie."

"Of course. I'll get his litter box and food packed up." Leaving her to talk with the sheriff, I make my way into the destroyed laundry room. Whoever did it dumped the litter box all over the floor, so I pick up the empty plastic box and slide it into a trash bag. Since I don't see any spare litter, I make a mental note to grab some on the way to the lighthouse.

My stomach churns with anger as I move through the wreckage of what was once a sort of second home for me. All the while, I consider how Edna would have handled having every single one of her possessions destroyed.

It would have infuriated her.

She wouldn't have broken though. No, Edna was as strong as they come, and her faith was to be admired. She would have stood strong through all of this, probably using it as an excuse to re-plant her entire garden. Honestly, she'd probably have prayed for those who broke in then hummed through the whole cleaning process.

A smile plays at the corners of my lips as I remember the woman I admired.

And then, one memory pops into my head.

"Please watch over her, Elijah. She's not as tough as she seems. She needs someone to watch out for her. You will, won't you?"

Edna made me promise to protect Andie. She'd been adamant about it. I'd brushed it off then, thinking it was just the ramblings of a woman on her deathbed. But what if it was more?

What did she know that we don't?

———

WITH A BAG OF FRESH LITTER IN HAND, I STEP INTO THE lighthouse, Andie and Aggie behind me. "The apartment is just up here." I start up the iron staircase that spirals to the apartment that I've been renting from Eliza for the last six months since she and Lance said their *I-do*s.

I take a minute to set up the litter box beneath the vanity sink then go back to the bedroom. Andie is standing on the porch overlooking the ocean while Aggie has already made my bed his home. Edna used to joke that the cat was bulletproof. He wasn't bothered by anything.

Now, I can safely say I agree with her.

I step onto the balcony beside Andie, trying my best to

ignore the wave of attraction at the sight of her standing here, the breeze ruffling her short, dark hair. She's a gorgeous woman—I'd be a liar if I didn't admit that.

But she's not for me.

Honestly, with my baggage? I'm not sure anyone is.

The sun is sinking below the horizon, casting the ocean in gorgeous shades of gold.

"This is a stunning view," she says.

"Thanks. I like it."

"How long have you been officing out of here?"

"We rented it from Lance's now-wife after they got married and moved in together. So, about six months."

"Eliza?"

I nod.

"I met her outside the church. She seems nice."

"She's great. Took her a while to warm up to us too." I make the joke then instantly want to kick myself.

Andie laughs. "Well, even if I do warm up, I have no intention of marrying any of you. No offense."

I grin back at her. "None taken. No one is available for you, anyway."

She arches a brow. "I didn't realize you had a significant other."

I laugh awkwardly. "Oh, I don't. But I'm not in a place where I can have a relationship. Lance is married as you know. And Michael is, well, it's complicated."

"Reyna," she says. "I grew up here, remember?"

"Fair point. Though they're not together."

"No. From what I hear, he royally messed things up."

"Understatement." I lean against the railing and inhale the scent of the salty sea air. It's so peaceful, being out here, high above the water as it crashes against the rocky cliff the lighthouse sits on.

"This place. It's lovely." She turns and surveys the bedroom. "Though that looks rather lived in."

"It's my apartment," I admit.

"You can't let me use your apartment."

"Sure I can. I won't be sleeping tonight anyway, remember?"

"Ahh, yes. You're on monitor duty."

"I'll be downstairs if you're comfortable with that. Otherwise, I can lock up and monitor the systems from Lance's place."

"Nah. It's okay. I'm fairly certain you're not a serial killer by now." The joke falls flat, given our current circumstances. "That was in bad taste."

I chuckle. "Maybe a little."

Her phone dings, and she reaches into her pocket. "My assistant," she tells me. "I booked her a room at the B&B since she's on her way out here in the morning. I'd told her about the state of my gran's house, but she insisted on coming out to help."

"Nice of her."

"She's a hard worker." But she doesn't elaborate further. "I cannot believe this is all happening. I barely had the chance to bury Gran, and now everything she ever owned…"

Without thinking, I reach over and cover her hand with mine. It's smaller than mine and warm.

So warm.

I fight the urge to curl my fingers around hers. "We'll get this figured out. You're not in it alone."

Her gaze focuses on our hands before lifting to mine. I'm momentarily captivated by her emerald eyes, frozen in place so that, even though I know I *should* remove my hand and pull away, I can't.

She's drawing me in like the moon attracts the tide.

A door slams, and Andie jumps.

"Yo! Elijah! You here?"

I pull my hand away as the moment is broken by Michael's terrible timing—as always. "I'll go deal with him and grab your suitcase. Feel free to get settled. There are clean sheets in the closet, and I'll come change them out in just a few." Before I can ramble anymore, I slip from the room and head down the stairs.

Michael is in the kitchen, prepping a cup of coffee. "Who's moving in?" he asks, gesturing to the suitcase.

"Andie," I say. "Only temporarily," I add when he studies me with an arched brow. "Edna's house was ransacked."

His humor vanishes, and the mask of a soldier slips into place. "Any idea who did it?"

"Not yet. But she's staying here until Felix can get the

windows replaced and we can get a system installed. I'm getting a security monitor up today. I want to know who is approaching the house."

"What can I do to help?"

"You're doing it." I take the coffee from him before he can protest and drink it.

He mutters something under his breath then preps another cup. "How is Andie holding up?"

"Surprisingly well."

"Not overly surprising though. She's Edna's granddaughter, and that woman was as strong as they come."

"Fair."

"I can't believe someone ransacked her house."

"Destroyed her garden too," I add. "Ripped up all the plants."

His gaze hardens. "So this is personal."

"That's certainly what it's looking like."

"You think Rebecca had anything to do with it?"

I glance out the front window at the darkening sky. "I don't think she's innocent," I say. "But what really worries me is that I don't think she's doing it alone."

CHAPTER 10

Andie

Sleep completely eludes me.

As I lie here, staring up at the ceiling fan while it whirrs above my head, all I can do is picture some faceless intruder destroying my gran's precious house. Shattering her collectibles and ripping her clothing from the closet.

The dresses she chose for church.

The clothes she'd gardened in.

Everything in it was a piece of her. And now, it feels like the memories surrounding my time there have been tainted.

I know what she'd say. *"Andie, they're just things. Things don't matter."* But they *did* matter. Because they were pieces of her.

The clock beside me reads two thirty. With a frustrated huff, I toss the thick comforter off then get an angry glare from the cat, who seems to have absolutely no issue falling asleep in a new place.

"Sorry," I mutter then push to my feet and grab the long cardigan I'd draped over the edge of the bed. Even though I changed the sheets, I can still smell Elijah on me as I move about the room. Every inch of this place smells like his cologne, and just breathing it in takes me back to the balcony.

To the feel of his hand on mine. The look of intense understanding in his eyes.

Gran, what in the world were you thinking, putting that house in both of our names? Then again, after what Felix said about her believing Elijah and I would be great together, I know exactly what was on that woman's mind. She loved playing matchmaker. So much so that it seems she was determined to do it even from the grave.

How could she have known that I'm too broken to risk another chance at heartbreak?

I step forward and run my fingers over the top of the wooden box I'd set on Elijah's dresser. I haven't had the heart to read her words since that last letter, the *"Are you still singing?"* haunting me even now.

How many times did I break that poor woman's heart? How many times did she long for me to come home, but I'd been too buried in my own past to realize just how much I needed her?

I start to open the box but change my mind at the last minute. Turning toward the door, I gently pull it open and head down the stairs. The spiral staircase comes around the corner, and I freeze in place, stunned by the sight below me.

Elijah, shirtless and coated in a thin layer of sweat, is doing push-ups in the middle of the floor. He spreads his legs farther apart and puts one arm behind his back, then goes down to the floor and comes back up.

He makes the movements look effortless, the only proof that they're not in the way his muscles coil and retract.

Oh.

My.

The man is *built*. Not in a "he spends his life at the gym" kind of way. But in the "has been steadily training for war" type of way. Every inch of his back is toned, as are his legs from what I can see.

My mouth goes dry, desire churning in my gut. *Nope. Shove it down, Andie. The man is good to look at. That's all.*

He jumps up then turns and nearly leaps out of his own skin when he sees me standing there. "Andie, sorry, I didn't hear you. Did I wake you up?"

I stare at his bare, sculpted chest. It's covered in scars— one of which runs the complete length of his abdomen and up to just under his armpit.

When he catches me staring, he rushes over and retrieves a white t-shirt to tug over his head.

It's almost a crime for him to cover it up.

"No. You didn't wake me." I wrap the cardigan more

tightly around myself and try to ignore the desire burning in my belly as he crosses into the little kitchen and withdraws a bottle of water from the fridge.

"Want one?"

"I'll take coffee if you have some."

"I do." He takes a drink then heads over toward the coffee machine. As he preps, I look at the computer screen. A bunch of red and green dots are lined up in rows on the left while names are positioned directly to the right.

"Is this what you watch all night?"

"I mainly listen," he says. "And look for any possible outages."

"Outages?"

The coffee begins brewing, so Elijah leaves the kitchen and comes to stand next to me. "The green are systems that are not armed. The red dots signify systems that are armed and ready. If there are any not working, they'll show up as yellow."

"What causes a system to not work?"

"Power outages mostly. Though we've had a handful over the years that have been cut by people trying to get inside."

"They cut the lines?"

He nods. "We have solar backups on nearly every system we install. Most of them aren't high powered enough to run it for long, but it will catch whoever thinks cutting the power will help them bypass the alert."

"So you just work out while you monitor."

"Not typically," he replies. "But I needed the release tonight."

"And what could you possibly have to be stressed about, Mr. Breeth?" I ask, mocking sweetness lacing my tone.

"More than you probably realize, Miss Montgomery."

Our gazes lock, and tension snaps in the air between us. There's something here, something that keeps me rooted where I stand despite the coffee beeping to let us know it's finished brewing.

His eyes—a light hazel—are breathtaking in their intensity. I've never met a man who wears his feelings quite so plainly. When he's angry, his gaze reflects it. Worried? Small lines appear at the corners of his eyes.

And right now—if I'm not mistaken—it's attraction I see written on his face.

Attraction that I absolutely feel in return.

Clearing my throat, I force myself to sever the connection. We were brought together by the sudden passing of my gran. And once we catch Rebecca sabotaging my house and fully transfer ownership to him, we will never see each other again.

"Let me grab your coffee." Elijah puts distance between us and slips into the kitchen. He pours a mug then glances over his shoulder. "Cream? Sugar?"

"Just black, please."

"Here you go."

"Thanks."

"Have you always drunk your coffee black?"

"No. I used to use—"

"Hazelnut creamer?" he interrupts.

I cock my head to the side to study him curiously. "Gran said you were great with background checks—or rather, cyberstalking as I call it—but that's next level, Mr. Breeth."

He chuckles. "That one is actually Edna. She told me the two of you used to go through creamer like it was water."

I smile, the memory of sitting with her before school, enjoying a mug that was more cream than coffee one of my favorites. "That we did. I remember—"

The monitor begins flashing as a low beeping fills my ears.

Elijah slips into business mode like most men slip into jeans. Effortlessly and without thought. He slides into his chair and rapidly types something onto the keyboard.

Seconds later, a screen pops up on his monitor—black and white camera footage of the back of gran's house. A person stands just outside the back door. Black pants, a black hoodie, face hidden from view.

The figure tilts their face up to the camera…and waves.

I scream.

———

MY HEART IS STILL POUNDING A COUPLE OF HOURS LATER while I sit in the front seat of my grandfather's old truck as Elijah talks to Sheriff Vick in front of my gran's house. It's five in the morning, and the entire property has been swept from top to bottom.

The police searched every inch of the place, along with Elijah and his boss, Lance. But no one has told me anything. Elijah made me wait here, and after seeing what I did in reaction to the monitor, I couldn't even make myself argue.

I've always prided myself on being strong. On rolling with the punches and maintaining my calm even when things get stressful. But tonight, I lost it.

All because I may have been able to outrun this town, but the nightmares still haunt me.

Elijah pulls the passenger side door open, his face grim.

Something is seriously wrong. I know it even before he says anything. "What is it?"

He hesitates, clearly not wanting to tell me whatever it is he has to say.

"Out with it. Did they break something else? Leave a creepy note? What is it?"

Elijah runs a hand over the back of his neck and sighs. "It's your mother."

Fury sings in my veins as I get out of the car and shove past him. "I knew it was her. I told you. I—" He doesn't follow, so I turn to look at him. "What is it? Tell me!"

"She's dead, Andie. We found her body behind a shrub in the backyard."

"Dead?" I choke on the word and stumble forward. Elijah manages to catch me before I could fall though, righting me and helping me lean against the car. "No. It was her this whole time. What happened? Did she overdose?"

He chews on his bottom lip for a moment. "She was killed. We don't know who yet. But—"

"The man on the screen. It had to be him."

"Andie."

"I want to see her." I shove past him and rush through the house. Lance steps in my path and holds up both hands.

"Miss Montgomery."

"I want to see Rebecca," I say. "It's my right. She's my —" I can't even get the word out. Guilt over my initial anger mixes with shock and disbelief. We've never been close. Truth is I can't stand the woman. But dead? Murdered?

"Andie, I'm not so sure that's a good idea," Sheriff Vick says as he removes his hat.

"That's not for you to decide, right? I get to see her."

"She is dead, Andie."

I turn slowly, facing Elijah. "I want to see her."

He exchanges looks with both Lance and the sheriff before reluctantly nodding and crossing over to take my arm. Floodlights illuminate the garden as crime scene investigators comb over the space. They check the flower beds, their blue jumpsuits crisp and clean.

Everything feels so surreal.

Like a twisted nightmare I can't wake up from.

Elijah guides me around the bushes and nods to a man kneeling beside a sheet-draped body.

The man slowly pulls the sheet down.

The dead never look like themselves. It's something I'd once thought was weird, but after attending my grandfather's open-casket funeral, Gran explained to me it's because our bodies are just shells. It's our souls that give us what those shells radiate.

My mother's eyes are wide open, her skin pale. Eyeliner is smeared down the sides of her face, and a red ring circles her throat.

Dead.

"How was she killed?" Tears threaten to fall now, but I shove them back down. I will not cry for her.

She abandoned me.

She scarred me.

She abused my gran.

So I will *not cry.*

"It looks like she was strangled," the man who'd removed the sheet says as he covers her again.

I look at Elijah. "How long has she been here?"

"It couldn't be more than a few hours," he replies. "We swept the place—back here included—when we put up the cameras."

"I'm going to guess she was killed somewhere else then brought here," Lance says.

"I agree," Sheriff Vick adds.

I hadn't even seen them approach, but they stand just behind me, both men wearing combined looks of pity when I face them.

My heart hammers in my chest. "So the guy in the mask did it. Okay. She probably made someone angry. It's not like she lived the best life. Excuse me." I walk around them and head straight for my gran's bedroom, somehow managing to move on legs that feel like jelly. How am I still standing?

People around me move like blurs, all while I do my best to keep my breathing steady. But I make it inside, closing the door and sliding down the wall beside it until I'm sitting on her carpet.

The walls begin to close in as images of that man in a ski mask surround me. I'm back in the house.

Back with *him*.

He jumps out. I scream. He laughs. Over and over again. A twisted, tormented game.

Suddenly, Elijah is kneeling directly in front of me, his hands on top of my knees. I didn't hear him come in.

"Breathe, Andie."

"I—" I suck in a breath as the edges of my vision blur. My chest feels heavy like a thousand bricks are crushing down on me.

"Breathe," he commands again. "God, please help her,"

he says aloud. "Please help Andie be strong. Help her find her breath." It's the prayer that brings me back.

"You prayed for me," I manage as I suck in another breath.

"You weren't doing it for yourself." He reaches up and brushes the hair from my face. "Better?"

"She's gone." It feels so surreal to say it out loud. To speak the words. Like I'm someone else, saying it about someone else. "This whole time, I thought it was her behind the damage. Maybe it was. Maybe she just made someone mad. But she's dead now, Elijah. My mother is—"

"Andie." He cups my face, thumbs stroking my cheeks. His touch is soft, though he has the calloused palms of someone who works with their hands. "Breathe." He pulls me in and rests his forehead to mine, and prays again, "Dear God, please help us through this. Please give us the strength, Lord, to find out who is behind this. Please give Andie Your peace. Lord, please remain beside her as she grieves. Amen."

I haven't prayed in years. Haven't asked God for anything.

But hearing Elijah praying on my behalf, asking for help, strengthens me just enough that I catch my breath. Even if I don't feel worthy of the love that I was taught our Creator has for me, I can appreciate Elijah's kindness. "Thank you."

"You're welcome." He releases my face, and the

moment his hands leave my skin, I long for his touch again. "Better?"

"Yes. I can get up now."

He stands and pulls me to my feet.

The moment we're on our feet, there's a knock at the door. Elijah looks back at it and says, "Come in."

Lance pushes it open. "You'd better come look at this."

CHAPTER 11

Elijah

There aren't many moments in my life where I've felt helpless.

Losing my parents was a big one, but I'd been a child then. Young enough that I didn't have any understanding of what it meant to not have Mom caring for me or Dad ready to play ball in the backyard.

When my grandmother died, it had been a shock, but she'd been struggling with her health for years, so it was an expected loss even if it did rip my heart out.

The day I nearly died alongside Michael and Lance was the first time I remember feeling absolutely and completely helpless. Bleeding to death as the men around me writhed in pain, the shrapnel burrowing deeper into my body with every single movement. The endless ringing in my ears. I'd been helpless and terrified.

Much like I am now. Only, this time, it's a different type of fear. And it's mixed with a whole lot of anger.

I'm unable to tear my gaze from the scene before me. A picture of Andie wearing a dark green, off-the-shoulder dress that probably cost more than my car has been daggered to the trunk of a tree in Edna's backyard.

The dagger is at the top of the photo, though whoever left it there ensured we knew exactly what the message meant. Because directly beneath it is another letter. One that details just what will happen if this psycho gets his hands on Andie.

He plans to do to her what he did to her mother.

What he will do to everyone she cares about because— according to him—old debts need to be paid.

My first thought was George's brother. Who better to carry out an act of revenge than the man who assaulted Andie in the diner? The way he'd grabbed her… I stifle a growl as I turn away from the image.

"You can bag it," I say to the deputy then nod to the sheriff. "I'm going to get Andie back to the office," I tell Lance, keeping my voice low just in case someone might be lurking somewhere they can hear me.

"Michael is there. Send him over. We need to move the camera, and I want to get another one somewhere a bit less obvious."

"You think whoever did this is going to come back?"

"I'm counting on it," he replies then glances over his shoulder.

Andie is standing on the back porch, arms wrapped around herself, emerald eyes wide and full of emotion. When we first met, I recall how stone-faced she'd been. How completely and utterly emotionless and almost robotic she'd seemed. However, right now, she looks every bit a terrified woman.

And it burns me up from the inside that I can't help her. That she's suffered yet another loss on the heels of losing her gran. Even if she and Rebecca hadn't been close, the woman was her mother.

"Find out who might have anything against her."

"You don't think it's someone Rebecca was involved with?"

"It's more likely," Lance replies. "But we need to cover all of our bases."

"Understood."

With one final nod, I leave Lance and cross toward Andie. He's right. We need to investigate anyone in Andie's background who might have motive and means, but the idea of pressuring her further makes me sick to my stomach.

"We need to get going. Is there anything you want to grab before we go?"

She shakes her head, so I guide her through the damaged house and out onto the street. It's still early, so the sun hasn't begun to rise just yet. As we move through the dark, I keep watch, one hand at my lower back, ready to draw my weapon at the first sign of trouble.

Thankfully, there is none, and we make it into the truck without incident.

The drive back to the lighthouse is silent, and by the time we're pulling into the drive, Michael is already standing on the porch, the door behind him cracked open. Aggie is in his arms, the fluffy cat enjoying scratches from the former Army Ranger.

"I'm sorry, Andie," he says as we approach.

"Thanks." She scoops Aggie from his arms and heads inside, taking the stairs slowly.

"She looks messed up."

"Rebecca was her mom. Regardless of how she felt, the woman gave birth to her."

"Fair enough. You two need anything?"

"No. Any issues with the systems?"

"Nope. I ran the footage of the guy outside Edna's house through the database, and nothing popped. His face was covered, so I wasn't sure it would, but I wanted to give it a try anyway."

"Thanks, man. Lance wants you on-scene."

"Sounds good. I'll head out now. Sure you're good?"

"Yeah. I need to see what info I can get from Andie."

A door above me opens, and I look up as Andie slips out onto the porch. She closes her eyes and tips her face up to the sky, the image of her stealing my breath.

"Yeah, you go see what's up with Andie," Michael quips, keeping his voice low. "I'll be back in a few to take over so you can get some sleep."

As he leaves, I continue standing exactly where I am, staring up at a woman who leaves me completely and utterly breathless in every possible way.

———

AFTER MAKING TWO CUPS OF CHAMOMILE TEA, MY GO-TO for the end of a long day—or, in this case, night—I head upstairs. The bedroom door is open, so I don't knock, just peek inside. Andie is seated on the balcony in one of the two small patio chairs that fit out there.

"I brought you some tea." I offer her a mug, handle first. She takes it, so I sit down in the chair beside her. "I know you don't really want to talk, but I need to know—"

"If anyone I know is capable of something like this?"

"Yes," I reply.

"I've seen plenty of crime shows, Mr. Breeth. I know how this goes." The way she says it tells me her shields are back in place. That cool façade she'd had when we first met has returned, and even as I feel pity for what she's going through, it irritates me.

"Great. Then I need a list of anyone who would have something to gain from hurting you like this."

"Already made it." She offers me her phone, and I scan the list she's typed out in her notes app.

"You made that quickly."

"I don't have many enemies, but when I make them, they stick." She stares out at the lightening sky. Rays of gold sneak out from behind the ocean, casting the world in a colorful glow.

"George isn't on here." She looks up at me, possibly annoyed that I brought him up. "Neither is his brother."

"Why would they be on there?" she asks.

"Because they have every motive to hurt you."

"George stands to gain nothing from hurting me. And neither does his brother."

"Andie—"

"No," she replies. "George left *me*. Years ago. He's getting remarried and has absolutely no reason to want to cause me any pain. And as for his brother—Stanley is a jerk. Always has been. But he won't gain anything from it either, and I doubt he'd risk his family just to get back at me."

"We still need to look into them."

She closes her eyes and leans her head back against the chair. "If you start digging into my past, you're going to uncover far more than I want to face." Exhaustion weighs down her tone.

"I'm sorry, Andie. I really am. But this isn't even just a matter of someone trashing your gran's house anymore. Someone—" I stop talking, sensing that a reminder is not something she needs.

"Was murdered. I get it. You can say it." She takes a sip of her tea. "Fine. Feel free to dig into whatever you want. I've given you a list of anyone who has ever made a threat against me, and when my assistant gets here, she can get you the letters I've been sent over the years. Though I'm not sure what good that will do since no one knew I was coming to Hope Springs."

"Edna's death is public record if anyone looks hard enough. The obituary might only have been printed in this county, but you were named. It's entirely possible someone is using her death to get to you now that they're here. Whoever killed Rebecca could have been waiting at the house for you and caught her trying to get in."

Andie's face pales. "I hadn't considered that."

"It's my job to consider all possibilities. So I am adding George and his brother to this list, and I will be digging until I find something to bring to the surface."

As I stand, Andie clears her throat.

"Then there's something you need to know, Elijah."

Slowly, I retake my seat, settling back and taking a sip from my tea. I wait because I sense that whatever she's trying to say is a battle to get out.

"My gran took me in when my father left, and my mom abandoned me." She looks down at her mug then back up. "I was young, and while I never had a great relationship with either of my parents, losing them hurt—bad. Having my mother blame me for all of her pain left a mark. I'd wanted nothing more than to make her proud, so when she came back and told my gran she was ready for me to come live with her again, I'd been beside myself excited."

"I didn't realize you went to live with her again."

She smiles, but it's hollow. "It wasn't for long. A

month, maybe. And it's not a time my gran or I ever talked about because, anytime she brought it up, I shut the conversation down."

I fall silent again, anger churning in my gut for the pain present on Andie's beautiful face. "Anyway, neither Gran nor I knew my mother had gotten remarried in the time she'd been away, so when I showed up at the trailer she was living in and a man was there, I'd first thought he was my dad. His back was turned, and I remember being so excited, thinking they'd gotten back together again and that his leaving might not have been my fault. Without thinking, I ran to him and wrapped both arms around his waist. The man wasn't my father, and he turned, ripped me off of him, and threw me off to the side. My mom had been furious with me because he was angry that I'd had the disrespect to touch him."

Because I'm genuinely worried I'll shatter my mug, I set it to the side and clench my hands into fists in my lap.

"When he saw how scared I was, he laughed. And after that day, he made it his mission—every single day for that month—to terrify me to the point I'd wet myself."

"Andie—"

"I don't want your pity, Elijah." She holds up her hand. "I moved on. It's in the past. And the only reason I'm telling you this is because his scaring preference of choice was jumping out at me while wearing a skull mask nearly identical to the one that man had on."

I pull out my own phone and open the note app. "What is his name?"

"Troy Hanover. But it's not him."

"How do you know? It could—"

"I know it's not him," she says, leveling her gaze on me, "because I killed him."

CHAPTER 12

Andie

S peaking the words out loud makes everything feel
so real.

I've never told anyone about what happened
that day I ran away to my gran's house for the final time.
I've never spoken the truth, and any time Gran tried to fish
for more information, I shut it down. I don't think she ever
knew there was a man there to begin with.

So when Elijah slowly puts his phone down and fully
faces me, I'm not entirely sure what's going to happen.

"What do you mean you killed him?"

"I got so tired of him scaring me that I did the same to
him. Except, when I did it, he fell over and died. Right
there on the floor of the trailer we were living in. I put on
his stupid skull mask and hid around the corner, then
jumped out at him right as he went to stumble toward the
couch."

"He died."

"Yes. He had a heart attack. But no one ever found out it was me who gave it to him." I stare down at my mug, wondering just how bad this makes me look in Elijah's eyes.

"So you've been blaming yourself for killing this man all these years?"

I look up at him, completely surprised to see there is no judgment in his gaze. "If I hadn't scared him, he might not have had a heart attack."

"You don't know that. What did your mother do?"

"I have no clue. When I realized what happened, I grabbed what little stuff I had and ran back to Gran's house."

"Did Edna ever ask? Did you tell her?"

"No. She asked why I left, but I told her that I just didn't want to live there anymore. I'm sure she had her suspicions as to why, but I doubt her only granddaughter murdering a man was one of them."

"You didn't murder him." Elijah pushes up from his chair and grips the railing. Jaw tight, he stares out over the ocean as a light breeze toys with the strands of his brown hair. I can sense the anger radiating off of him, but where every other man I've ever known would have likely laughed at me or been horrified by my bitter admission, Elijah is the picture of control.

"You were a child defending herself."

"I killed a man and never reported it. I left him dead on the floor."

"That doesn't make it murder."

I shake my head. This secret is a weight I've carried for far too long, and saying it out loud feels an awful lot like letting it go—even if I know I never will be able to fully release the guilt.

"I may not have used a weapon, Elijah, but I'm the reason he's dead."

"You've been shouldering the weight of this for a long time, Andie. Could you have called for help? Sure. But the bottom line is that you were a tormented child who was afraid. You can't expect to react to certain situations as an adult would have."

But even as he speaks words I know to be true, a thought creeps into my head that has haunted me. I'm the reason a man is dead. I killed him. That makes me a murderer, regardless of the circumstances surrounding the incident.

"You need to pray," he tells me.

"Pray?" I nearly laugh. "That's your answer to me telling you I killed someone?"

"You need to talk to God, Andie. He's the only one who is going to be able to help you with what you're battling."

"I've managed to bury it this long." The truth is I'm afraid. I do believe in God. I always have. Do I doubt my worth? Yes. Do I fight against the thoughts that I'm somehow a mistake? Absolutely. But neither of those even comes close to the guilt I carry from knowing I have sinned so vastly I could drown beneath the weight of it.

My throat constricts, and I try to stand. Elijah reaches out and gently grips my arm. I pause in place, breathing in the scent of the salty sea air wrapping around us like a blanket. The tension between us as we stand here, his hand on my arm, our gazes locked, is potent.

"You have to let go of the past, Andie. Otherwise, it's going to drag you down. You don't stand a chance at breaking through the storm if you have your past shackled around your ankles."

When I don't respond, he releases me. I slip back inside and head into the bathroom. As I stand there, hidden behind a closed door, a single tear slips down my cheek.

———

"Miss Montgomery," Mia greets as she steps up to the porch.

"How was the trip?" Despite the seven-hour drive here from New York, she looks completely pressed. A dark sleek skirt outlines her hips, and a bright pink, long-sleeved shirt hugs her torso. The heels she wears are taller than anything I would even wear, and not a single strand of her dark hair is out of place.

"It was pleasant." She offers me a binder. "Here are the letters you messaged me about."

"How did you get these printed already?"

"Wi-Fi in the car," she replies. "And I never go anywhere without a printer."

"Efficient."

"It makes no sense to be anything but," she replies. As always, Mia is all business, but as she turns toward the ocean view from the front of the lighthouse, even she looks impressed.

"It's beautiful, isn't it?"

"Not a bad view," she replies. "Where would you like to get started?"

"The sheriff is going to send a deputy with us over to my gran's house."

The door opens behind me.

"Change of plans, I'm going with you." Michael bites into an apple and grins at the both of us. He's handsome, ruggedly so, and beyond charming. But even as I can appreciate both of those facts about him, it's the former Army Ranger currently sleeping upstairs who holds all my attention.

Even as I wish I could keep my thoughts off of him.

Especially after everything I told him last night. We haven't spoken since, and the vulnerability I'm feeling is not sitting easy with me.

"Sheriff Vick said he was sending a deputy."

"He did. But I called and said I'd go. Lance is monitoring the systems from his place while Elijah sleeps, so you're getting me as your bodyguard." He grins again, and

I glance over at Mia, who actually looks flustered beneath the veteran's charming smile.

"Bodyguard? You really think I need one?" But even as I say the words, I know it's true. The stabbed image of me was a direct threat.

"It's what I do," he replies. "I'll grab my jacket and drive you both over."

"Did you bring anything but heels and business clothes?" I ask Mia. The thought of her walking through the destruction of Gran's house in three-inch heels makes my feet hurt even though I'm wearing tennis shoes.

"I did. Slacks and flats."

"Great. Then you should probably change. You're going to make me hurt just watching you."

She looks down at her outfit then back at me. "Okay. I can head back to the B&B. You can send me your grand-mother's address, and I can meet you both there."

"Sounds good. An hour?" Hopefully, that will buy me some time to go through another letter before we leave.

"That seems like an appropriate amount of time. I will see you both then." She saunters down the path toward her car. I face Michael and offer him the binder.

"What are these?" He bites into the apple to hold it in his mouth as he opens the binder. Then he pulls the fruit away and chews the piece left in his mouth.

"Letters I've received over the years. Threats."

"Great. Thanks." He looks up as Mia backs her sedan out of the drive. "She's all work, huh?"

"Always. It's what makes her such a great assistant."

"Hmm." But he doesn't say anything else, just turns and heads back into the lighthouse.

I follow then slip up the stairs. Elijah is asleep, but if I can get in and grab the box, I can slip back out without waking him. Just outside the door, I remove my shoes then slowly open the door.

He's sleeping soundly on the bed, and I'm glad to see it since we argued over him trying to sleep on the floor. Slowly and soundlessly, I make my way over to the dresser and grab the box. But just as I'm reaching for it, Elijah lets out a distressed cry that tears the heart out of my chest.

I turn toward him, expecting him to be awake in whatever grief he's suffering, but his eyes are closed. Sweat shimmers on his body in the dim light sneaking in from outside, and his expression is contorted in anguish.

Both hands fist in the covers, and he groans again.

He shoves the covers down from his chest, and I suck in a breath when I get an up close and personal look at the torn but healed flesh. Thick, gnarly scars climb up his side. Some are punctures; others look like tears. And the largest is a burn of some kind. What happened to him?

He cries out again, and I step forward.

"Elijah?" I reach out and gently touch his exposed shoulder.

His eyes fly open, but the look in them is one of fury. He throws himself up and slams me to the floor. My vision blurs as my head hits, and I scream.

"What are you doing here!" he bellows. There are no traces of the man I've come to know in the furious gaze staring down at me.

"Elijah!" Michael rushes in and grabs him around the waist. He yanks him back, and Elijah lands like a predator, bouncing back up. "You are at home," he tells him as he keeps his distance, placing himself between me and Elijah. "Brother. You're home," he says again, maintaining his calm tone.

Elijah's breath begins to wheeze, and he leans back against the wall, slumping down and drawing his knees up to his chest. He puts his head between his knees and breathes deeply. In and out. In and out.

"Come here," Michael orders me.

I remain where I am.

"Andie. He's fine now."

"I'm sorry. I'm so sorry." Elijah's shoulders shudder, and Michael turns away from me to wrap both arms around his friend.

"Our Father, who art in Heaven, hallowed be Your name," Michael starts.

Elijah's voice is shaky as he says, "Thy kingdom come, Thy will be done, on earth as it is in heaven."

"Give us this day, our daily bread," Michael continues.

"And forgive us our trespasses, as we forgive those who trespass against us," I say, crossing over to Elijah's side. I reach out and touch his arm, but he doesn't look at me. Michael's appreciative smile says it all though.

"Lead us not into temptation, but deliver us from evil," Michael says.

"For Thine is the kingdom, and the power, and the glory, forever and ever," I say.

"Amen," we all say at the same time.

We sit in silence for a few minutes. Then Michael stands. "I'm going to get you some water." He looks at me, so I nod, letting him know I'm okay.

As soon as he's gone, I move around to kneel in front of Elijah. "I'm sorry I woke you."

Elijah shakes his head.

"I didn't know."

"It's fine." He's angry. Though I get the sense he's not mad at me.

"It's not. I should have left you alone so you could sleep." Even though I'm still afraid to touch him, I reach up and run my hands down his muscled arms.

"I could have hurt you."

"But you didn't."

He shakes his head. "I'm sorry. I'm so sorry. I didn't mean to. I can't—"

"Elijah, it's fine." My heart still pounds, but I wrap my arms around him anyway, pulling him in for a hug that feels just as foreign to me as I imagine it does to him. But within seconds, his arms come around me.

I sink into the embrace, enjoying these moments of quiet before he pulls away.

"Are you okay?" he asks.

"Fine."

"You hit the ground." He reaches out and runs a hand over the back of my head. I hiss through clenched teeth then let out an uncomfortable laugh when he withdraws his hand like he just touched a live wire.

"Just a bump," I insist.

Elijah pushes off the floor and pulls me up. My gaze travels over his scarred torso and the burn marks on the left side of his abdomen.

"IED," he replies. "My last tour."

"I'm so sorry, Elijah."

"I survived," he says then reaches into his closet and withdraws a shirt. After tugging it over his head, he pulls me toward the door.

"You need to get back into bed. Michael went to get you water."

"You need ice," he replies.

We get downstairs right as Michael hangs up his phone. "Sorry, was headed up."

"She needs an ice pack."

"Head?" he asks.

"It's just a bump," I insist.

Elijah heads into the kitchen and opens the freezer, removing a wound care ice pack. After wrapping it in a napkin, he offers it to me. "Keep it on your head. We should call Doc."

"I don't need Doc," I insist. "I promise."

"She seems fine," Michael says.

"Why were you upstairs?" Elijah asks.

"I was getting my gran's letters. I wanted to read some before we head over to her house. I'm sorry. It was foolish. Selfish."

"It's fine," Elijah says, but his tone is different now than it's been the last few days. He's closer to the man I met in the parking lot of the church. Cool. Detached.

"I'll just go get the box." Leaving the two of them downstairs, I go up and grab the box. Once I've picked it up, I turn and nearly jump out of my own skin when I see Michael standing in the doorway.

"Elijah's been through things," he says. "We all have. But for him, it's all still very, very real." When I don't respond, he walks farther into the room. "Aside from me and Lance, Edna was the only person he's ever been close to. Until you."

"We're not close."

"You're close enough," he says. "I'm sorry you had to see that. But I hope it doesn't change the way you see him. He deserves to not be seen only as his suffering."

He leaves, not giving me a chance to respond.

The fact is that I don't see Elijah as his suffering.

If anything, knowing that he struggles with his past only makes me feel as though we might actually have things in common.

Because the thing is—I'm haunted too.

CHAPTER 13

Elijah

I mages on my screen paint a picture of the man who convinced Andie to leave her home and everyone she'd ever known behind. For anyone taking him at face value, George Johnson looks like any other normal member of society.

His blond hair is neatly cut while his eyes are framed by dark glasses. He's even smiling widely as though he's not a predator who preys on young girls.

High school girls.

I shake my head and lean back in my chair. The woman he's marrying now is barely over nineteen, and based on social media posts, they've been together for a couple of years. Meaning he met her before she'd even turned eighteen.

What am I missing?

I study the documents and pictures that make up his

entire life, hoping for something that will allow me to paint a massive bull's-eye on his back for no other reason than I am desperate to take out some of my anger somewhere— even if that's not a Christian way to handle problems.

I feel like a can of soda that's been shaken.

And I'm not sure how to relieve the pressure.

The gym certainly hasn't helped. Since I wasn't able to get any sleep after Andie and Michael left, I'd gone in, hoping to wear myself out, but it only made things worse.

I've prayed. I feel like I'm always praying these days. Seeking strength in my weakness. Power in moments where I'm powerless. But right now, as I sort through Andie's past, I can't get my thoughts away from her.

I'd been out of my mind when my nightmare-fueled rage had Michael wrenching me off of her, and all I can think about is how dangerous it would have been if he'd not been here. I like to think I would have come out of it on my own, but I'm not so sure.

Even now, I can smell the blood tingeing the air. The fuel that dripped from the tank of our overturned Humvee. The screams of the dying fill my ears as do the pleas from my fellow soldiers as they begged to be spared.

I suck in a breath and try to slow the heart hammering in my chest.

I've spent the last three years trying to outrun the demons that have clung to me ever since that day. I've fought for control, for some semblance of peace. Yet, I struggle to find either. There hasn't been a single night I've slept dreamlessly, and I know that there will be no future family for me unless I can get it under control.

What happened this morning when Andie woke me is a stark reminder of that impossibility.

The feel of her arms wrapped around me sneaks up and shoves all other thoughts out of my head. It was as though the entire world fell quiet in that moment. And it was just me and Andie.

Just the two of us.

No darkness plaguing me.

No nightmares echoing in my mind.

Just the smell of her delicate perfume and the feel of her body pressed against mine.

I pinch the bridge of my nose, trying to move past it. The absolute last thing I need to do is lose myself in thoughts of a woman I vowed to protect.

God, please help me focus.

Shoving my past aside, I focus on the screen once more. What am I not seeing? The letters Andie's assistant brought didn't contain anything that gets red-boxed. Mainly angry models, jealous designers, and a handful of peers furious that Andie's designs took off and theirs haven't.

Nothing that holds any actual weight, though I did run extensive background checks on every single one of them, including her assistant.

Terrified I'm going to miss something, I start over again, scanning the list Andie gave me. Of everyone, George's brother is the only one who might actually be a genuine threat. Stanley's the only one who has shown any actual desire to harm Andie. And after the way he grabbed her in that diner, it wouldn't surprise me if he were capable of far more.

Trashing a house? Absolutely.

Murder? Possibly. Either way, he's the only one who fits the profile I built.

The door opens, and Lance steps in. "How's it going?"

"Fantastic," I reply sarcastically.

He chuckles. "I love it when you sugarcoat things."

"I've got nothing so far. Aside from Stanley Johnson, I don't see anyone who stands out as a clear threat."

"What about in Rebecca's past?"

"Still digging into her." I minimize the window pertaining to George and pull up the file I've got going on Edna's daughter. "I've pulled financial records, her travel over the last few years, places she's lived, and anyone connected with her or her previous husbands. So far, nothing is jumping out at me."

"It will." Lance takes a seat across from me. "Eliza and I are postponing our trip to Boston tonight. My parents will be in town for a couple of weeks this time, and with everything going on, I asked to reschedule."

I let out a frustrated sigh because I know what him canceling means. He may not be our commander anymore, but Lance Knight is a leader. And he's worried about me. "Michael talk to you?"

"He sent me a text. Are you okay?"

"Fine."

"You can talk about it, Elijah. Sometimes it helps."

"What's there to talk about? We lived, didn't we?"

"Elijah." He says my name in the same tone he used back when I saluted him. Then, he'd used my last name, and we'd barely known each other, friends by circumstance, given our assignments.

"I'm fine," I tell him even as flashbacks of the past assault me. It was Lance's quick thinking that saved our lives that day, and he took seven bullets to the chest for his trouble. God kept us alive. Why? I'm not sure. But even as grateful as I am that He saved us, I can't help but hate the fact that the others died.

Three of us out of a dozen men.

I shake my head. "We need to get this figured out so Andie can get on with her life."

He arches a brow. "She leaving town afterward?"

"That's the plan."

"How do you feel about that?"

I glare at him. "Fine. Why wouldn't I be okay with it?"

"You two just seem to have a connection." He shrugs.

"We're not you and Eliza," I remind him. Lance's wife was being stalked, and he'd felt a calling to protect her. But this is nothing like that. "Andie is in town because her grandmother passed. Trouble followed her here, and I made a promise to Edna. That's all this is."

"Okay." He shrugs. "Then let's get it solved. I checked in with the sheriff. He's got nothing new. Rebecca's blood work should be back tomorrow, so hopefully we'll know something more."

"Will he turn over her phone?"

Lance reaches into his pocket and pulls out an evidence bag before offering it to me. "Gave it to me this morning. He said you can crack it faster than any of his guys."

"Thanks." After slipping on a pair of gloves, I break the seal and tip the phone out. Checking the port type, I reach into my drawer and pull out the fit I need then plug it into the computer.

A few keystrokes later, I have access to Rebecca Montgomery's cell phone. "In."

"And that's why you're the computer guy," Lance jokes and rolls a chair over to sit beside me so he can see the screen too.

I open up her texts first, and we're immediately greeted with more naked pictures of Andie's mother than I ever needed to see. Quickly, I scroll past them, trying to get to the actual message portion.

"It looks like she was in a couple of relationships," I say. "There's a lot of inappropriate messages, but aside from that, nothing that mentions Andie."

As soon as I've cleared those, I exit out and head into her call history. Nearly every call is to or from the same number. Which is a massive red flag, given the multiple text threads she had open.

"Read me this number." I hand Lance the phone and open my search program. He rattles it off, so I hit send and wait a few seconds for the results. "A burner. Not registered."

"So Rebecca was talking to someone who was using a burner."

"This number was not among the text recipients either," I say, leaning back in my chair.

Lance pulls out his cell and fires off a message.

"Sheriff?"

He nods. "I'll take the phone over once you're done copying the contents, but I wanted to give him somewhere to start."

I set up the computer to copy the contents of Rebecca's phone then stand and head into the kitchen for a coffee. I feel dead on my feet, beyond exhausted, but I'm not sure how I'll manage to sleep when my mind is entirely focused on Andie and the fact that the only woman who seems to have the answers we need is currently in the morgue.

"You need to talk to Pastor Redding," Lance says.

"Why?"

"You're struggling."

"Nothing I can't handle."

"Elijah."

As soon as the coffee begins brewing, I turn to face him. "Look, what happened is over. And my focusing on it is only going to continue making things worse. Besides, I don't have the time to go over and sit at the church while he tells me a bunch of things I already know."

Lance doesn't argue—he never does. Mainly because

he likely knows I'll end up on a church pew before this is all said and done anyway. Lance's faith is something I have always envied. Even before I was a believer.

My grandmother never made it a big deal for us to go to church, and neither did my parents before they passed. So I didn't grow up in an environment that taught faith. By the time I was in the Army, I gave God very little thought. Until the day I nearly died. Lance prayed with me. I prayed. Michael prayed.

It was the first time I'd really felt a presence in my life, and while I never told anyone before, I truly believe I witnessed God reaching down and pulling me from the depths of darkness as I lay dying.

A massive hand reaching toward me, a bright light surrounding me—both of those images are burned into my brain forever. It was a turning point for me. A second chance. And I've done everything I can not to waste it.

But the pain is still so fresh. So potent. I can't figure out how to let go. Especially since that was not the first IED I survived. The one just before that... I close my eyes and take a deep breath.

"I'm always here if you need to talk," Lance says.

"I'll be fine."

"Focused?" he asks, and I know he's worried about me slipping up and making a mistake.

"Always."

CHAPTER 14

Andie

Broken.

It's the word for today. A theme, if you will. Everything in my gran's house is broken. My heart is broken. Whatever had begun between Elijah and me is broken now. The latter is just me throwing a pity party for myself after reading into something that clearly wasn't there. But in the recesses of my mind, I let myself have it.

It sucks.

I slide into a booth at the diner, and Mia takes the seat across from me. As she answers yet another phone call, I turn my attention to the front picture window, my gaze landing on the stormy sea.

Dark clouds are coming in, rolling over the ocean, and in the distance, lightning flashes. A storm is brewing. And not just the one in my heart. As though my thoughts brought him to the door, Elijah strolls past the window and crosses the street, heading down to the dock.

I watch him move, my gaze drawn to him like a moth to flame.

Never in my entire life have I felt so completely connected to someone. Even when we despised each other at first. Though there are still moments where I want to ring his neck, there's something about him. A type of charming strength that draws me closer.

I get it now—why Gran thought we'd hit it off. And while it's likely not in the way I imagine she'd hoped for, I can see myself being friends with the former Army Ranger.

"I'll be right back," I tell Mia as she hangs up the phone.

"Okay. Would you like me to order you something?"

"Water, please. And some soup. Whatever the soup of the day is."

Mia nods and studies the menu as I slip from the booth. Outside, the wind whips at my hair as salty sea air fills my lungs. Whatever is coming is going to be a doozy, that's for sure.

My heart pounds as I walk toward the water.

Up ahead, a few overly cautious shop owners are boarding up their windows. The pharmacist covers his with plywood while the church closes its metal shutters. Pastor Redding offers me a wave as I pass, and I return the gesture before making my way onto the wooden dock.

Elijah stands at the end, his hands on the railing, face turned up to the sky.

As I get closer, I nearly kick myself for coming out here in the first place. I hadn't even considered that he might be praying. Or simply seeking solitude after what happened earlier. I start to turn around, but the desire to be close to him grows stronger, and I find myself moving in closer rather than putting distance between us.

I step up to his side and grip the railing, then look over at him.

Elijah's gaze meets mine. Gorgeous hazel pools that have toppled the walls I so carefully built after what George put me through.

Lightning cracks in the distance.

Thunder booms. I jump, ready to run back inside. Anywhere I can shield my hearing from the storm.

"Are you okay?" I call out over the sound of more thunder.

"Fine. I just needed a minute."

"Oh. I can leave." Embarrassed, I step away, but Elijah's hand covers mine, so I still, turning back toward the water.

"Please don't."

"Okay," I say, nearly whispering the word.

"When you're close, the world isn't so loud." He closes his eyes and drops his head forward.

The words break my heart and stir something in my soul. A feeling that this is exactly where I am supposed to be. Right here. Right now. I sidle in closer, hoping that my body language will tell him that he quiets the world for me too.

———

"I REALLY DON'T HAVE TO SLEEP UP HERE," ELIJAH TELLS me for the dozenth time.

"I would prefer if you did," I tell him as I toss a pillow over to the pallet he's making on the floor. Outside, the storm rages. Rain hammers the side of the lighthouse; wind whips at the trees. Their branches scrape against the side of the building like nails against a chalkboard.

"After what happened earlier—"

"I promise not to wake you up this time," I tell him.

But he still looks nervous. Afraid, maybe.

"Elijah. I promise you, it's going to be fine. But if you're that worried about it—"

Thunder crashes outside, startling me. I've never been one for thunderstorms. *Ever.* Honestly, I'm not entirely sure why, but every time I hear the sound of it cracking, it's like I'm thrown back into my childhood, listening to the table splinter as my mom's husband fell into it.

Over and over again.

No matter how many years have passed.

Elijah watches me closely. "I'll stay. Just…please don't try to wake me up. Unless it's an emergency."

"Okay. I promise." Victorious, I pluck Aggie from the

floor and climb into the bed. I stare up at the ceiling, the cat purring on my chest as I pet him. Of course, that position isn't comfortable enough though, so he spins and puts his butt in my face.

I roll to the side, and he begrudgingly moves to the foot of the bed.

Elijah is still, lying on his back on his bed of blankets. I stare down at him as he looks up at the ceiling, unable to help but wonder just what it is he's thinking about. Does he spend his nights thinking of his past?

Or running through what's to come tomorrow?

"I've been reading my gran's letters."

He focuses on me. "And?"

"I hurt her. A lot. When I left."

His expression softens a bit, noticeable even in the dim light cast by the cracked bathroom door. "You didn't know."

"You thought I did though."

He looks away. "I was wrong."

"What did she tell you about me? Did she talk about me at all?" When he doesn't immediately respond, I sigh. "Was it really that bad?" The joke falls flat though, and he rolls onto his side, expression serious.

"She talked about how proud she was. How amazing you were doing in New York and how grateful she was you'd found your calling."

"My calling." I snort, unable to help myself.

"You don't think what you're doing is your calling?"

I remain quiet, unsure how to vocalize what I'm feeling. What I've been feeling for longer than I care to admit. "Have you ever stopped to look at your life then wonder just how you got there?"

"A few times, I suppose," he replies.

"I never had any clear direction of what I wanted to do. My mother certainly wasn't any help in figuring it out, and Gran tried to guide me, but I'd been so angry that I hadn't wanted to pay any attention to any of it."

"I get that."

"It was George who told me I should go into fashion." Once more, I roll onto my back to stare up at the ceiling. I don't want to see the disappointment in his eyes or the pity that may accompany it.

Gran gave me every penny she could spare to send me to design school in New York. She'd fought to get me the future I'd told her I wanted, and it hadn't even been my dream.

"I didn't know that."

"No one did," I tell him. "I realize now that it was just part of the flattery portion of his grooming, but back then, it felt so good to have a man tell me I looked nice. That I knew how to dress. That I should build my adult life around it."

"It's wrong what he did to you."

"I get that now. And looking back, I can't believe how foolish I was. But in the moment, after spending my life being rejected by my father and the men my mother brought home, after being told over and over again that I wasn't good enough, having someone look at me like that was...nice. As twisted as that is." I laugh uncomfortably, unsure why I'm word vomiting like this.

We don't even know each other that well.

"If you hadn't done design, what do you think you would have gone into?"

"I honestly wish I had a clue. Don't get me wrong, I enjoy what I do, but I can't help but wonder what would have happened if I'd never given George the time of day. Who knows? Maybe I would have stuck around town and we could have met under better circumstances."

And what a dream that would be. To have met this man when I was unburdened by the mistakes I made. What would it have been like? To look upon him with eyes that weren't haunted?

Elijah is silent for so long that I wonder if he's fallen asleep, but then he clears his throat. "It's easy to allow ourselves to be weighed down by the past. The difficult thing is forgiving ourselves and moving forward."

"What do you have to forgive yourself for, Mr. Breeth?" I say it lightly because I can't imagine this man, who stepped up to help an elderly woman without question, would have done anything in need of forgiveness.

"You'd be surprised at the weight I carry, Miss Mont-gomery. Good night." Elijah's tone is serious and leaves no room for further conversation.

He falls silent, so I lie there, staring up at the ceiling,

my mind reeling as I go over everything I know about Elijah. Which I realize is not much.

Curious, I roll onto my side and draw the covers up over my head to shield Elijah from the light of my cell phone. I've just typed his name into the search bar of my browser when an explosion rattles the lighthouse and sends my heart rate skyrocketing.

CHAPTER 15

Elijah

Gun in hand, I creep down the stairs, bare feet silent on the steel staircase. Andie is behind me, despite my arguments that she remain in the room, though I'm thankful she doesn't make a sound as we descend into the dark office.

Lance is monitoring remotely tonight, which means that the place is empty. It also means he likely knows what's happening right now and is already on his way. Something I'm counting on depending on what just happened outside. The sheriff should already be on his way also, but with the weather outside, he'll likely be delayed.

I turn on no lights, just head straight for my desk where I duck down and flip on the monitor. Andie crouches down behind me, her phone clutched in her hand.

The moment the monitor comes on and my exterior security cameras are on screen, I know we're in trouble.

Andie's car is on fire, orange flames lighting up the dark night sky even as rain hammers down on top of it.

But that's not even the worst of it.

Five men in matching skull masks stand just outside. They're tall, bulky, and not at all rushed despite the fact that the explosion would have drawn immense attention. They stare up at the cameras, almost challenging me to come outside.

"What is happening?" Andie whispers. I look back at her. She's terrified. Visibly shaking where she kneels. "Why is this happening?"

After reaching into the top drawer of my desk and withdrawing my knife, I tug her to her feet and rush over to the corner of the living area.

We have a minute before they breach the doors. Maybe two if we're lucky. So I rip the rug back and open the hatch leading down to a basement not included on any building schematics.

"Get inside. Call the sheriff again. Tell them what's happening."

She stares back at me, emerald eyes wide with terror. "What are you going to do?"

"I'm going to buy us time."

"Elijah—"

"Please, Andie." Desperate to touch her, I reach up and run my hand over her cheek. "Get inside. Stay quiet. Do not come out until you hear me say it's okay."

I turn back to the camera as the one in front gives hand

signals and three of the men break off from the group, likely flanking around the back while the other two rush toward the front door—mere feet away.

"Now, Andie. We're out of time."

"I can't leave you."

"I'll be fine," I insist. Someone hits the door. "But I can't do what I need to if I'm worried about you!"

After one final moment of hesitation, Andie climbs down the stairs and disappears into the dark. I close it then cover the entrance with the rug once more. I only need to keep them occupied long enough for help to arrive.

Then everything will be fine.

Lord, please let her survive. Take me if it's my time, but let Andie walk out of this.

The world around me goes quiet, and I breathe in deeply, letting adrenaline fuel my muscles but not take over my mind. I play out the scenarios in my head within seconds, determining the best line of attack is to hit them before they see it coming.

Another hit against the door.

It's reinforced, but it won't hold for long.

My cell rings.

I answer and press it to my ear.

"We're on our way," Lance says, panic in his voice.

"Get her out safe," I tell him. "Promise me. No matter what. You get her out."

"We will get both of you out," he says.

"Promise me, Lance."

"I promise. Michael should be there in—" The door splinters, and an explosion rings my ears. I'm knocked off my feet and slammed into the wall behind me with such force I can hardly see straight.

Two men rush in, and I lunge to my feet, charging forward and slamming my shoulder into the nearest one. The impact has pain shooting through my side, but I shove it down. Years of fighting in alleyways, basements, and abandoned buildings have raised my pain tolerance. I've taken many hits in my life.

And this one will not be my last.

I raise my fist and slam it into his face then raise my gun and fire it at the man trying to sneak up behind me. He goes down, stumbling back and splintering my desk.

I jump to my feet as another attacker races down the hall, having gotten in through the back door. He fires his weapon, and I roll to the side then fire my own. He lets out a yell as the bullet tears through the meat of his leg, dropping him to the ground. I leap over the desk I'd taken shelter behind and knock the firearm from his hand.

"Stay down," I growl, my foot on his throat, gun aimed at his head. I don't want to kill him, but I won't hesitate if he moves. The window breaks as a canister is thrown inside.

Adrenaline pulses as I dive to the side, seeking cover.

It goes off, and burning pain shoots through my side. I suck in a ragged breath and fight the urge to yell in agony. Shrapnel.

My mind reverts—the scene around me shifting from the lighthouse I call home to a blood-stained desert surrounded by the enemy. Pain eats up my side, the very oxygen around me feeling like a thousand needles being pressed into my injury.

"Stay down!" Lance orders.

I try to move. To get to my brothers as they lie dying. Please, let me get to them. I crawl, dirt ripping at my already torn flesh, but just as I reach Corporal Sandoval, another explosion rocks the ground.

A woman screams.

I cover my nose and mouth as best I can, but the smoke burns my eyes. Keeping low, I move along the floor, searching for the entrance to the basement. If they got her —I can't fail her. Not like I failed them.

"Elijah!" *Michael.*

"Down here!" I choke out, lungs burning.

Hands go to my shoulders, and I don't fight the help because I know it's Michael. He pulls me from the room and out into the fresh air. I suck in my first, unhindered breath, my lungs burning from the thick smoke still billowing out of the lighthouse.

Sirens wail in the distance.

"I need to get Andie," I choke out, hissing in pain as Michael rips the shirt from my body. "Basement."

"Lance got her," he replies. "You're a mess. Could be worse," he says then takes my torn shirt and presses it to the wounds in my side.

Seconds later, Andie stumbles out alongside Lance, Aggie in her arms. Relief floods me, the sight of her a salve to my broken soul.

"And it looks like they went up for the cat too," he adds.

"Elijah!" She rushes over toward me and throws herself at my side. I stare up at her, vision blurry from smoke and probably blood loss, depending on how bad the shrapnel is. Her eyes go wide, and she turns to Michael. "What can I do?"

"Keep pressure here. I'll stick Aggie in the car." He takes the cat from her, and she presses my shirt against my side as Michael walks away.

"Don't die, Elijah," she says. "I'm not done disliking you yet."

I laugh, but it's agony. "I. Don't. Plan. On. It." I suck in a ragged breath. "Are you all right?"

"A couple scrapes, but I'm fine."

Lance tosses an empty metal canister to the ground. "Crudely made," he growls, pulling his gas mask off. "Nails and sharpened bolts. Along with some homemade tear gas. God is the only reason you're not dead," he says.

He's right. The only place I'd managed to get to before it exploded was my already splintered desk. I'd shielded my face and neck, but if there were nails in there, the force of that explosion could have sent them straight through the wood.

I could be dead.

I should be dead.

Again.

Why does He keep saving me?

The sheriff pulls in first, followed by an ambulance and the fire department.

"These guys weren't amateurs," I wheeze. Every breath is like fire in my veins. "They knew what they were doing."

"We'll deal with them," Lance says. "Right now, we need to make sure you survive."

CHAPTER 16

Andie

The church is quiet today.

Then again, I'm not sure what else I would be expecting given it's only seven in the morning. Elijah is in surgery, a collapsed lung and internal bleeding thanks to the shrapnel from that bomb they threw into the house.

He's the one who suffered the damage, but I can barely breathe.

The image of him bleeding on the ground, barely conscious and struggling to breathe, is one I'm not sure I'll ever get out of my head. I'd remained strong and held pressure until the paramedics arrived, but when it came time to get into the ambulance, I'd refused to go.

I told myself I had to see to Aggie.

But really, it was because I couldn't handle the

strongest man I've ever met looking so weak. And just how pathetic does that make me?

Playing with my hands, I try to breathe through the heaviness in my chest.

Two of the men died from their injuries, and two fled from the scene. Lance and Michael saved the man Elijah shot in the leg, and with him in custody, they claim we'll have answers. But I can see they're just as afraid for Elijah as I am.

Just as terrified he won't pull through.

"How are you holding up?" Pastor Redding asks as he takes a seat beside me. The man's hair is graying at the temples, but he still looks exactly the same as he did when I was little.

It's strange how some things change and others remain exactly the same.

"Not great," I reply honestly. "It's been a long time since I had anyone but myself or Gran to be worried about."

The pastor reaches over to take one of my hands in his. The contact is comforting, but I consider pulling my hand away. Why do I deserve comfort when Elijah is in surgery, having metal removed from his abdomen?

"Elijah is strong."

"Strength isn't always enough." I know it's ridiculous, but my mind drifts back to that man my mother had been married to. He'd always seemed so strong—physically anyway—and all it took was one scare, and he'd fallen like a house of cards.

Elijah ended up with only God knows how many nails and other metal shards throughout his body. And that was after he'd fought off three attackers all by himself.

"Have you prayed about it?"

I shake my head. I should have. "I don't even know that He will listen," I cry, my shoulders shaking. "If you knew what I'd done. If you had any idea…" I close my eyes and try my best to breathe through the pain.

"Then let's do it together." He doesn't start right away though, just waits for me to nod. I do then close my eyes. "Dear Heavenly Father, please wrap your light around Elijah. Give him the strength he needs to recover, and guide the hands of the doctors tending to him. Please, God, grant us the courage we need to remain strong for him during this time of healing, and lead us with Your light and Your Word. Amen."

"Amen." My throat burns as I try so hard to keep it together.

"You've had a rough return home."

I laugh, but there's no humor in it. "You think?"

"Want to talk about it?"

"What is there to talk about? You already know what's happened."

"I do," he admits. "But not how it has affected you."

I glare at the cross straight ahead, even though it's not God's fault. Bad things happen because people commit bad acts against each other. The free will we were granted is a gift that is abused by many, but even as I know that, I struggle with the knowledge that Elijah did nothing to deserve what just happened to him, yet he's fighting for his life.

"I don't understand why these things have happened. What happened to Gran, to Rebecca, to Elijah—"

"And to you," he says. "Don't forget that you've been hurt too."

"I don't matter," I say.

"You do."

"No," I snap. "I don't."

"Why don't you think you matter?"

I get to my feet, pulling my hand from his. "Because I'm still breathing! No matter what I went through, I'm still here! What right do I have to complain? Most of what happened to me, I brought on myself."

Pastor Redding simply watches me. He's always been someone easy to talk to. Someone who, even if you didn't know him well, you'd feel safe telling your deepest, darkest secrets to.

"Elijah is still here too," he says softly.

I close my eyes. "Those men attacked him because of me. They came for him because of me. And I don't even know what I did. I have no idea why they were after me. Is it because of my mother? Because of something I did? I don't know. All Elijah wanted was to be a good person to my gran. That's all he ever cared about. Yet, he got wrapped up with me, and now he's—they all die around me. Everyone around me dies."

Pastor Redding gets to his feet and takes my hands. "Andie." I refuse to open my eyes and look at him though. "Who dies around you?"

"I killed someone," I whisper. "When I was a kid."

"Tell me what happened." There's no judgment in his tone, no fear. No anger.

"My mother married a man after she and my father split. He used to love to scare me. Tormenting me with a mask. So, one day, I got tired of it, and I tried to do the same to him." I meet Pastor Redding's gaze. "I jumped out, and he had a heart attack."

"That's not murder, Andie."

"I left him there. I didn't try CPR, I didn't call 9-1-1. I grabbed my things and ran. What does that make me?"

"A scared child," he replies.

I shake my head. "Everything I've ever done has hurt others. I left Gran to chase after a man I had no business being with, and it broke her heart. Then I was so ashamed I stayed away, hurting her further. And now Elijah—he could die because of me. Why is he being punished for my sins?"

"Oh, child." Pastor Redding guides me back to the pew. "No one is being punished. You are redeemed. Forgiven by His love."

"How? I don't deserve it. I don't—"

"None of us deserve it, Andie. But Christ died so that we might find our way into an eternity of peace. That doesn't mean we won't suffer while we're here; it just means we have a better place reserved for us when we pass from this life. But you have to fight for that salvation, child. You have to fight against the enemy telling you that you aren't enough. That you shouldn't even bother trying to leave the sin behind because you will be forgotten. You won't be. And you *are* enough. No matter what."

"I don't know." I shake my head. "I just don't see how. I'm so lost." Pain crushes down on me, fear for Elijah, anger at myself, and—if I'm being honest—at God for allowing him to get hurt in the first place.

"Then let me help you find the way back." It's such a simple request, spoken with soft authority and confidence.

"I'm not a Sunday girl anymore, Pastor."

"Then don't come on Sundays." He stands and nods at someone standing behind me. I turn, my heart jumping when I see Michael standing there. I push up, but before I head toward him, I turn back to the Pastor.

"Not on Sundays."

"Pick whatever day you want, Andie, and just show up."

I glance back at the cross, and something shifts in me. Not substantial but enough that I feel a bit lighter. So I nod. "I've always been fond of Wednesdays."

He smiles. "Then, I'll see you then."

———

I stand outside Elijah's hospital room, staring at the closed door. A gift shop teddy bear is clutched in one hand, but now I'm feeling incredibly dumb about the gesture. I mean, what does one say to a person who just saved their life?

Here's a stuffed animal?

The door opens, and Lance and his wife Eliza step out of the room. They both stop when they see me, so I try to smile. Based on their expressions of pity, it comes out looking half-hearted at best.

"How is he?"

"Awake," Lance says. "Looking terrible, but that's not anything new."

Eliza elbows him in the side. "He could have died."

"Fair enough." He chuckles and wraps his arm around her shoulders. "How are you?"

"I'm okay. I'm not the one who was blown up." The shrapnel exploded outward rather than down. Only God knows why. Even Lance and Michael both seemed shocked by it. Either way, I was safe in the basement while Elijah fought for his life above me.

"Good. The sheriff has our guy sweating in an interrogation room, so as soon as we know anything, I'll let you know. Have you called your assistant? Elijah said she was in town?"

"I did. She's on her way back to New York. I told her we would pick up stuff from my gran's house later. That it wasn't safe right now."

"Smart."

Eliza steps forward and pulls me in for a quick hug. "Let us know if you need anything, okay?"

"Okay, thanks." I pull away then slip past them and into the room. Machines beep, and the room is dark aside from a bright light above Elijah's head. It illuminates the damage to his face, the bruising and bandages on his nose.

I stifle a sob, covering my mouth with a shaking hand.

"Do I look that bad?" he manages, voice gravelly.

Tears blur my vision, and I shake my head. "Can hardly tell a difference," I choke out.

He tries to laugh, but it comes out more like a strangled cough, so I move closer to the bed. "Is that for me?" he asks, gaze dropping to the bear.

"Yes. Sorry. It's all I could find." I set the bear on the bed beside him. His eyes are bloodshot, his forehead stitched just beneath the hairline.

"I'm okay," he says. "It looks worse than it is."

I close my eyes as a tear slips free.

"I've never seen you cry," he says. "Not at the funeral, not with Rebecca."

I should be embarrassed. Angry with myself for crying because the tears make me weak. But I can't seem to stop. Elijah nearly died. Because of me.

He brushes a tear from my cheek, and I lean into the touch, not ashamed that it feels good to have him touching me. Elijah has slipped right past the walls I built, breaking through the boundaries I'd set for myself.

I don't know how to stop what's happening between us. Whether it's merely attachment given the circumstances, friendship, or something deeper. But I do know that I'm terrified it's going to end with him just like everyone else… dead.

CHAPTER 17

Elijah

I've never been a fan of hospitals. Even before I'd been in one the first time, there was just something about the stark white walls and the overwhelming smell of cleaner that grated against me. So, by day three, I've gotten enough of a handle on my pain that I'm ready to go home.

Andie is asleep in a chair in the corner where she's been nearly every day since the attack. Apparently, Michael took the cat back to his place, and with the clothes Lilly dropped off, Andie hasn't had to leave my side.

I won't admit it out loud, but having her here has meant more to me than anything.

The door opens, and Doc slips in, his graying hair wild as though he's been running his hands through it. Then again, he's always looked a bit like Albert Einstein to me.

"Elijah, good to see you awake," he says with a smile.

"Can I leave now?" I ask, bypassing all greetings.

"You don't like our food?" he asks, gesturing to the uneaten sandwich on the tray in front of me.

"Not even a little."

He chuckles. "Well, I'm going to say yes. You can go home, but I'm going to order bed rest. At least, for the time being. In a few days, you can get up and try to move around, but you need to let your body heal."

"I'll be fine." I sit up and suck in a pained breath when my abdomen aches with the movement.

Doc doesn't say anything, just arches a brow.

"See? Fine," I growl.

"What are you doing?" Andie rushes over to my side, her soft hands on my arm. "You need to stay in bed. Doesn't he need to stay in bed?" she asks Doc.

He chuckles. "I feel good about leaving you in her care," he says. "Bed rest for him. At least two days of only being on your feet for a max of thirty minutes a day. After that, you can move as needed. No stairs though. You're going to need to find somewhere else to stay."

"Okay. No stairs. Got it." She chews on her bottom lip. "Felix said the windows for Gran's house have been installed. But—"

I know what she's thinking. The guy in custody hasn't said a word. No matter how much they've tried to sweat him out. He hasn't rolled over on anyone and hasn't even called for a lawyer. Given that two of them got away, we're not safe at Edna's house. Not yet.

"I have a house we can go to," I tell her.

"No stairs?" she asks.

"No stairs." I turn to Doc. "When can I get out of here?"

"Bed. Rest, Elijah. I mean it. You can get up for thirty minutes a day, and they don't have to be all at the same time, but you need to take it easy so you don't tear anything. Two days. Bed. Rest. Then easy movements. They removed nearly a hundred metal shards from your gut. Don't play with this one, Elijah."

"I understand," I tell him. "And I promise not to break your rules."

"Then you can leave in just a few. They're drawing up your discharge paperwork now."

Relief floods me. "Good." I start to reach for my phone but hesitate when another wave of pain washes over me. "Can you hand me my phone? I need to check in with Lance."

"I can." Andie retrieves my phone and offers it to me.

"What's up?" he asks, answering on the first ring.

"Doc's letting me out. Think you can give us a ride?"

"Be there in thirty."

I end the call. "He'll be here in half an hour."

"Then I'll go check on that paperwork." Doc smiles at me then Andie before leaving.

She comes around to stand in front of me and crosses her arms. "This feels too soon."

"It feels like it's been forever," I counter.

"Elijah, you were nearly blown up."

"I'm still breathing." I lean back in the bed, trying not to look too relieved that the pressure is off my stomach. "Besides, this recovery is nothing like the last one." The moment the words are out of my mouth, I want to kick myself. I don't talk about it with anyone...ever. So why I blurted it out now, I'm not sure.

"This has happened before?"

"Sort of."

"The burns on your side."

I crack open an eye and stare up at her. The blankets are pulled up to my abdomen, but just enough of the scarred flesh from the burns remains in view. "Yes."

"Did it happen while you were in the Army?" When I don't answer, she sighs. "You know everything about me, Elijah, and I know very little about you."

"Everything?" I ask, meaning it as a joke.

"Yes. I haven't hidden anything from you."

I know she's right. About her honesty and my lack of being forthcoming about my own past. "I told you it's from an IED."

"How bad?"

I sigh. "It was hidden beneath the sand and blew up when we drove over it. I was on the side of the truck that hit it, so I got most of the burns. It ate away at my side and left me full of shrapnel and bleeding to death on the side of a road. Michael and Lance were there too, and both were injured, but we were the lucky ones because we walked away."

"Oh—Elijah."

I shake my head, uncomfortable with the turn of conversation. "Lance held back the enemy fire when they came for us, but hearing the dying cries of my brothers—" I suck in a breath. "I haven't forgotten them."

"I am so sorry, Elijah."

"It happens in war. Good men die. Lesser men survive."

"You are *not* a lesser man," she says.

I turn my attention out the window. "Some would argue."

"Had you not survived that day, I wouldn't be alive today."

"You don't know that."

She closes the distance between us and cups my face. Her touch is tender, and it warms a part of my heart I hadn't realized was cold. "I do know that," she says, "and I need you to know it too."

The expression on her face is so intense, so unguarded, that it steals the breath from my chest. Which, given the collapsed lung I suffered from due to the explosion, is probably not a good thing. My gaze drops to her full lips, and I can't help but wonder how they might taste.

Andie's breath catches, and I see the same attraction burning inside of me reflected in her gaze.

She leans in.

My heart hammers.

"All right, who needs a ride?"

Andie pulls back so abruptly it leaves me wondering if I'd imagined her standing that close to begin with. I turn to Lance. "As soon as they get me discharged, we will."

———

THE CLOSEST SAFE HOUSE TO HOPE SPRINGS IS ABOUT fifteen minutes outside of town, situated right on the beach. It was the first house Knight Security purchased—under a separate LLC of course—and needed to be completely renovated from top to bottom.

Thankfully, Lance has a buddy who lives in Boston and runs his own construction company. They had the place up and running within a few months, and we've used it off and on for clients who needed a safe place to get away until the threat was neutralized.

A metal gate opens when Lance presses a remote, and we take the short driveway to the house. Blue shutters contrast against white siding, but it's the bright red flowers in the boxes that catch my eye.

I'd forgotten Edna helped me pick them out at the beginning of spring.

Grief sneaks up on me, pain that has me closing my eyes until I can swallow it down. In the craziness of the last week, I'd nearly forgotten that she was gone. What kind of person does that make me?

"Here we are." Lance puts the car into Park and gets

out, then opens the door for me. Before he can offer me assistance, I climb out and lean against the car to catch my breath.

Andie takes my arm, looping it over her shoulders without waiting for my approval, and begins walking. The grin Lance shoots me is one massive "I knew it was more than you thought it was," and I wish I could knock the smile off his face.

Of course, I wouldn't because I love him like a brother, but the fleeting thought is there.

"This is beautiful," Andie breathes as we enter the house. The amount of natural light is beyond breathtaking, especially since someone was here, adding personal touches to the couches and stocking the glass refrigerator.

"Eliza brought some food out while we were waiting," Lance says. "She's going to bring out some dinners as soon as she finishes prepping them. The word lasagna was thrown around a time or two."

"That's so kind of her. She doesn't have to do that," Andie says.

"She likes to." Pride laces his tone.

"Well, we really appreciate it."

I don't miss that Andie answers for me, nor can I ignore the twisting in my gut that comes like a warning. We're getting too close. Things are getting too complicated. I need to pull back. Need to put distance between us.

But as she guides me over to the couch and helps me sit, I realize just how deep I am. Because she only stopped touching me seconds ago, and I'm already desperate for her touch again.

Lance's cell rings. After working with him for as long as I have and serving alongside him before this, I can read the shift in his body language as he listens to the call. The way he stiffens and his brows draw together.

Something is wrong.

"Thanks for letting me know." He hangs up and faces me. "The guy we had in custody is dead."

"Dead?" Andie chokes out. "How? He was in jail?"

"The sheriff sent him to county, hoping it would get him talking, and three inmates jumped him in gen pop."

"Gen pop?"

"General population," I answer. "How big is this thing?" Between the guys jumping us at the lighthouse and now this, I'm starting to think there's a whole lot more to it than we thought.

"I don't know," Lance admits as he shoves his cell back into his pocket. "But either his murder is one massive coincidence, or—"

"There is a lot more at play than we thought," I finish. When confusion sets in, my general rule of thumb is to go back to the beginning. I need my laptop. I try to stand, and fresh pain sears my abdomen.

"Whoa. Sit," Andie orders.

"I need my laptop. We need to go back to the beginning."

"It's in the office," Lance tells me, gesturing to a bedroom right off the main living room. It's where we set up surveillance when we're here. "But you need rest, Elijah."

"I can get rest when this is over. Right now, Andie is in danger, and we need to figure out why."

"Not just Andie," he says.

I narrow my gaze and cross my arms. "Being in the wrong place at the wrong time doesn't make me a target."

"No. But this does." He reaches into his back pocket and withdraws an evidence bag that he hands me.

I reach inside and withdraw a cell phone. Going through my usual steps, I check the calls first, notice a bunch to and from the same number—likely another burner —then move to the messages.

TARGET: ELIJAH BREETH. KNIGHT SECURITY. TAKE HIM OUT. LEAVE THE WOMAN ALIVE.

It seems so surreal. So completely outrageous that, for a moment, I wonder if it's not Lance and Michael messing with me. Except, logically, I know they wouldn't. Not with this. "They were after me."

"This time. Yes," Lance says.

"But why? What could I have possibly done to draw attention like this?"

Andie crosses her arms, walls back up. It's a defense mechanism and one she wields with the precision of an expert assassin. Kill all feelings. Leave no weakness. It would be impressive if I weren't already so on edge.

"I'm not sure. But I'm wondering if this has something to do with Edna."

"Edna?" I nearly laugh. "There's no way she could have been involved in anything like this."

"My gran wouldn't be wrapped up in anything that would lead to murder," Andie adds.

"It's unlikely, I admit that, but—" Lance sighs.

"We need to investigate every possible lead," I reply, knowing he's right. Investigations hinge on collecting *every* fact. Not just the ones that seem plausible. "But it's not her."

"Do some digging. Find me facts," he says. "Until then, you're both lying low."

"Is Aggie doing okay?" Andie asks.

"According to Michael, he's the laziest cat he's ever met."

She smiles softly.

"He's not here?" I'm surprised she let the cat out of her sight.

"No. We thought it best he stay with Michael just in case you both need to get out fast," Lance says. "All right, I'm heading back in. I need to get some things handled back at the office. Call if you need me. Your cells are off and in the office safe, but the landline is secure." He gestures to a phone on the kitchen counter.

"I know the drill," I say, honestly agitated that I'm the one forced to remain inside. I don't do well with inaction, and while I normally love the research side of things, this time, it's personal.

This time, I want to be out on the front lines.

Even if, given that someone wants me dead, that's the last place I should be.

CHAPTER 18

Andie

S ketch pad in hand, I sit on the porch overlooking the ocean, drawing the gorgeous view as I see it in front of me. Bright rays from the sun, a seemingly endless waterscape that draws my eye and makes me long to fly like a bird.

Just so I can see where it goes.

My feet are bare, my pink toenails bright against the wooden porch railing. A once steaming mug of tea sits beside me, though it's long gone cold and still sits barely touched. Gran used to hang every single doodle I'd draw on her fridge. There was often not a single spare inch of blank space. And when she ran out, she'd move them to a folder to make room for more.

I'd drawn everything from horses to butterflies. Flowery landscapes and rocky mountains. Maybe that's what helped George convince me that I wanted a future in fashion. God knows I drew a lot of outfits while I'd been pretending to pay attention in class.

It's been years since I drew anything *but* clothing now.

I add a bird to the sky on my drawing then shift my attention to the partially drawn person standing, back to the viewer, on the page. The beach spans out to both sides of him while he stares out at the ocean. Back bare, I can see every single scar, every ragged injury left behind—a roadmap of his trauma.

Elijah captivates every ounce of my attention. More so now that I know some of what he's gone through.

"Lesser men survive."

The fact that he can think of himself as lesser than anyone is dumbfounding. He's the strongest man I've ever met—not that the bar for that is particularly high. But even if it were, I've no doubt he'd still exceed it.

So why does he think so low of himself? And who are those he said would argue?

The door behind me slides open, so I shut the sketch pad quickly then glance over my shoulder as Elijah steps out onto the porch. He's moving easier today, likely the night's sleep and another round of pain meds helping him stand straighter and walk taller.

The black shirt he wears covers most of his injuries, so if you were looking at him, you'd never know he nearly died a few days ago. Though the fading bruising on his face is evidence of some of the pain he suffered.

"You're supposed to be on bed rest."

"Thirty minutes a day," he replies, taking a seat and staring out at the ocean. "This is part of my thirty minutes." His tone is sharp, and he's been a bit off since Lance left yesterday. But after our near—whatever that was—in the hospital, I have to admit it feels a bit like rejection.

Even if I know we're nothing more than two people thrown together due to unfortunate circumstances.

"Okay. Need anything? Coffee? Tea?"

"No." He closes his eyes and leans back against the chair.

Did he have another nightmare? I didn't hear anything, but that doesn't mean he wasn't suffering in silence. "Are you sure, I can—"

"I'm fine, Andie," he snaps. Before I can respond, he hisses between clenched teeth. "I'm sorry. It was a long night."

I'd gone to bed somewhere around eleven, but he'd been wide awake and sitting up in bed on his laptop. He'd barely grunted when I told him I was heading to my room.

"How late did you stay up?"

"Late enough." He turns to me. "Did you sleep okay?"

No. "Good enough," I reply with a smile. He doesn't need to know I'd spent nearly the entire night dreaming of him and what it might feel like to have his lips on mine. The intensity of that look we'd shared in the hospital flashes through my mind again, and my cheeks heat.

I turn back to the ocean. That's something I understand. The breaking of waves. The draw of the tide. But this connection between Elijah and me is completely foreign. It goes well past attraction and settles far deeper than simple friendship.

"Anything in the letters?" he questions.

He'd offered to help me read through Gran's letters, but I told him no. I'm not ready to share what is likely the last personal moments my gran and I will have together. Even if it means unlocking the puzzle sooner.

That may change at some point, but not now. Not today.

"Not yet. I read quite a few last night, but they're all updates about the town, things she's thinking about. Her missing me." My throat constricts on that last part. I'd been unable to keep myself from crying while I thought Elijah was dying, and while I don't want to dissect the reason behind him being my breaking point, I do know that I don't want to lose the fight in front of him again.

"Great. Let me know if that changes." He gets up from the chair with a slight groan, so I stand too.

"Do you want some food? I can make some eggs."

"No. I'll have a protein shake." He slips into the kitchen, and I follow.

"I really don't mind, Elijah. I'm making some for me anyway."

"I don't need you to take care of me!" he nearly yells it, the tone of his voice so frustrated it catches me off guard.

"I'm not trying to take care of you."

"Yes," he argues, "you are. You fought me going into that cellar because you were worried about me. Then there's the answering for me yesterday, cooking me dinner, trying to get me to stop working and get sleep last night, and now the eggs! I don't need a caretaker! You are my client—that is all. I am the one who is taking care of you." His cheeks are red, his hazel eyes furious.

But there's something else in them, too. Hidden behind the anger. Fear?

"First of all," I snarl, my own anger meeting his. "I was afraid for you. And I will not apologize for being the kind of person who didn't want to sit down there and listen to you die. As for the dinner, Eliza technically cooked that. I merely heated it in the oven. I thought I was saving you time by heating it up since I was hungry too. But, hey, I tell you what. Next time, I'll be sure to cut the lasagna in half and put *your* portion in the refrigerator before heating up mine."

I move in closer, glaring up at him. "As for you getting sleep, you can't exactly protect either of us if you're dead on your feet. And the eggs? I couldn't care less what you eat for breakfast, but it seemed a friendly gesture to offer to make you some too when I'm already going to feed myself and it's literally no extra effort." I turn on my heel.

"Andie—"

"No. Don't worry, *Mr. Breeth.* Going forward, I will ensure that I only look out for myself. You can starve for all I care." I slam the bedroom door behind me and cross over to the letters.

As I take a seat on the bed, I half expect him to knock

on the door, so when he doesn't, I'm a bit let down. *Men.* Taking a letter from the box, I settle back against the head-board and break the envelope's seal.

> Dearest Andie,
>
> Today started out as a hard day. But as I was preparing to lose my grip on three bags of groceries, a young man rushed over and grabbed them from me. He kept my feet firmly on the ground, and when I got the first full look at his face, I was nearly struck down to the ground. He looks so much like my Charlie. Nearly a spitting image, even. Though, as I spent a few more minutes with him, I noticed that his eyes are a different color, and they are far more haunted than Charlie's ever were.
>
> He's new to town, a former Army Ranger, from what he told me. And he's working over at Knight Security. Remember my last letter? I told you that they opened up in our tiny town? I nearly laughed when I found out! Can you imagine any danger in our small town?
>
> Anyway, he was kind, and I do hope our paths cross again. I think you would like him.

Missing you more every day,
Gran

Elijah. I'd been wondering when he'd make an appearance in the letters. Seeing him here, on the page, somehow eases some of my anger. I'm not sure why—but I can't deny that it does. *His eyes are far more haunted than Charlie's ever were.*

Haunted is a good word for it.

Would Gran say the same thing about mine if she could see me now?

CHAPTER 19

Elijah

"Elijah, you really didn't have to do that."

"I wanted to." I push Edna's lawn mower into her garden shed then shut and lock the door. After removing my gloves and shoving them into the back pocket of my jeans, I face her.

"Well... Then come in for some lemonade."

I really don't have time. With a system update to perform remotely and some emails to respond to, I shouldn't even have come back today. But after seeing just how long her lawn was getting, and knowing she was going to try to mow her own yard to save money, I didn't see a choice.

"I'm okay. I need to get in to work."

"You need to come in for some lemonade, boy. Don't make an old woman drink an entire pitcher alone."

I smile, unable to bring myself to argue further. "All right. A few minutes."

She beams. "Good. Come on. Take your shoes off outside."

I do as she says, leaving my boots just outside the door and setting my gloves on top of them. After washing my hands, I take a few minutes to look around her living room. My stomach flips when my gaze lands on a picture of a gorgeous brunette, her dark hair cut just above her shoulders. She smiles from the photo, though I note that it doesn't quite reach her eyes.

"Who is this?"

"Ahh, yes. That is my granddaughter, Andrea. Andie for short. She's in New York. A big-time fashion designer now." Her words are full of pride, but her tone is heavy. Almost sad.

"Do you not see her often?"

"Not nearly as often as I'd like. Here." She offers me the glass then gestures for me to take my seat on the couch. "Now, you've been in Hope Springs for a few months, haven't you?"

"Yes, ma'am."

"Former military?"

"Army," I reply.

"And you're working at the security firm?"

"Word gets around in this town, doesn't it?"

"That it does," she replies with a laugh.

I take a drink of the lemonade then stare down at the

glass. "You made this?"

She arches a brow. "Is there a problem with it?"

"No. It's—it just reminds me of my grandmother's," I say, nearly choking on the wave of grief that hits me from nowhere. She's been gone a little while now, but the wound is still so fresh. And the pain from that particular hurt is far more difficult to manage than the injuries I sustained overseas.

"I'll take that as a compliment."

"You should."

"Tell me, are you close with your family?"

Ouch. "I don't have any. My parents passed when I was little, and my grandmother raised me. She's gone now."

"I am so sorry. Siblings? Cousins?"

"Only child. And since my father was also an only child and my mother lost contact with her family long before I was born, I never knew any cousins. It's just me."

"I'm sorry about that. I suppose I shouldn't have pried, but I was curious."

Her candid nature is somewhat calming to me. Which is strange, seeing as how I can't stand talking to anyone about anything deeper than the weather.

"I really appreciate your help with my lawn," she says.

"I appreciate the lemonade."

"Good." She smiles. "I have one final question for you, Elijah. Then, I promise to ease up on the interrogation."

"Okay." I'm a bit worried about what's coming next.

Edna narrows her gaze on me. "How do you feel about

pot roast?"

———

By the time Wednesday morning rolls around, I'm still no closer to finding anything of value. I've scoured through my old files, scrubbed my own personal history, and doubled down on Andie's. No matter how much I dig, there is nothing to be found.

Add to that the tension between us these past two days, and you could say I'm beyond frustrated and desperate for a swim or some time at the gym. A run. A fight. Anything to help me burn off this frustration.

Unfortunately, I'm still *technically* supposed to be taking it easy. The pain might be manageable and dulled to an ache, and I'm officially off bed rest, but my body is still nowhere near where it's supposed to be.

Andie's door opens, and she steps out wearing dark jeans and a cream-colored t-shirt. Her dark hair has been pulled back from her face with a clip of some kind, and instead of being barefoot like she's been every day since we got here, she's wearing tennis shoes.

"Where are you going?" I ask.

"Michael is on his way to pick me up." Her tone is clipped as she lifts her purse and slings it over her shoulder.

"You can't leave."

"I'm not a prisoner, Elijah."

"It's not safe," I insist, the idea of her leaving this

haven suffocating.

"Michael will be with me. I have an appointment. I skipped last week, but I'm not missing this one."

"With who?"

She turns toward me. "You can't have this both ways." She gestures between us. "Either you want to be friends, or you don't. If you don't want to be friends, then you have no reason to know where I'm going as it has nothing to do with what's happening."

"You leaving has everything to do with what's happening."

I can tell by her reaction that my answer was not the one she wanted. But how am I supposed to give that to her if I can't even seem to figure out how I'm feeling?

"I'll be back in a few hours, Elijah." She turns to leave, so I reach out and grab her arm. The touch ignites a fire in my soul, a burning desire to draw her closer, so I let go.

"Please tell me where you're going."

She glares up at me, and I note small, barely visible freckles dusting her nose and cheekbones. How did I miss those before?

"Church," she says.

The doorbell rings, and she moves away from me to answer it.

"Ready?" Michael asks, breezing in as though nothing's wrong. That's his special ability though, to diffuse tension in the room without even trying. Or so he thinks. Having him here now only makes me more anxious.

"Let me grab something really quick, and then I will be." She smiles at him, though her gaze completely avoids me.

I hate the burning jealousy that sparks to life inside me.

"A heart at peace gives life to the body, but envy rots the bones." I repeat Proverbs 14:30 in my head, over and over again, as a reminder that jealousy is not something I need to allow to fester.

Especially when Andie isn't even mine to feel jealous over.

"You okay?"

"She doesn't need to be leaving," I snap.

He holds his hands up in mock surrender. "I go where I'm called, Elijah."

"You know it's not smart."

"Which is exactly what I told her. But she is insistent on keeping this meeting with Pastor Redding."

"What are they meeting about?"

"Again, I don't know. Why don't you ask her? You two are here playing house after all."

"It's not like that, and you know it," I growl.

"That why you're so peachy today? Because you want it to be that way and it's not?"

I don't even have time to respond because Andie steps out with the box of letters in her hands. I can't let her walk out without me. "I'm coming with you. Don't leave without me."

"You shouldn't be going anywhere," she insists.

"Neither should you," I call back as I head into the bedroom I've been using and grab my wallet and keys.

————

THE DRIVE TO TOWN IS A QUIET ONE WITH MICHAEL singing along to Skillet and Andie staring out the window. My side aches just a bit, but I haven't had pain medicine in two days, so I'm considering it a win.

Hope Springs is a welcome sight as we head down Main Street and pull up outside the church. I all but jump out of the back seat to pull open Andie's door. She glares at me as she gets out, the box of letters in her hands.

I long to know what she wants to talk to the pastor about even though it's none of my business. The walls between us are stifling, but I'm the one who put them there.

Michael opens the large wooden door to the sanctuary and peers inside. I do the same, ensuring the only person in there is Pastor Redding. He smiles and waves at us as he crosses the room.

"Please keep the doors locked," Michael asks him.

"No one will harm her while she's here," he assures us, his gaze lingering on me as though the assurance was meant specifically for me.

I fight the urge to squirm where I stand.

"We'll be across the street in the diner," Michael says. "Call before you unlock those doors, and if there's any trouble—"

"We'll call," Andie answers.

"Perfect," he says.

"Thanks." Without a word to me, she heads inside, letting the door shut firmly behind her.

"Well, you did something," Michael comments with a laugh as he clasps me on the back. Together, we walk across the street, though, with every foot of distance between me and Andie, my anxiety grows.

We choose a booth right by the window with a clear view of the church. There are no cars in the parking lot aside from Michael's and the pastor's. So when Lilly comes over to take our order, I spare her a few moments.

"You're here!" she exclaims. "We've all been so worried."

"Thanks. I'm fine."

"We've been praying for you," she adds. "How are you?"

"I appreciate the prayers," I say. "And I'm doing much better."

"Great. Well, whatever you want is on the house."

"That's not—"

"Isn't it, Alex?" she calls out to her husband.

"On the house!" he yells from behind the counter.

"You saved my best friend," she tells me, eyes misting. "This is the least I can do."

Knowing that any further argument will still lead to the same outcome, I concede. "Thanks. I really appreciate it. A coffee for now, please."

"Same," Michael adds.

"You got it." With a smile, she heads toward the kitchen, so I turn my attention back to the church.

"Are you going to tell me what happened or make me annoy you until you finally cave?"

"I drew lines in the sand, and I don't think she likes them."

"What kind of lines?"

"The kind that leave no room for misinterpretation," I reply.

Michael nods in understanding. "Ahh, so in true Elijah fashion, you pulled her closer then shoved her out the door as soon as she got comfortable."

My temper flares. "What's that supposed to mean?"

"Well, you always start out with the best of intentions. And being yourself—kind, reliable—you draw people in. However, when you sense someone getting too close, you throw the walls up."

"I don't do that."

"You do. Draw them in then shove them out the door as soon as they decide to come through it. I'm honestly surprised you let Edna get as close as she was. Then again, you had no romantic interest in her."

"I am not romantically interested in Andie."

"Here you go." Lilly breezes over and places the steaming cups in front of us. "Do you know what you want to eat?"

"Nothing yet," Michael replies. "But thanks."

"Anytime. Just wave me down when you decide." She slips away and heads toward another table with four teens.

"A lie to yourself is still a lie," he says. "And I know you better than you know yourself most days. I've seen the way you look at her. More importantly, I've seen the way she looks at you."

The mere idea that Andie could possibly feel anything beyond tolerance for me is far more thrilling than it should be. "You're projecting your own complicated feelings onto me."

Michael brushes off the mention of his ex-fiancée and the torch he still carries for her. "You can tell yourself all the lies you want, but it's not going to change the facts. Sooner or later, you're going to have to learn to let someone in, Elijah."

"I have no time for relationships."

"No. You're just afraid of what having one would mean."

"Please, continue to enlighten me on the inner workings of my own self."

"Fine." He leans back and crosses his arms. "You want enlightenment? Here it is. You've spent the last few years doing everything you can to avoid any kind of attachment because you're still angry that you survived."

His words hit. Hard.

"Angry I survived?"

"Yes. You carry guilt for the man you were before you joined the military, and even though that man died a long time ago, you're acting like it was him who walked out of the fire. Not the man you became after finding your faith."

"There were so many others who should have survived," I tell him. "Better men. Stronger men."

Michael leans in. "God saved *you*. He saved me. Lance. I won't even pretend to know why, but I do know that you have to stop beating yourself up over something you couldn't change even if you wanted to. Every single day you let yourself suffer with the loneliness as your own personal punishment is one more day you're wasting the gift you were given."

"I don't know why He saved me." Saying the words out loud alleviates a bit of the weight. It's true though—of all the men He could have rescued, allowing me to survive feels like a mistake.

"I have no idea why He saved me either, but I do know that it was for a reason."

Taking a drink of my coffee, I study the front of the church. Andie is just inside, talking about who knows what. Is she hurting? Grieving in silence?

"Stop wasting your second chance, Elijah."

"You're acting like I've been tossing out dating invitations and living in a hole."

"Not the dating invitations," Michael replies with a half-smile, "but the small apartment above the lighthouse is as good a hole as any, wouldn't you say?"

CHAPTER 20

Andie

My gran's letters are beside me as I stare at the cross just ahead. "I guess I'm struggling with everything I've done," I say honestly.

"Your past?"

"Yes. The things I did after I left this place. The people I was with." I swallow hard, trying to ease the blow of those particular words. For so long, I sought physical companionship just so I wouldn't have to be alone. Often trading it for a warm bed to sleep in during the year I was homeless. There was no connection aside from my need for something.

I couldn't even say I was attracted to some of the men I ended up with. And all the while, I knew in the pit of my stomach I was making mistake after mistake.

No matter how long I've been abstinent since, no matter

how many showers I've taken, there is still a part of me that feels…unclean.

Pastor Redding nods, clearly understanding what I'm trying to say. "Your sins are forgiven," he says. "You have been washed clean with the blood of Christ. Because of his sacrifice, your sins carry no sentence."

"How am I supposed to let go and believe that I'm forgiven? That what I did doesn't matter anymore?"

"Pray about it," he replies. "Ask for guidance. Turn to the Word. I can tell you what I know as a pastor and a follower of Christ, but only you can make yourself truly understand."

We fall into silence, and I consider what he's said. Gran always said that every problem she'd ever had, from the smallest to the largest, was solved by turning to the Bible. I've read mine, sure, but have I really sought the truth written on those thin pages?

"How are things with Elijah? Is he doing better?"

I sigh. "Physically, he seems to be doing better."

"But you're worried. I can see it all over your face."

"He's just been short. I can't seem to get a read on him. I couldn't stand him when we first met. Honestly, I struggled with the idea that my gran liked him at all. He just seemed like such a grouch. Then I got to know him a little better and started thinking that maybe we could be friends."

"And now?" he asks when I take a longer pause than usual.

"Now he's put the walls back up and is getting mad when I try to help him."

Pastor Redding chuckles. "Elijah doesn't strike me as someone who asks for help very often."

"He let my gran in," I admit. "And I think that's what's frustrating me the most. I *want* to be friends. I want to know what he and Gran talked about because he's one of the only living connections I have to who she was after I left."

Pastor Redding pats the top of the box. "It looks to me like she left you another connection," he replies. "Follow it and see where it leads you. And, if you're looking for advice on Elijah—not that you are—let me offer this. Sometimes, we have to open ourselves up before we can reach those who need us the most."

———

"WHERE IS MICHAEL?" I ASK AS I EXIT THE CHURCH. Elijah pushes off the truck he'd been leaning against. I hate the way my heart jumps when I see him. The way my body comes to life in his presence.

"He got a call about one of our systems," Elijah replies. "But he left us the truck."

"Should you be driving?" I ask.

"I've been left with instructions to let you take the wheel," he says with a half-smile as he holds up the keys. It's honestly the lightest I've seen him since he was hurt.

"Good." I set the box on the hood as I reach for the keys. Elijah pulls them just out of reach.

"I'm sorry for the way I've been acting."

His apology catches me off guard, and I find myself staring up at him, unable to break eye contact with him.

"I—okay."

"I've done things that make me less than proud and because of that, I carry a lot of guilt. As someone just pointed out to me recently, I have a habit of pushing people away. I'm sorry that you've taken the brunt of my frustrations lately."

His words so closely mirror what I'd been talking to Pastor Redding about that I can't help but wonder if we weren't put together for this specific reason. We're both struggling to let go of the previous versions of ourselves.

"Thank you for your apology. But I'm still driving." I jump up and grab the keys from him.

He laughs, the first genuinely happy sound I think I've ever heard from him, then opens the driver's side door for me. He grabs the box of letters from the hood and walks around to the passenger's side.

Once we're seated, Elijah sets the box of letters in his lap and buckles in.

I'm just backing out when a man steps behind the truck.

My first reaction is annoyance—why didn't he look before stepping out? And then I get a look at the man's face, and my stomach lurches.

"Stay here," Elijah orders as he climbs out of the truck.

Nope. I will not have my past view me as weak.

"Care to explain why you just stepped behind my truck?" Elijah demands.

George doesn't even look at him. His eyes are locked on me. "You are so beautiful," he says softly. "Just like I remembered you."

He looks almost the same. Hair slightly wavy on top, thick glasses perched on his straight nose. His clothes are even the same style he wore back when we left this town.

"Why are you here?" I ask.

"I—my fiancée left me, so I came home. My brother said you were here. How long have you been here?" He takes a step closer, and Elijah slides in front of me. "I've missed you. I tried to reach out a few months ago, but your assistant wouldn't let me through. I knew I had to see you. And here you are."

"You don't get to talk to her."

For the first time, George directs his attention to Elijah, and his expression hardens. "This is not between you and me, Breeth. Surprised I know who you are? My brother told me all about you."

Is that jealousy in George's tone?

"Then he would have told you that I don't tolerate predators," Elijah snarls, taking another step closer.

George's cheeks flush. "I am not a predator. She was—"

"Eighteen when you left, sure. But how old was she when you started grooming her? Sixteen? Seventeen?

Younger?" Elijah moves in closer, his hands clenching into fists. I reach forward and grab his arm.

"This is not the place for this, and he's not worth it." I tug Elijah back, and thankfully, he lets me. I've no doubt if he wanted to pull free, he could do so without so much as a grunt. Even injured as he is.

"Please, Annie, can we just talk? I know what happened to your grandmother and your mother. My brother told me. I want to be there for you. To help you."

Annie. He'd loved to call me that. Said it was more feminine than Andie. That it fit me better. "My name is Andie. And no, we can't talk. I have nothing to say to you." I nudge Elijah. "Come on."

"I will keep trying until you talk to me, Annie!" he calls out.

Elijah and I climb into the truck, and I try to steady my shaking hands as I turn it on and put the truck in reverse. After a quick check to make sure George is no longer behind me—although running him over would be ridiculously satisfying—I back out of the spot.

George is standing on the sidewalk in front of the church, staring after me, and I can barely breathe as I round the corner and leave town. But no matter the distance, I can still feel his piercing gaze on me.

———

WHEN WE ARRIVE AT THE HOUSE, I JUMP OUT, LEAVING THE box with my gran's letters—and Elijah—in the truck. Going around the side of the house, I make my way down the old wooden stairs toward the beach, stopping only to remove my shoes so I can feel my toes sink into the sand.

It grounds me in a way nothing else does. I reach the water's edge and take my first full breath. Aside from keeping up with his whereabouts for my own sanity, I haven't seen or talked to George since the night before he left me.

We'd shared a bed, and he'd told me he loved me. Then I woke up in the morning, cold, broke, and alone.

Wrapping my arms tighter around myself, I try not to think about the fact that, somehow, he still makes me feel so small. So naïve.

Elijah steps up beside me. "Are you all right?"

"I'll be fine. I'm just angry."

"With who?"

"Myself mainly. I can't even be mad at him. It's so like him to seek me out at my lowest point."

"You don't look like you're low to me," he says softly.

I look over at him. "I gave that man every part of me. Even the pieces I should have kept to myself. And he used me then threw me away, just like everyone else has."

"Your gran didn't."

I turn to face him. "But I used her, didn't I?" A tear slips down my cheek. "I used her and then threw her away.

The woman raised me, and I left her for him. For empty promises."

"Andie." Elijah reaches up and cups my cheek. His thumb caresses my skin, and the touch is so tender it soothes my soul. "You didn't throw her away."

"You aren't reading her letters, Elijah." I move away and face the ocean. Elijah drops his hand. "In every single one of them, she tells me that she misses me. That she wishes I would come home. And I didn't. I stayed away because I was ashamed of who I was—of what I'd done."

"You've done nothing that deserves shame."

"You don't even know me. You don't know what I did for that year. The things I traded for a warm place to sleep. If you did, you'd let whoever is after me have me."

He forces me to face him. "There is nothing you could have done that would have me turning my back on you."

"It's only a matter of time." Panic claws at my chest, anxiety gripping me with iron claws. Seeing George pales in comparison to everything else I'm dealing with, so why is it that I'm spiraling like this? But I know the answer. It's one more thing. One more ghost haunting me.

"Listen to me. No, it's not. I am not going to leave you. I'm not going anywhere. You and I are in this together. Are you hearing me?"

"You already tried to shove me out the door." The words are out before I can stop them, and I wish I could take them back. He apologized. I don't need to hurt him with my insecurities.

"You scare me," he whispers.

"What?" His words shove my anxiety to the back burner. "Why would I scare you?"

"I've been in more combat zones than I can count. I did things I wish I could forget. I've been shot, stabbed, tortured—" He closes his eyes and takes a deep breath before opening them again. "Blown up. And it's you who terrifies me."

"Why would I terrify you?"

"Because you make me—" He inhales again and keeps his gaze trained on me. The sunlight makes his eyes even brighter, bringing the colors to life. "You are constantly on my mind, Andie. I wake thinking of you. When I go to bed, I dream about you." He steps in closer, and my heart skips. "You've seen what happens to me. The demons I struggle with."

I know he's talking about his PTSD. About attacking me before he was fully awake. Or, at least, he sees it as an attack. I recall the fear beneath the anger. The twisted terror in his expression. And that's not violence. It's pain.

"You didn't hurt me, Elijah," I remind him.

"But I could have. I could have…" It's the most vulnerable I've ever seen him, and I'm afraid that saying anything right now will stop him from telling me what he's thinking. "It makes any kind of relationship impossible. But you make me wish—" He bends down and leans his forehead against mine. We're a breath apart with only the crashing waves as company. "You make me wish I deserved you."

I tilt my face enough to offer the mouth I so desperately want him to kiss. "You told me that you thought of yourself as a lesser man," I say. "But I don't see you as anything less than everything I've always been afraid to want."

Elijah snakes a hand around the back of my neck and pulls me in. He hesitates just a moment, our lips a breath apart as the wind wraps around us. And just when I worry he's going to back away, his lips touch mine—gently at first. A tender taste of what we've both been desiring.

But that simple meeting of lips only leaves me craving so much more. I lose myself in the kiss, warmth surging through me as need sings in my blood. I crave him. This kiss. His mouth moves effortlessly on mine as though the two of us were formed for each other.

Wrapping both arms around his waist, I tug him closer, and he deepens the kiss. The breeze continues to surround us, cocooning us in our own private reality where there's no death. No danger. Just him and me.

For now.

CHAPTER 21

Elijah

Hours later, I'm still thinking about that kiss.

Even as I sit here beside Andie with Eliza, Lance, Michael, and the sheriff, I can't get my thoughts straight. Which, given our current predicament, is probably not a good thing. Especially since, the deeper I get, the more I realize that I'm not sure how I'll let her go when it's all over.

"Thank you all for being willing to meet me," Sheriff Vick says as he reaches into his pocket and withdraws a notepad then turns his attention to Andie. "We received a call from the anonymous tip line about someone who claimed to have seen George Johnson dragging something large into the backyard of your gran's house on the night your mother was murdered."

Her green eyes go wide. "What?" she whispers.

I know she's thinking of the fact that we just saw him

earlier today, and probably about a million other things, so I reach under the table and take her hand. It's warm, and she threads her fingers through mine, squeezing gently as though she needs the comfort.

"Since he doesn't live here in Hope Springs anymore, we wanted to verify the information and make sure it wasn't just someone using your past to lead us astray."

"And?" I ask when he doesn't immediately respond.

"According to his parent's neighbors, he got into town just after your gran's funeral and has been here ever since."

"So it's possible?" Andie whispers.

"He won't tell us where he was. Says he didn't do it, of course, but he has no alibi for the night of your mother's murder."

Andie pulls her hand away and stands so abruptly she nearly knocks her chair over. "He killed her?"

"We have no evidence to prove he didn't and only the call that places him at the scene."

"What about the guys at the lighthouse?" I ask. "George wasn't there."

"How do you know?" Andie asks. "They were all masked. He could have been one that got away."

"He doesn't fit the build," I tell her. "Those men were hired muscle there for a single purpose."

"What about the library?" Eliza asks.

"He could have been using that and the damage to Edna's house to scare you," Lance tells Andie. "Groomers will do that. Scare their victims into a corner until they feel as though they have nowhere else to turn."

"It's also possible they aren't connected," the sheriff says.

"But unlikely," Michael replies.

"I will agree with that." Sheriff Vick reaches into the folder he brought and hands me a stack of papers. "Here are the rap sheets for the men who died at the scene and the one we arrested."

I already have them, but I don't tell him since the way I got them wasn't necessarily aboveboard. Aggravated assault. Armed robbery. After giving them a brief look over, I offer them to Lance and Michael.

"Any idea who the others are?"

"No. All of these men ran in different crowds before this attack. As far as we can tell, none of them even knew each other."

"So this was incredibly organized," I comment. The person who set it up didn't just hire a crew and go with it, they handpicked each and every member.

"Which makes the idea that George is involved with them even more unlikely." Lance turns to me. "Is there *anyone* from your past who might have a reason to come after you now?"

I spare a look at Andie, but she's facing away from me, Eliza standing at her side.

"I looked into it. But the crew I ran with before is either all in prison or dead." I swallow hard, hating the words even as I speak them. Andie turns to me, and I know I'll have to talk about this a second time.

In more detail.

"What about any relatives of theirs? Close friends?"

I shake my head. "I don't see how. As far as anyone knows, I'm already dead too." Honestly, that part of me died a long time ago.

"There has to be something we're missing," Michael comments as he sets the background checks to the side. "Can we get in to talk to George?"

"I want to do it," Andie says quickly.

"What? No. You don't need to do that."

"He's in custody, which means he's not a threat. If he's not talking, then let me try. Maybe he'll tell me."

"Andie, that's a terrible idea," I tell her, recalling how she'd behaved today.

"I deserve to try to get answers, Elijah."

I swallow hard. She's right. I know that. Everyone here does. And it's entirely possible that George will confess to her. That she's an obsession he hasn't been able to kick, and when he saw that her grandmother passed away, he knew she'd be here and he'd have a chance to capture her attention.

People have done worse things for less.

"I want to talk to him," she insists. "Can I?"

"I don't see what it will hurt," the sheriff says. "Honestly, I'd be grateful for a break in this so I can put it to bed. The town is already restless over having one dead body. Even if no one cared much for her, the murder is making everyone nervous." He smiles apologetically. "I'm sorry to be so callous."

"No need to apologize," she replies. "It's the truth."

———

As soon as everyone is gone and the place is locked down, I head into the office to check our security monitors. Everyone who came here today knows how to check for a tail, but I still worry they'd be followed.

"What type of crew did you run with?"

Andie's leaning against the doorjamb, staring at me. I knew this was coming, but I hate that it's a piece of my past that will stain her view of me. "After my parents died, my grandmother tried hard to raise me to be a good person. But I fell in with a bad crowd."

"What did you do?"

"I fought," I tell her. "Bare-knuckled brawls for money. In basements, garages, warehouses, alleys—wherever we could get into on short notice."

"Like underground fight clubs?"

"Exactly like underground fight clubs. I was fast, and because I could take a hit and get back up, I made good money doing it. Was able to pay off most of the hospital debt from my parents' accident."

Andie stares at me, but if she's surprised, I can't tell. "So you fought for money."

"Yes."

"When my grandmother found out about it, she was furious." I can still see her face. Her reddened cheeks as she glared up at me. The shame I'd felt then is just as heavy now.

"How did she not already know? A teenage boy coming home with bruises would raise a lot of red flags."

"I was fast," I tell Andie. There's no arrogance in the statement because it's a fact. "I rarely got hit. The times I did, I explained that I'd been roughhousing with some of the guys at school. No big deal and all that. Boys will be boys. That's what she'd say anytime I came home with a bruise. Anyway, a few days later, she had a stroke. It was the second one she'd ever had, and she made me promise to do something more with my life, so as soon as she was healthy and back home, I joined the military."

"Why did you choose to leave her?"

"I had too many connections in Los Angeles—that's where I'm originally from." I swallow hard, recalling just how difficult it was to make the decision to leave. "I knew she'd never leave the friends she had there, so I made the choice to take myself out of that life as soon as I'd gradu-ated high school."

"And you never looked back?"

"No. Once I got in, I realized that I loved the structure. That I was good at doing what needed to be done. So I put everything into that and became a Ranger."

"How long did you fight for?"

"Two years."

"I never would have pegged you as the type."

"Not many do," I admit. "Lance was a homeschooled genius. Michael, the town's golden football star. I craved the violence that came from fighting. It was like breathing oxygen for me. The thrill of the battle, the blood staining my fists. That's not something I care to advertise."

"You're not that man anymore though."

"I still fight." I think back to the men who attacked me. To the way my heart hammered in my chest, my blood pounded in my ears.

"But now you fight for something more than money," she replies. "When you said that lesser men survived, you think you're lesser because of what you've done?"

"The men who died that day deserved to live. They'd never done anything worse than get a speeding ticket."

"And you think because you were a troubled teenager, who took out his anger on a willing participant, you deserved to die?"

When she says it, it sounds foolish. I feel foolish for thinking that way. But I can't help the guilt I carry. "In a way, yes."

Andie straightens and crosses toward me. She stops right in front of me and tilts her face up to look into my eyes. "I stand by what I said, Elijah. You are not a lesser man. You did bad things. So have I. Maybe that's why we get along so well," she adds with a half-smile.

"You have no idea the anger I felt when George was standing behind the truck. I wanted to hurt him."

"Then that makes two of us. But the thing is, Elijah, we didn't. And that means something." She stares up at me, and I move closer, dropping my head down to kiss her. The feel of her soft lips beneath mine jump-starts the desire in my veins.

I cup her face, tilting it up so I can deepen the kiss.

Never, in my entire life, have I felt such heat for someone. Andie makes me want to be a better man. She makes me want to risk everything for a single lifetime at her side.

The phone rings, and we break apart.

With my gaze on hers, I back toward the desk and retrieve the landline. "Hello?"

"I need to speak with Miss Montgomery." The tone is clipped, to the point. And instantly recognizable even though I only met her once.

"How did you get this number?" I ask her assistant.

"She gave it to me when she called me earlier. I need to speak with her. Now, please."

Pulling the phone away from my ear, I offer it to her. "It's your assistant."

She takes the phone, gaze never leaving mine. "What is it?" Andie's face pales, and her eyes widen. "Okay. I'll be there as soon as I can. Please do what you can."

"What is it?" I ask when she hangs up the phone. "Be where?"

"My investors are all backing out," she replies. "Apparently, I'm being accused of stealing designs." Her brows draw together as she processes. "It doesn't make any sense. I've never stolen anything. I swear."

The pit in my stomach grows because I know this is no coincidence. "You're being drawn out," I tell her. "It's a trap."

"But this is my life, Elijah. My livelihood. I have to defend it. There's a meeting the day after tomorrow with my investors. I need to be back in New York for it."

"Andie—"

"I have to go, Elijah." She steps past me, so I reach out and grab her hand.

"Then let me come too."

"Fine. You can come. Just—" She takes a deep breath. "I can't believe this is happening. Everything is burning to the ground. My gran. My mother. Now this? What else can they try to take from me?"

Your life.

The words pop into my head, but I don't dare say them out loud.

They'll be echoing in my brain until the day we stop whoever is after her.

———

WITH MICHAEL AT THE HOUSE, I STEP INTO THE CHURCH.

Andie was still asleep when I left this morning, and thankfully, he'd been more than willing to come sit so I could make this trip into town. Honestly, he was probably grateful to hear I was going at all.

It's still dark outside, but Pastor Redding always makes it into the church before sunrise. Edna told me that. She'd spent nearly every morning here, praying and having coffee with the pastor's wife.

A door at the side of the sanctuary opens, and Pastor Redding steps out. He seems surprised when he sees me, but that shock turns to delight.

"Elijah. Is everything okay?" His expression turns concerned, so I nod quickly.

"Everything's fine." *But is it?* I take a seat on a pew toward the middle of the sanctuary. When I'd come with Edna, she'd have me sitting front row. I still remember the first Sunday after I'd helped her with the groceries.

I'd been sitting in a back pew, and she'd grabbed my hand, practically dragging me to the front.

Pastor Redding sits down beside me. "What's on your mind?"

"Nothing new. That's not true," I admit quickly. I just lied. In church. To a pastor. Shaking my head, I sigh. "Andie Montgomery."

He chuckles. "Ahh, yes."

"She's just—she's a force of nature." I can't imagine any other way of describing the way I'm feeling. I'd been set in my ways before she showed up. Content with my loneliness. But now, the idea of losing her terrifies me.

Especially since I know how quickly everything can be lost.

"Andie is that," he says. "She was always quiet, but there is a storm in her."

"I think I'm falling in love with her, and I've only known her a week."

"You've known of her a lot longer than that," he replies.

"Fair enough. But I didn't care much for what I'd heard."

He laughs. "Edna loved her. You loved Edna. It stands to reason you saw some good in her even before you met."

"So you're saying I only love her because of my connection with Edna?"

"No. I'm saying that you likely are feeling a connection that is partially rooted in your shared affection for Edna. Everything you've built with her is you, Elijah. Why are you so afraid of it?"

I clasp my hands in my lap.

"How is your PTSD?" he asks when I don't respond.

I've spent more than a few days in these pews after a nightmare, and sometimes just vocalizing what I'm feeling has helped me move past it and get a few easy nights of sleep. But the demons always return. They cling to me in that desert. Granules of sand that sear my skin.

"It's been worse lately."

"Because of what's going on with Andie?"

"Possibly."

He grunts in understanding.

"Lately, I've been so angry. I've wanted to cause pain to everyone who hurt her. I feel the desire to hunt them down and make them pay. I've always struggled with a violent heart," I tell him. "It's what I fed back when I was fighting. Every hit I took, every fist I landed, was like a balm for me."

"You're worried that you're reverting?"

"I know I am. I don't know how else to explain it. Those men in the lighthouse—"

"They were there to hurt you. To hurt Andie. Do you regret stopping them?"

"No," I tell him truthfully. "But—"

"Before you found God, before the military, what would you have done to George Johnson after learning what he'd done to Andie? Or Stanley—I heard what he did to her in that diner," he adds. "So tell me, what would you have done to them?"

My gaze lands on the stained-glass window behind the crucifix. "I don't feel comfortable speaking it aloud in church," I say with a half laugh.

"God already knows what you're thinking, Elijah."

"Fair enough." I shrug. "I would have made them bleed. Taken vengeance for her without thinking about it."

"And what did you do when Stanley Johnson grabbed her arm?"

I take a deep breath. "I threatened him."

Pastor Redding laughs. "But you didn't make him bleed, did you? You didn't attack him."

"If he hadn't let her go, I would have." Just thinking of that day infuriates me. The terror on her beautiful face, the fury on his. "If he hadn't let her go, I would have ripped him apart."

"Elijah." He touches my arm. "Just the simple fact that you hesitated shows your growth. You may have had a violent heart before, I won't argue that point, but you're changed now. Reborn in your faith. The man you were before has died."

As he says it, Michael's words also echo in my mind.

"You carry guilt for the man you were before you joined the military, and even though that man died a long time ago, you're acting like it was him who walked out of the fire. Not the man you became after finding your faith."

Both men offer reminders that I've desperately needed. I *am* different.

But that doesn't mean I won't still struggle.

In fact, choosing to change who I was means the battles will only get harder.

"Thank you," I say to Pastor Redding.

"I hope I helped," he says as he stands. "My door is always open. And might I suggest you visit Romans chapters seven and eight? I think the message there is going to resonate today. Have a good day, Elijah. And tell Andie I said hi. I'm praying for you both."

CHAPTER 22

Andie

I never wanted to face off with my past. I wanted to bury it. Somewhere deep down in the dark, where it would never resurface.

But here I am, walking into the sheriff's office, Elijah at my side. He's been quiet since we left the house this morning, and I can't tell if it's because of this meeting or the fact that we'll be making the flight to New York this afternoon.

I risk a glance up at him, my gaze traveling over the strength of his stubble-covered jaw, the soft lips I've begun to crave. How am I falling so hard so fast? Didn't I learn my lesson?

"Are you okay?"

"Not particularly." I press a hand to my stomach. "I feel like I might be sick."

He threads his fingers through mine but doesn't say

anything aloud. Yet, the message is so powerful it's as though he spoke it. *You are not alone. I am here.*

He has to release my hand as we move through the metal detector and he turns in his firearm. Then he takes my hand again as we make our way over to Lance, who is standing outside a door, talking to Sheriff Vick.

A uniformed officer stands just outside a white door.

"He's in there," Lance says, gesturing to it.

"There's a viewing window so we can watch," the sheriff tells me then points to a door directly to the left of the guarded one. "You won't be alone."

My stomach twists, nerves burning me up. He probably killed my mother. Was possibly behind the trashing of my gran's house. Yet, here I go, stepping into a room—alone—with him. What could go wrong?

"I will be fine." I take a deep breath.

Lance offers me a tight smile then walks through a door alongside the sheriff while I remain outside the white door that separates me from the man who derailed my life with a charming smile and empty promises.

"Are you sure you don't want me to go in there with you?" Elijah asks.

"He won't talk if you're in there. He's threatened by you."

"Good."

I swallow hard. "Before yesterday, I hadn't seen him since the night before he left me."

"You don't have to do this," he says.

Tilting my face, I look up into his kind, hazel eyes. "I do need to do this."

Elijah grips my chin then leans down and presses his lips tenderly to mine. "I'll be just on the other side of that glass. One word and I'll be there."

"Thank you."

With a final nod, he slips into the viewing room. As I approach the door, the deputy smiles kindly.

"Yell and I'll come in," he says. "One loud word and it'll only take me seconds to get to you."

"Thank you. I'm ready."

He opens it to let me inside.

The room has bright white walls with LED lights overhead, and a table sits in the center, bolted to the floor, George's hands cuffed to the top. As I make my way over to the chairs across from him, my legs turn to jelly.

His eyes are on me.

Focused intently on every move I make, but I don't meet his gaze until I'm seated.

"Annie, I'm so glad you're here."

"Andie," I correct him.

"That's not fitting for you," he says softly, using the cajoling tone he always employed when I was in school. He'd spoken so softly to me, making me think that he was the only one who cared about me. "You're too feminine. To soft. Haven't I told you that?"

"I'm not soft," I reply, honestly surprised that I believe it. "Did you kill my mother?"

His brows draw together. "You know I'm not capable of violence."

It's true. In the entire time I knew him, he never once had an outburst of anger. No, George was always too calm for that. His words were too carefully chosen. "You were seen at the place she was later found dead."

"I would never hurt your mother. I would never do anything to hurt you."

"Except saddle me with a mountain of debt and an apartment I couldn't afford."

He drops his head to stare down at his lap a moment before looking back at me, expression twisted in shame. It was a look that worked on me whenever I began to question his whereabouts or asked to go home to visit. The man could control me with a single glance.

"Annie, you'll never know how sorry I am for what I did. I was so afraid though. So worried about you seeing that you were too good for me. So I ran. I got scared, and I ran."

"You ran because you're a predator," I tell him. "And I got too old for you."

George's mask slips for just a second—long enough that I see pure rage on his face. In that moment, he reminds me more of his brother than ever. "If I'm a predator, then you're a home-wrecker. Just like they always said you were. Showing up in class, wearing tight jeans. What was I supposed to do? I'm a man!"

"I was young!" I yell, slamming my hands on the table.

He jumps. "I was fifteen when you first whispered into my ear. Do you remember that?" My stomach rolls. "A fifteen-year-old sophomore who should have been safe with her teachers. But you told me how mature I looked. How grown I was and that I should leave my hair down because it was so beautiful." I gesture to the hair I've never kept longer than my shoulders since. "You're the reason I keep it short. Because I know you loved it long." Tears burn in the corners of my eyes. Shed for the girl I'd been.

"I didn't touch you until you were eighteen," he counters.

"No. We didn't share a bed until I was eighteen. But you did plenty before then." I want to vomit. To scream. To slam my fist into his face over and over again until he's no longer handsome enough to charm anyone. *Dear God, be with me. Give me strength.* I take a deep breath.

"I'm not here to debate any of that with you. The fact is I made my choices, and I live with the consequences." I meet his gaze. "What I want to know is whether or not you killed my mother or had anything to do with the library or my grandmother's house being trashed."

"He's going to leave you too, you know."

"What?"

"Breeth. He's going to get tired of you. And when he does, he's going to leave you too. And you'll be all alone, wishing that you'd come running to me when I opened my arms."

Anger sings in my veins, so I lean in closer. "I don't see

you opening your arms, George, because they're currently handcuffed to a table. Have you forgotten you're being charged with the murder of my mother?" I shove my own insecurities over this newfound—whatever it is—with Elijah and focus intently on George.

He glares at me, the mask he's worn for so many years slipping off. "I didn't kill anyone."

"Then why were you at my grandmother's house?"

"I told you. I've been looking for you. I called a few months ago, and your assistant wouldn't put me through. I tried to get ahold of you through your grandmother, but that old woman wouldn't give me the time of day."

Old woman. "You better watch your tongue." I can practically feel Elijah simmering from the other side of the glass.

"That librarian too. She caught me—outside your gran's house. Told me that I was a predator and that, if she didn't know what God would do to me would be far worse than anything she could deal out, she'd handle me herself." He snorts. "Stanley and I let her know what we thought about that."

"So you trashed the library."

"We demolished it," he replies. "It was Stanley's idea."

"And the brick through my window?"

His cheeks redden. "That was Stanley. I told him not to do it. That I didn't want to hurt you." The mask slips back into place. "I only felt bad for leaving the way I did, and I just wanted to find a way to make it up to you. I've missed you." He tries to touch my hand with his, but the handcuffs keep him in place.

"So you trashed the library and threw a brick through my window."

"Stanley threw the brick," he retorts.

"Why would you trash the place that mattered most to me in this world if you only wanted to make up?"

"I didn't trash her house. The front window was Stanley. I don't know who did the rest. And I didn't kill Rebecca. Why would I? She was only ever supportive of us."

I can feel the color drain from my face. "What did you just say?"

"Our paths crossed when she first got to town. She told me that she would never have kept us apart. That, if you would have listened, she'd have told you that I was good for you. That we were good for each other."

I don't know why I'm so shocked that she would hand me over to a man like him.

But I am.

"Fine. If you didn't kill Rebecca, then where were you that night? Before and after you went to my grandmother's house?"

"I was…" He sighs and shakes his head.

"Tell me, or you're going to go away for murder, George. You've already confessed to multiple crimes. Don't add murder to the list." I try to use a bit of his game against him. "I don't want to see you penalized for something you didn't do."

He smiles. "I knew you still cared."

"Tell me," I insist.

"I met someone online. She wanted to meet, so I went to meet her."

"How old?" He doesn't answer. "How old is she, George?"

"Seventeen. But it doesn't matter because she didn't show up anyway. I sat alone in a parking lot, waiting for her. When she didn't arrive, I knew that I needed to follow my heart. So I went to find you."

"Seventeen." I shake my head angrily, trying to battle back the nausea. "You're sick."

"I want to love and be loved. What's so wrong with that?"

I don't even justify it with a response. "What about after?"

"I went to my brother's. We had a few beers with one of his neighbors."

His story about being with his brother and a neighbor can be easily checked, but the parking lot one will be a bit more difficult.

"So you're saying that you didn't kill Rebecca."

"No. Of course not. I didn't kill anyone. There was no one there when I showed up, and after I peeked through the window and saw all the damage, I took off. I've been so worried about you. Why wouldn't you talk to me? Why wouldn't anyone let me through? What did you tell them about me?"

"The truth." I take a deep breath. "My assistant didn't put you through because you're on a no-contact list. As for my grandmother, as far as I'm concerned, you should be grateful she didn't press charges against you." I push up from the chair. "And as for me? I want nothing to do with you, George. You're a sick, twisted man who preys on girls, and I'll no longer fall victim to your game. In fact, I'll find every way I can to keep you behind bars."

"Don't leave me!" he calls out. "I'm not done talking to you!"

"I'm done with you, George. If you ever manage to get out of here, don't bother trying to contact me." I slam the door behind me.

Elijah steps out from the viewing room alongside Lance and the sheriff. He holds me against him, wrapping an arm around my shoulders. The nearness soothes my pain.

"Do you believe him?" Lance asks Sheriff Vick.

"We need to verify his alibis."

"Can you get him on the admission of soliciting a minor on top of the damage to the library?"

"We can. We'll get a warrant, search his home and computer. Gather as much evidence as we can. He'll do time."

"Stanley too?" I ask.

"We'll get him for breaking and entering plus vandalism," he replies.

I swallow hard, feeling a sense of victory that he will not be able to target any other young girls.

"Are you all right?"

It takes Elijah's words to break me out of my thoughts. I'm surprised to see that it's just the two of us standing outside the interrogation room. When did Lance and the sheriff walk away?

"I'll be okay. Thanks." I smile. "I'm surprised you didn't come barreling through the door."

"I considered it, believe me." He runs a hand through his hair. "But you seemed to have it pretty well handled."

"I did okay."

"You did great. You got his alibis. And uncovered the damage to the library and the brick through your window."

"Not a confession for murder, though."

"If he didn't do it, a confession is useless because it doesn't stop what is really going on." Elijah reaches down and threads his fingers through mine. "But this is a win, Andie."

As I smile up at him, the door to the interrogation room opens, and George walks out beside two uniformed officers. He sees Elijah beside me, his gaze traveling down to our joined hands, and his expression turns deadly.

It's that change that has me doubting his insistence that he didn't kill Rebecca. Because the way he's looking at us makes me think that it's possible he's capable of murder after all.

———

"THIS ISN'T NECESSARY," I SAY WITH A SMILE AS ELIZA offers me a mug of tea and takes a seat on the couch. Elijah, Michael, and Lance are all working on installing an even better security system in Gran's house, so Eliza is keeping me company while they work outside.

"I know it's not. But after hanging around with those three, I imagine you could use a little girl time."

I laugh. "Honestly, aside from Lilly, I haven't had many friends. Girl time is not something I'm overly familiar with."

"Fair enough. If it helps, I'm the same way."

I take a sip of my tea. "How long have you been in Hope Springs?"

"Almost two years," she replies. "I came here from L.A."

"That's where Elijah is from, isn't it?"

"It is," she replies. "But we didn't know each other from before. They're a good bunch of men, you know."

"They seem to be."

"It's hard to trust when you've been hurt." The way she says it makes me wonder just what this woman has seen. "But the three of them will do anything for the people they care about. You seem to be someone they care about."

"I hardly know them."

"You and Elijah seem close."

My cheeks heat. "I'm not sure what's going on between

me and Elijah," I admit. "There's something there, but it's new. And he doesn't seem overly thrilled with the idea of a relationship."

"I wasn't either. When I came here. Lance installed my water heater." She chuckles. "I was so awful to him at first —I'd just gotten out of a terrible marriage and didn't want anything to do with anyone."

"Understandable."

"But he was there when I needed him. Took a bullet for me—literally."

I'd heard something about the stalker she'd dealt with, along with the near-death experience, but Elijah hadn't gone into details. "You two are great together."

"I never believed in soul mates," she says. "But I do think God made us for each other." Her grin is infectious, and I'm still smiling when Elijah steps into the room.

Our gazes meet and hold, the silent exchange between us worth well over a thousand words. Is he feeling this too? This stirring of the soul? "It's done. No one is getting within ten feet of this house without us knowing. And the cameras are high resolution, so we'll be able to make out features. As long as—"

"They aren't wearing a mask," I finish.

"Yes."

Michael breezes in and takes a seat on the couch beside Eliza. "While you two are living it up in the big city, we'll monitor the place and let you know if there's any activity."

"Thanks."

"Anytime."

Lance comes into the room and walks toward Eliza. He leans down and presses his lips to the top of her head. "Ready to go, my love?"

"I am." She stands. "We're headed to Boston so Lance can check in with some of the clients and I can go shopping with his mother."

"Sounds fun."

"It is. If you need anything, you can call me. Elijah has my number. Be safe."

As she says the words, I get this sinking feeling in my gut that whatever has been happening is only the beginning of what we'll have to face before it's all over.

CHAPTER 23

Elijah

Bags in hand, I follow Andie into her apartment. After setting them on the floor just inside the door then locking it behind me, I stare in complete awe at the place before me. The walls are a pale yellow, the couches white with splashes of color in the form of throw pillows.

A queen-sized bed sits against one wall, a dresser beside it, and a second bookshelf—this one with actual books—is situated beside the only interior door. A bathroom would be my guess since I see no other place for one.

She has plants in nearly every corner and a bookshelf overflowing with a type of ivy plant and succulents. It makes me smile because, even though Andie doesn't have an outdoor space like Edna did, she managed to create her own garden.

"You are your grandmother's granddaughter."

She laughs. "I'm just glad to see that they're all still alive. My neighbor was watering them for me." After crossing her living room, she pulls open the patio doors, and a light breeze carries in through the open space. Even as late as it is, cars honk, people yell, but the serene view of Central Park just outside her apartment somehow mutes everything else.

"This is stunning." I step out onto the patio then stare out at the partially illuminated park. Streetlights down below cast just enough illumination that you can see trees and bushes while the light from buildings all over the city lessens the weight of the darkness.

"It's not the ocean though," she replies. "I miss Hope Springs already. I cannot believe I miss it."

"The place grows on you. I'm going to do a quick sweep of the apartment. Check the windows and the bathroom and place some sensors."

"Okay. Coffee? I know it's late, but I could use some."

"Yeah. Sounds good." As she gets to work on the coffee, I inspect the apartment. Since most of the place is one massive room, it thankfully doesn't take long, and I get to watch her while we work. As soon as her apartment is set up with my wireless system, I take a seat on the couch to finish the setup on the panel.

"How are we looking?" she asks, offering me a mug.

"All set."

"Great." Andie sits on the other end of the couch and

kicks her sandals off. She rolls her neck, and I note the exhaustion on her face.

"Here." Setting the panel and my coffee on the table in front of me, I reach out and place her feet in my lap.

"What—no—you don't have to—oh, please never stop." She groans as I massage her right foot, digging the pads of my thumbs into the bottom. I slowly work my hands down her foot then back up, all while she keeps her eyes closed, head rolled back. "That feels amazing," she says.

It shoots straight through me—thoughts that have no business in my head. And even though I know I should stop to give myself a chance at maintaining the moral code that I've defined for myself, I can't.

So I switch to the other foot.

"Elijah. Seriously. You missed your calling."

I laugh. "You look tired."

"Exhausted. But so are you. You're the one with metal in your gut."

"Not anymore. They got it out, remember?"

"Still. You should be taking it easy."

"Massaging your feet is taking it easy," I tell her. "Touching you is—therapeutic for me."

She opens her eyes. "You are far more charming than I gave you credit for the first time we met."

"I'm not trying to be charming. It's the truth."

Her cheeks turn pink. "I like it when you touch me. A lot more than I should."

Just hearing her say it stirs my feelings all over again. "I can't have a relationship. And I am not the type of man to sleep around."

"I'm not looking for one either," she admits. "And I don't sleep around either. Not anymore."

"Then we agree that whatever is between us needs to remain…"

"PG?"

"Agreed," I reply, though I hate myself for it. The truth is I want this woman more than I've ever wanted anyone. But not just in bed. I am intrigued by her strength, by the heart that she tries so hard to keep hidden. And the fact that what I'm feeling goes so far beyond mere attraction terrifies me.

———

*F*LAMES LICK AT MY SKIN.

Ears ringing, I can't hear anything Captain Knight says as he drags me away from the destroyed Humvee. Michael is lying on his back, his hand pressed to a wound on the side of his neck.

And then everything slams into me.

The sounds.

The smell of burning flesh and rubber.

The heat of the sun above us.

"Keep pressure!" Knight yells as he presses my hand to my side. "Don't touch the other side, okay?"

I nod.

A bullet sings through the air and hits the ground with a puff of dirt.

"Dear God, please help us," Lance whispers then rushes away and kneels behind what little cover we have. He aims his rifle and fires.

"You gotta live, man," Michael chokes out. "You gonna live?"

"Are you?" I ask.

He laughs, but it's a strangled sound. "Maybe. Can you — I need you to do something for me if I don't." With the hand not currently pressed to the side of his neck, he reaches into his pocket, struggling with each movement.

"Stay still."

"I need you to give this to her." I know who he means, the woman he left behind. The one he hopes is still waiting for him at home. The paper is smeared with his blood as he tries to offer it to me.

"Keep it on you so you can give it to her yourself. If you don't make it, I'll know where to find it."

He nods, tears in his eyes.

A man groans. I tilt my head. "Corporal?" I ask then try to scoot closer to him. He turns his face to me, half of it burned beyond recognition. Bile rises in my gut.

"I don't want to die," he chokes out.

"You're going to be okay. Do you hear me?"

More bullets fly. Knight jerks back and groans, falling

*to his knees. Fear ices my veins, and I reach for the pistol
at my side. They won't get us.*

They won't get me.

Not again.

———

I SHOOT AWAKE, SWEAT BEADING ON MY SKIN. THE CEILING
fan above me whirrs slowly, chilling me as I throw the
blanket off and place both feet on the floor.

"Hey, are you okay?"

I glance up, surprised to see Andie sitting up in bed, her
dim lamp on beside her. "Fine," I say, tone more clipped
than I meant. "Nightmare."

"You need a distraction." She climbs off of her bed and
carries the box of Edna's letters over to me. She sits on the
couch and offers me the one in her hand.

"Are you sure?" When I'd offered to read them before,
she'd been almost angry at the idea of me touching what
her grandmother had left behind for her, but now, she offers
it freely. Do I truly look that pitiful?

"I wouldn't be holding it out to you if I wasn't sure.
Besides, this one has you in it."

"What? She wrote about me?" I'm honestly surprised.

She nods. "In her later letters, she does."

Curiosity shoving my nightmare aside, I take the letter.
The sight of Edna's familiar handwriting brings a fresh
wave of grief crashing down on me.

"Dearest Andie," I read aloud, "You will never believe it, but I finally got internet in my house! I know that I'd been so against it—" I chuckle as I recall just how excited she'd been when it was up and running.

"But Elijah insisted I get it. He says it will be useful and that he can show me how to pay my bills online instead of mailing in checks. How are things going with you? I hope you are having all of your dreams come true. You deserve nothing but happiness, my dear girl. All my love, come home soon, Gran."

I finish reading and look up at Andie. Her eyes are a bit misty, but no tears fall.

"I'd tried so hard to get her to get internet at her house, but it was you who convinced her."

"It took me a while," I reply. "I'd wanted to install an alarm at her house and get her hooked up so that, if she fell again, I could—"

"Again?"

"She fell once. Hit her head on the table. She said she wasn't out long, but when I got to the house, there was quite a bit of blood on the floor." I was so afraid after that, worried that she'd get hurt and no one would know.

"I didn't know that."

"She never wanted you to worry. She made me promise never to contact you unless it was something life-threatening. I considered it, but—"

"You don't break promises." She points to the letter. "She mentions that too. How, when you say you'll do or won't do something, you follow through. That was one of the things she admired most about you."

I swallow hard, emotion burning in my throat. "She made me promise to protect you."

"What?"

"When she was in the hospital that final time. She made me promise to keep you safe."

Andie's eyes widen. "That's why you stepped in like you did."

"I would have done it even if I hadn't promised her. Honestly, before I knew you were in any real danger, I considered breaking the promise and just parting ways so I would never have to think about you again."

Instead of being offended, she laughs. "If it helps, I couldn't stand you either."

"You think? You accused me of trying to seduce an eighty-year-old woman."

She winces. "I did do that, didn't I?"

"You did."

"Well, to be fair, I had no idea who you were, only that you were spending a lot of time with my gran. It seemed weird at first."

"She was such a good person. A light."

"She really was." Andie reaches into the box and pulls out another letter. "Care to read more?"

"Those are yours."

She shoves it into my hands. "It's clear to me that you

loved her as much as I did, Elijah. You need this connection just as much as I do."

"Are you sure?"

She wraps a hand around the back of my neck then pulls my mouth down to hers for a quick kiss. It only lasts a heartbeat, but the feel of her is branded onto my heart.

"I'm sure, Elijah."

She curls into my side and pulls out another letter while I break the seal on the one she gave me. And together, in the middle of the night, we allow ourselves to be swept away by the words of someone we both loved, all while I come to the stunning realization that I am falling for Andie Montgomery.

I'm falling hard.

CHAPTER 24

Andie

I should be exhausted. At some point around four in the morning, I fell asleep leaning against Elijah, only to wake two hours later with him still reading. I'm surprised he looks as alert as he does given he'd been mumbling in his sleep long before the nightmare finally woke him.

But here we are, walking into my office, him in dark jeans, black boots that look like they were made for combat, and a button-down shirt. The business skirt and jacket I'm wearing fit me like a glove, but since I've been living in jeans and a t-shirt, it feels almost alien to me.

Unwelcome.

"Good morning, Miss Montgomery," Mia greets as she walks toward me on heels as high as stilts. Her gaze lands on Elijah. "Why are you here?"

"We're dating," I say quickly. It's not entirely a lie—I don't think—and telling her I need a bodyguard is attention I don't particularly care for. When I told her to leave Hope Springs, I'd only said I needed more time to get the vandalism cleaned up. I'd left off most of the danger, not wanting word to spread.

While I don't think Mia is a gossip, I didn't feel like risking it. If the tabloids got word of what was going on, they'd be all over Hope Springs. And my hometown is a place I've wanted to keep private for a reason.

Many reasons, actually.

"How nice. I can get Mr. Breeth set up in your office if you'd like?"

"I will show him. Are they here?"

"Not all of them," she replies. "Mr. Malik, Mrs. Velena, and Mrs. Sierra still have not arrived."

"Perfect." I breathe a sigh of relief. The last thing I want is to have kept them waiting. "Can you get us both coffees?"

"Of course. Mr. Breeth, how do you take yours?"

"Elijah," he corrects. "And black is fine, thanks."

She nods and strides off, so I lead Elijah to my office, passing what I call the production room in the process. Inside, it's unusually quiet, likely because Mia sent everyone home as soon as the allegations came in.

No need for there to be an audience for this meeting.

Once we're in the safety of my office, I shut the door

and set my bag down. "I'm sorry. I didn't mean to just blurt that out, but I didn't want her to know."

"I'm not bothered," he replies. "Honestly, I'm relieved."

"You are?"

"I want this to go somewhere, Andie. Once the dust settles and everything is clear, I'd like to revisit how we feel about each other." He takes my hands, and my heart begins to race. What does it say that just a simple touch from this man can turn me inside out? "I know I said I wasn't one for relationships, but—"

"I feel the same," I interrupt. "And I would love to see where this is going."

Elijah beams at me. A true, unhindered smile that steals my breath. Then he leans down and presses his lips to mine. I wrap both arms around his neck and lean into the kiss. If any of the few employees still in the office were wondering who he is, there would be no question about it now.

Someone clears their throat, so I pull back and face the doorway, expecting Mia. Unfortunately, it's not her.

Alec Malik is dressed to impress in a three-piece suit, his blond hair styled by someone who probably charged him a few hundred dollars. The man looks like money, and sadly, he thinks his finances give him superiority over everyone.

He'd been after a date with me the last year when he

came on board representing an unknown donor but backed off a couple of months ago. Based on the jealous fury on his face, he was hoping I'd cave one day.

"Alec. It's good to see you."

"You too." He breezes into the room and all but rips me from Elijah's arms to pull me in for an embrace. Then, before releasing me, he kisses me noisily on the cheek.

Behind me, Elijah is practically vibrating with anger.

"This is Elijah Breeth. My—uh—boyfriend."

"Mr. Breeth." Alec holds out his hand, and Elijah takes it. "Pleasure."

"Yeah," he replies as he withdraws his hand.

"We've been worried about you," Alec says as he refocuses on me. "When we got the call about your grandmother, we were all so upset. I never met the woman, but I felt like I knew her. I grieved with you, Andie, even though you couldn't see me. I hope you know I was there."

Has he always been this obvious? Or am I just seeing it clearly now?

"Thank you. Your words are kind."

"I mean every one of them." He tows me to his side then guides me toward the door. "Everyone is waiting for you. Let's go clear up this nonsense so you can get back to doing what you do best."

"I'll be there in a minute." I back away. "Please, go and wait for me."

"We can walk together when you're ready."

"She said you can wait for her," Elijah growls.

Alec glares at him. "We're friends," he says. "And I am going to be there for my friend."

"Go," I say with a forced smile. Unfortunately, Alec is one of the people who hold the cards of my business in his hands. If he chooses to say anything to the man he works for, he could withdraw his support. The others will follow, and I'll have no funding. I might be doing well for myself, but if I lose financial support, my business will tumble like a house of cards.

"Very well. I'll see you in there." He turns and leaves the room.

"Well, that was—" I turn toward Elijah.

"He has a thing for you."

"I know. He's been asking me out for years. I think seeing us together must have triggered his jealousy. He's not normally that bad."

But as I speak the words, I can already see Elijah's wheels turning.

"You're going to run a background check on him, aren't you?"

"I am. In fact, I need the names of everyone in that room."

"I'll have Mia give them to you."

The door opens, and the very person we'd been talking about strolls in with two coffees. "Here you go."

"Great, thanks. Listen, can you get Elijah the names of our investors? He's starting a file system for me."

If she's suspicious, she doesn't show it. "Sure. I can

bring you a list once I get the rest of the coffee delivered to the conference room."

"Great, thanks." I turn back to Elijah. "I'll be back as soon as I can." I set my coffee down beside his then lean in and give him a chaste kiss before retrieving the coffee again.

"Are you sure you don't want me in there?" he asks.

"I'll be fine, Elijah. This is what I do. Well, part of it, anyway."

After leaving the office, I head down the hall to the conference room and take a deep breath. Every one of the people in this room believed in a vision I had before I ever brought any of it to life. I couldn't get a business loan to save my life, but one of the instructors I'd had at the design institute set me up with a meeting so I could pitch my ideas. She'd believed in me when no one else did.

And because of her, I built what I have.

Now, I might lose it all.

Keep it together. With a smile on my face, I enter the room. The round table has eight seats, and half of them are filled. Alec has taken the chair closest to where I will sit while Pria Hardin sits beside him, and the other two investors—Emma Velena and Poppy Sierra—are in chairs across from him.

The mood is somber, their expressions grim.

"It's great to see you all, even if it is under such horrible circumstances."

"We hope to clear up any confusion," Poppy says.

"Great. Because that's what I'm hoping for." I set my folder down and take my seat. "Mia didn't give me many details over the phone, though she said someone called and made a false accusation about my designs?"

"Yes. We received word that you'd stolen the designs from a young woman who shadowed you for a time."

"I've never had anyone shadow me," I tell them truthfully. "You can ask anyone who works for me. I work alone. Always have."

"That's not what she said." Emma withdraws a written letter from a folder in front of her, followed by a handful of designs too similar to some of the ones in my current sketchbook.

"This makes no sense." My heart begins to pound. "These are my drawings. A near exact match."

"That's what we were worried about." Pria shakes his head. "We put our trust in you. Helped you build everything you have. And then this happens? I will not have my name tied to a company that cannot be trusted. I've been in this industry far too long to allow a virtual No Name to take me down."

"But that isn't me," I insist. "I didn't steal them because these are mine."

"Is it possible she got ahold of your work before it was designed?" Alec asks.

"No. Unless she was helping me physically put it

together, no one sees my sketches until the first outfit is ready to be worn. I keep everything in hand."

"Then how can you explain the fact that she brought these to us before you ever sent the final photos over?"

My body goes cold. "What?"

"We've had these images for months now," Alec says. "Before your last show."

"Months? And you said nothing?"

"Why would we? We wanted to see if it was true." Pria replies. "As it turns out, it is. She warned us you'd be showing us that exact dress. The design is truly one of a kind—it was easily recognizable when we saw it at the showcase before you left."

"Yes, then you take off suddenly, claiming a death in the family—"

I shoot up from my chair. "Are you saying that I made up my grandmother's death?" I growl, fury lacing every single word.

"No one is saying that." Alec reaches out and touches my hand. "Are we?"

My vision blurs, and heat creeps up my neck. The room begins to spin, and I can feel every single beat of my heart straight down to my toes. *Anger. It's just anger.* "My grandmother died," I say. "I did not make any of it up. This is a lie. I don't know how, but it's a—"

I stop speaking as the spinning room tilts and plant my feet to remain standing.

My breathing grows labored, each inhale more difficult than the last.

"Andie?" Alec asks, standing.

"I—get Elijah." I fall over, and my head slams into something—though I'm already so far gone that I'm not sure what.

And then everything goes black.

CHAPTER 25

Elijah

I 've just finished looking into Alec Maliki when someone screams.

Gun drawn, I race into the conference room to find Alec attempting horrible CPR on Andie. Mia stands, eyes wide, hands pressed to her heart as she stares down at her boss. Panic fuels me, and I sheath my weapon then shove him aside.

I lean down and listen for breathing but hear none.

No pulse either.

"Call 9-1-1!" I order Mia then take over chest compressions. "Please, God, don't let her die." I pray aloud, over and over again, repeating the same thing as I continue trying to keep her heart pumping.

"What happened?" Alec demands. "Why is this happening?" He's hysterical. Completely and totally out of his mind as he paces back and forth. The other investors remain where they are, staring down at the clinically dead woman on the floor.

"Shut up!" I order him.

"The ambulance is here!" someone calls out.

I remain focused, doing my best to keep her blood pumping through her heart as the paramedics arrive. It's only when they tell me to step away that I listen and watch as they try to bring the woman I love back to life.

Please, God. Please don't let her die.

———

"SOMEONE DRUGGED HER?" MICHAEL ASKS THROUGH THE phone.

"Yes." Andie is asleep now, eyes closed, an oxygen mask on her face. She looks so pale. So weak.

"When? How?" he asks.

"My guess is her coffee. Her assistant was prepping it, but she'd been busy getting everyone's ready, so she claims to have left it sitting for just a few minutes. Anyone in the office could have gotten to it—including her. The police said they would be having it tested. I called Jaxson. He's going to be flying out."

The LAPD detective and former Marine helped us out last year, and when I'd called this time, he'd agreed to cut his vacation short and fly to New York to help me sort this out. I can't be in two places at once, and right now, Lance and Michael are needed to keep our business afloat.

"This is getting ridiculous. Is she going to be okay?"

"The paramedics managed to start her heart, and the doctors pumped her stomach. They think she'll be okay. But for how much longer?"

"We've narrowed it down to someone at that office. So that's a start."

"None of the pieces make sense though," I remind him. "This person killed her mother, trashed her grandmother's house, sent people after me, and now tries to poison her? How does all of this fit?"

"I don't know, brother, but we'll figure it out."

"I feel so helpless. So completely useless."

"You're there for her. You saved her."

"I love her." The words are out of my mouth before I can stop them.

"So glad you've caught up with what the rest of us have known since you first met her." Michael chuckles. "You saved her life, Elijah. She's going to be fine."

I take a deep, steadying breath then reach forward with my free hand to take hers. "I'll let you know when we find something out. Any movement on Edna's place?"

"Nothing but silence. Seems to me the danger followed you to New York."

"Good to know. Talk soon." I end the call and lean forward to press my forehead to the top of her hand. So close. I'd been so close to losing her.

"Hey," Andie chokes out.

I look up to find her watching me. "How are you feeling?" She tries to move her oxygen mask, but I shake my head. "You have to leave it on."

"What happened?" she asks, her words muted through it.

"You were drugged."

"I don't understand. How?"

"The doctors said someone must have crushed a bunch of pills up and put them in your coffee."

She groans. "So it is all connected. The accusations were a way to draw me out."

"We knew that was likely what they were for. And now that's what it's looking like. Though it did help us narrow it down to someone who has access to your office."

"Who? I do thorough background checks on everyone I hire."

"Someone slipped through," I tell her. "And today, it nearly cost you your life."

She closes her eyes. "Everything hurts."

"I had to give you CPR for a while to keep your heart pumping. You'll be sore for some time."

"CPR?"

"You died, Andie. Your heart stopped for three minutes." Just saying the words nearly breaks me. The image of her lifeless body is far more haunting than any nightmare I've ever had.

"I don't remember anything but hitting the ground," she says. Her words are barely audible. Her eyes shoot open. "The investors. The meeting."

"Your death put the meeting on hold. Seriously, everyone understands."

"They were accusing me of plagiarizing my designs." She closes her eyes again. "I don't know how they would think that. No one has access to my designs."

"Someone got them somehow. But I'll get it figured out. You need to rest."

"Are you okay?" she questions. "Your coffee was okay?"

"Mine was fine." I wish it had been mine though. I wish it were me lying in that bed right now. Except then, there would be no one to protect Andie. "I have a friend coming into town. A detective out of LA"

"Your old stomping grounds," she replies with a half-smile.

"Ironically, it was Lance who introduced us."

She looks up at me, emerald eyes glossy. "I'm sorry I scared you."

"You keep scaring me." I take her hand in mine and press my lips to the top of her palm.

"I've never had anyone look at me the way you do."

I open my mouth to respond, to tell her that she matters more to me than anyone else in the entire world, even though I barely know her, but someone knocks on the door, and Andie closes her eyes.

"Get some sleep." I kiss her on the forehead then cross the room and open the door. Jaxson is a sight for sore eyes. His dark hair is graying at the temples, his gaze stern.

"How is she?" he asks as I step aside and let him in. The LAPD detective sets his duffel bag down on the floor then crosses his arms as he looks at Andie.

"Tired," I reply, keeping my voice right at a whisper.

"You look tired too," Jaxson comments.

"I was blown up less than a week ago."

He nods. "Lance told me about that. You're lucky to be alive."

"You don't have to tell me that." I run a hand through my hair.

"There a shower in there?" he asks, gesturing to the bathroom.

"Yeah. You bring me some clothes?"

"Check the bag. I figured you didn't have much with you here, so I grabbed an extra set before I left my apartment. We're about the same size."

Relieved, I open the bag and withdraw a pair of jeans and a t-shirt. "These them?"

"Yep. Go grab a shower. I'll keep an eye on her." He takes a seat in the chair in the corner. "I've put out feelers with my contacts here in New York, so as soon as they get back to me, I might have more information to offer."

"Thank you." Since he's an actual officer, he can get information a whole lot easier than any of us. The former Marine has helped us out on more than one occasion when we've needed something our security company cannot legally obtain. I slip into the shower and turn on the hot water.

It begins steaming as I strip out of my old clothes and toss them to the side.

Hot water hits my back as I climb in and rest both palms against the tile wall. It stings when it hits my still-healing injuries, but I don't yield. The pain serves as a reminder that I'm alive. That no matter how many steps ahead this person seems to be, we keep winning.

Otherwise, Andie would be dead.

Bowing my head, I pray. *God, please give me the strength to keep going and the knowledge to piece this entire thing together. Please let her survive, God. No matter what, please let Andie make it through this.*

FRESHLY SHOWERED, I TAKE A SEAT ON THE CHAIR BESIDE the bed. I'm just leaning back when the door opens and a man walks in. His nearly obsidian hair is sprinkled with gray, and his green eyes are stern as they survey the room.

"Can I help you?" I demand, getting to my feet.

Jaxson remains sitting though I know he'll get involved the second it's needed.

"I doubt it," the man replies, though he shuts the door behind him. His suit alludes to someone with a lot of money, and I realize that he might be one of her investors here to try to make even more accusations.

"Whatever you have to say to Andie can wait." I nearly

growl the words. "As you can see, she's not in the shape to discuss business."

"I'm not leaving," he tells me.

"Yes, you are." I get in his face, ready to shove him out the door if necessary. But then Andie groans.

I look over at her and note the shock on her face.

"Dad?"

CHAPTER 26

Andie

I haven't seen my father since the day he walked out on me and Rebecca. Honestly, if it weren't for the one photograph I managed to save of the three of us while my mother had been burning all evidence of him, I probably wouldn't even recognize him. So to find him staring down at where I lie in the hospital bed is nearly as much of a shock as learning I was technically dead for three minutes.

"What are you doing here?"

"I heard what happened." He remains where he is, standing nose to nose with Elijah, who looks about ready to tear him apart.

"But how?"

"I'm an investor in your company. When they made the announcement that you were in the hospital, I caught a flight, and now I'm here."

"An investor?" He could have told me he could fly, and I would have been less shocked. "Since when?"

"Since your grandmother contacted me and told me what you were doing."

"What— Elijah, please." He looks ready to rip my father's head off, which is making it hard to fully process everything that's happening.

How is he here?

Why is he here?

Elijah takes a step back, and I note a third man in the room—one I definitely don't recognize but imagine is probably the detective Elijah told me was coming.

One stranger at a time.

I shift my gaze back to my father, who is watching me intently. "Gran contacted you?"

"Yes. We stayed in touch throughout the years."

The words are a traitorous dagger. "She never mentioned you. Not once."

"I asked her not to." His gaze flicks nervously to Elijah. "Can we talk in private?"

"No," I snap before Elijah has a chance to answer for me. "In case you haven't noticed, someone is trying to kill me. They are here for my protection."

His cheeks flush. "You don't need protection from me. I'm your—"

"You're a stranger," I interrupt. "We may share blood, but that doesn't make us family." My words land, and his expression softens before he nods.

"I am a stranger." He takes a deep breath then turns to Elijah. "My name is Jack Gannon. I am Andie's father."

"Elijah Breeth."

"Jaxson Payne," the man in the corner says.

"Thank you both for keeping her safe." He turns back to me. "I contacted your gran a few years after your mother and I split. I apologized to her for running, and she told me that she didn't think it was good for you to have any contact with me. I imagine it was out of protection because she didn't trust me not to disappear again. Since I couldn't blame her, I agreed and begged to be kept up to date about anything going on in your life. After you graduated college and were trying to get your own design firm off the ground, she contacted me, and I have been supporting you anonymously ever since. A silent investor. Alec works for me," he says.

"Alec." I nearly laugh.

"Yes. He is my assistant. He intervenes on my behalf and attends all meetings for me."

"So you just write the checks and send him in to handle everything else?"

"I didn't know what else to do. Your gran made me promise to stay out of your life."

"I'm an adult!" I yell. Tears sting the corners of my eyes. "For the last nine years, I've been an adult. You couldn't reach out to me once in any of those years?"

He closes his eyes and takes a deep breath. I don't remember much about my father. I know he wasn't a yeller, that he let my mom do whatever she wanted and spent more time drunk than sober. But right now, he looks like an exhausted man, one weighed down by the choices he's made.

"I can only say I'm sorry," he finally says. "I can't make up for what I did, though I can make plenty of excuses as to why I left."

"Rebecca is dead." For the first time in my adult life, tears stream down my cheeks. "Did you know that? Gran is gone."

"I know. I heard about your mother. It's a shame."

"A shame?" I try to sit up, but exhaustion pulls me down. "A shame? Someone murdered her." I know it's not his fault, but I spit the words out.

"It is a shame. Your mother and I didn't have a great relationship, I'm sure you know that. It was toxic, and I thought you would both be better without me."

"Don't hand me that load of bull," I tell him. "You thought *you* would be better off without her. You didn't consider what would be best for me. And it looks like you were better off." I gesture to the suit. "Where exactly did you get all that money you've been donating?" I snap. "We were broke when you were married to Mom, so where did it come from? Drugs?"

He winces like I struck him. "That's fair. But no. I've been clean and sober for nineteen years now. I started working for a trucking company then left five years later and opened my own."

"Did you remarry?"

He hesitates. "I did."

"Kids?"

"Two."

The hurt starts all over again, the feeling of abandonment rooting in my soul. "So you started all over again. Just left us behind for newer models."

"Your mother and I met when we were both so young," he insists. "We never should have gotten married. I knew it, but when we found out about you..." He looks away. "I'm sorry, Andrea, I didn't mean it like that."

"My name is Andie," I snap. My heart rate spikes, and the monitor beeps. I close my eyes and try to steady my breathing before opening them again.

"You need to leave," Elijah tells him. "She's healing, and this is too much stress."

"I want to know that she's safe."

"She is. And when she's ready to contact you, she will." To my surprise, Elijah keeps his tone level, his expression neutral.

"I want to talk to you about your employee, Alec," Jaxson says then pulls out a notepad and a pen. "Let's do it in the hall."

My father starts to follow then hesitates. "I'm sorry, Andie. I never stopped loving you. If you don't believe anything else I say, please know that I hate myself for leaving you."

Without another word, he follows Jaxson out of the

room. I lean back, my adrenaline pumping, tears streaming down my cheeks.

The bed dips as Elijah climbs on beside me, and I curl up against him, resting my head on his chest. The heavy beating of his heart serves as a grounding mechanism for me, and as I time my breathing to his own, I'm able to ease my frayed nerves.

"Are you okay?" he finally asks.

"No."

"Understandable."

"The nerve of him. To show up like this after all these years."

Elijah presses a kiss to the top of my head but doesn't say anything.

"It's like he thinks that, just because he waltzes in here and says he's been investing money in my company, it makes up for all the years he left me alone." I shake my head and then tighten my grip on Elijah.

"I'm sorry, Andie."

"It's not your fault. I just—I can't believe he showed up."

"In his way, he loves you."

I look up at him. "You sound almost sorry for him."

"I am sorry for him," he replies. "He missed out on getting to know you."

"I'M DOING MUCH BETTER, THANK YOU," I TELL MIA AS she calls and checks in yet again. The hospital released me first thing this morning, and we wasted no time leaving New York. We rented a car and opted to make the nearly eight-hour drive back rather than take a flight. Since planes make me nauseous on a good day, I'm grateful.

With Jaxson in the back seat of our rented SUV, we're headed back to Hope Springs, and although I'd once left this place behind and never looked back, I'm ready to return.

I miss the ocean. The smell of the salty air. The people.

"I'm so glad to hear it. You gave everyone quite a scare."

I look over at Elijah, who is staring straight ahead as he drives. Does he know how crazy about him I am? "That's what I heard."

"When are you coming back in? The investors have been trying to nail down a time to re-schedule."

"Once I get everything handled with my grandmother's house," I tell her. "Right now, we're on our way back to town."

"How far out are you?"

"About fifteen minutes," I reply.

"Well, let me know if there's anything you need me to handle. I'm here."

"Will do, thanks. Goodbye, Mia."

"Goodbye, Miss Montgomery."

I set my phone back in the cupholder.

"Everything okay?" Elijah asks.

"It will be. Once all of this is over, I can figure out who stole my designs and pawned them off as their own. Then I can put the investors' minds at ease, and everything can go back to normal. Well, as normal as it can be."

"Speaking of," Jaxson says. "When did you say you revealed the design they claim was stolen?"

"Right before my gran's funeral. It was part of our spring collection."

"And who had access to it?"

"No one. I made the outfit myself. I always make the first one. No one saw it until it was revealed at that show."

"Do you ever leave your things unaccounted for?"

"No. The only one with a key to my office is Mia, but even then, the designs are kept in my private safe at home."

"Who has access to that?" Elijah questions.

"My neighbor has a key to my apartment. But—"

The car comes out of nowhere. Everything happens so quickly.

The screeching of tires.

Twisting metal.

Glass shattering.

Pain. Mind-numbing agony.

"Andie!" Elijah bellows, and then, for the second time in as many days, the world around me goes black.

CHAPTER 27
Elijah

"I have to get out of here!" I yell as I try to stand again.

"Sit down before I have to start all over again," Doc scolds as Lance shoves me back down onto the bed. His hands hold my shoulders, and even though logically I know I can't go hunt for Andie when my forehead is bleeding, I also know we've already been here too long.

She could be anywhere.

Jaxson and I were both out for three hours before someone found us in that ditch. Three hours, and there's no telling where Andie is. The other driver is gone, the car abandoned and wiped clean of prints, so I know whoever was in it had to have taken her.

But who?

And why leave us alive?

Jaxson stands in the corner, silent as he has been since

Doc finished his exam and determined he has a mild concussion. Which, given the fact that the rental has been smashed into smithereens, is a pretty good prognosis.

We should both be dead.

Andie. Her seatbelt had been cut, and we found one of her shoes at the scene. Where is she? How badly is she hurt? Is she even still alive? Millions of scenarios run through my mind on repeat.

"Okay, there." Doc steps back, so Lance releases me. I push to my feet, ignoring the aches that shoot through my body. "I don't know how you're still on your feet," he says. "But if you take any more hits right now, I'm not sure you'll be able to stand."

"I'll be fine." I start toward the door.

Michael moves in front of me, hand up. "Why don't you let us take the lead on this."

I turn toward Lance. "If it were Eliza, would you stop?"

We both know he wouldn't. Didn't, in fact, when she was in the crosshairs of a stalker. "No."

"Then get out of my way," I tell Michael.

He moves, and I practically run out of the hospital, ignoring the fact that every step brings fresh pain.

"What is the next move?" Lance asks as he, Michael, and Jaxson catch up to me right as we climb into Lance's truck.

"I need to get to the office and start piecing this together."

We pull out of the parking lot and start the drive to the lighthouse.

"I contacted the sheriff. He's searching for any traffic camera footage in the area. Most of it is empty highway, but we might get lucky."

Please, God, let them find something.

"I don't know. But there's got to be something somewhere that ties all this together. Did you contact her father? Any word on Alec?" Jaxson had wanted to set up an interview but hadn't had any luck.

"He hasn't been seen or heard from since Andie's collapse."

Lance guides his truck into the parking lot, and I'm surprised to see the sheriff's car there, him leaning against the hood. When he sees us, he pushes off and waits near the porch as we climb out.

"How are you both feeling?" he asks Jaxson and me.

"Fine. Any new evidence?"

"We actually did find something I think you'll want to take a look at." He gestures toward the door, so Lance unlocks it, and we go inside. Then he hands me a thumb drive. "This was taken about a mile from the accident. Caught on a traffic cam just outside of town."

I fire up my computer, heart pounding.

This is her.

It has to be Andie.

Right?

After sticking it into the USB port on my computer, I

open the file and watch closely. I scan every person on the sidewalk, every car that passes until—

"That's Mia." Andie's assistant is behind the wheel of a large white SUV.

"I thought you said she was still in New York," Lance says.

"She was. Andie was talking to her—" And then the pieces begin to fit. Not all of them but enough that I can make out a clear picture. The coffee. The text message that directly ordered those men to take me out.

What if I'd been the target in New York too?

"Did you run a background check on her?" Jaxson asks.

"Of course." I roll over to my laptop and fire it up, then open the file I have on her assistant. "Twenty-four, never been married. Grew up in a house with both parents and two other siblings. Went to college at the same school Andie did, studied design."

"The woman in the car is Diana Pallum," the sheriff says. "I had someone run her face through facial recognition."

"No. That's Mia Harper. She's Andie's assistant."

"Diana Pallum is a ninety-seven percent match," he insists. "And Mia Harper is currently living alive and well in Paris, France, working on a new design line for some big designer over there. I can't even pronounce the name. I called and spoke with her before I headed over here."

"That can't be right." I double-click on the photograph attached to the file I built on Mia Harper.

Blue eyes.

Blonde hair.

I zoom in. And spot a small, crescent-shaped scar at the corner of her right eye.

After doing a quick search in a database I probably shouldn't be using, especially in police company, I open a photograph of Diana Pallum. Same general facial features, though her eyes are brown, and her hair is a strawberry blonde versus the platinum in Mia's photo.

No scar.

Closing my eyes, I picture Mia's face when I'd seen her last. She'd screamed when Andie collapsed, her expression almost hysterical.

Had there been a scar?

"What is it?"

"The scar. You met her assistant. Do you remember there being a scar on her face?"

"No," Michael tells me. "I actually don't. But it's such a minor detail—"

"Not in this, it isn't. It's not her. She was using a false identity." I lean back in my chair, furious that I missed it. How did I miss it? But I know the answer to that, don't I? I've been grieving the loss of Edna, all while trying to actively fight the growing feelings I have for Andie.

And now the price of my distraction might just be Andie's life.

CHAPTER 28
Andie

My body aches. Every single muscle and joint burns like they're on fire.

But the pain is nothing compared to the bone-chilling fear as I sit tied to a dining room chair. The structure is practically falling down around us, and the stench of decay clings to the air. The wallpaper has yellowed and is peeling, the floor sunken in some places, shag carpet worn, torn, and stained.

Alec sits across from me, though he's unconscious, his chin touching his chest. His breathing is steady, but based on the bruising on his face, he could have some internal injuries as well. What he's doing here, I've no idea because our *host* has yet to say a word to me.

"Alec," I whisper loudly. I tried to kick him under the table earlier, but my legs are tied to the chair I'm sitting in. "Alec!"

I glance into the kitchen.

Mia has her back turned as she hums and cooks something on the stove. It smells pungent like a mixture of wet dog food and vinegar. She hasn't spoken a word to me since I woke up, even when I tried to get her attention, she just remained in the kitchen, humming along to nonexistent music as she cooked.

It's as though she's in her own world, completely separated from us.

Heart hammering, I close my eyes and take a deep breath. The rope tied around my throat bites into my skin. I struggle against it, but it's secured to the ceiling by what looks like an old plant hook. Nausea churns in my gut, and bile sears my throat.

Elijah.

I have no idea where he is. No idea whether he or Jaxson survived the accident. If she brought them here. I have no way of knowing because I woke up tied to this chair.

Is he alive? The mere thought of his death is even more suffocating than the stench in the air. His face swims into view, rare smiles, bright eyes…

Please, God, let him be alive. Please give me the strength to get out of this. I need to see him. Just one more time. Please.

"Praying will do you no good," Mia says. I open my eyes to find her staring down at me, two plates in her hands. "If that's what you're doing." She grins and sets one down in front of me.

I gag, bile rising in my gut as I stare down at the lump of jellified food on the plate. But then I notice the design on the dinner plate.

Gran. "These are my grandmother's plates."

"Possession is nine-tenths of the law, you know. So these are mine now. Besides, it's not like dear Granny Edna is using them anymore."

I bite back my anger. I need to stay calm. Keep a level head. "Where is Elijah?"

"Where is Elijah?" she repeats in a mocking tone. "Always about Elijah. Elijah this. Elijah that. You just met the man! He should already be dead," she sneers. "That coffee was meant to be *his.* But you went and switched it."

She'd tried to kill him and gotten me instead. The image of him lying in a hospital bed assaults me. "Why are you doing this, Mia?"

"My name is Diana!" she yells, face turning red. Seconds later, she laughs. "Though you wouldn't know that, would you?" After dropping Alec's plate in front of him, she takes my bound hand. "Nice to meet you, officially, Andrea Montgomery."

She releases me and goes back into the kitchen, moving around a massive hole in the floor.

"Diana. I don't understand what's going on. Can you tell me why you're doing this?" How did I not pick up on her being an imposter?

She ignores me and sets a third plate on the table then walks over and slaps Alec in the face. He groans, eyelids fluttering. "Wakey-wakey, eggs and bakey!" she calls out then giggles like a mad woman.

He opens his eyes and stares down at the food.

"Okay, maybe not eggs and bacon," she comments. "But what can I say? Eating on a budget over here." She drops down into the seat at the end of the table. "Now. Dig in!"

Given that we're both secured to our chairs, neither of us can reach for the forks beside the plates.

"Oh!" She laughs wildly. "I guess you need a hand, don't you? Here. Let me help." She starts with Alec and scoops up a heaping amount of food on the fork. "Open up."

He clamps his mouth shut and shakes his head.

"Open wide, here comes the choo-choo train!" She stabs it into his lips, and he screams.

Blood pools from the areas where the tines penetrated his skin, but she doesn't stop. With his mouth open on a pained cry, she shoves the fork in.

He gags, and she claps, dropping the fork to the floor. "Good? It's good, isn't it?" She laughs then comes over to me.

I swallow hard. "I really would rather not eat right now. Unless, of course, you want vomit all over your table."

Mia—or rather Diana—narrows her gaze on me. For a moment, I wonder if she's going to argue, but instead, she takes her own seat and eats a bite of the food in front of her.

I risk a glance at Alec. His mouth is bleeding, his face pale. "Why is he here? Why am I here? Who are you?"

"Do you recognize where we are?" she asks, holding out both hands.

"No."

She stares at me as though her glare alone will be enough to make it click. "You know, I knew you were self-centered, but this is next-level. Here, maybe this will jog your memory." She gets up and moves into the living room where she pretends to fall over and hit her head on the table.

It hits me.

"This is my old house."

"Correction!" she yells, getting to her feet. "This is my father's old house. You and that slut of a mother just lived here for a time. You know, until you killed him."

Dread burns in my gut.

Impossible.

He didn't have any kids...did he?

"My father never came home. I found out far too late that it had everything to do with the fact that your mother found him and dug her gold-digging nails into him." She kicks her feet up on the table and takes another bite.

"I didn't know he had any kids."

"How would you have known? Self-centered brat. You were the apple of everyone's eye, weren't you? I wonder what everyone would think if they found out you were a murderer?"

"I didn't murder your father."

"Yes, you did. I know you did. Because I was here when he died. I watched the whole thing. Do you know that? I came here, looking for him, and he hid me like I was something to be ashamed of. Right over there, even—" She gestures to the closet.

Its slatted doors have been broken in, but I can picture it the way it was before.

"It was an accident. He'd been terrorizing me, and I just wanted to scare him back. I didn't mean to kill him."

"You left him there. You left him to rot. I sat there, waiting for him to get up. Waiting. Waiting. All the while, you were packing a bag and running back to your perfect life."

"I—"

"Shut up! I don't care what you have to say! Don't you get it? I don't care!"

I bite back my words. "What does Alec have to do with anything?"

"He was my way in. He helped me find you. He knew the plan. And then he grew attached." She gets up and grips his hair, yanking his head back. He winces. "Pathetic men. They just can't seem to keep their heads around you women, can they?"

"Diana, I am so sorry for what happened, but I was a child. I was scared. That's why I ran."

"Your granny seemed to think everyone would hate you for what you did."

"Gran? Did you talk to her?" My mind races. "Did you —did you kill her?"

"No." Diana waves her hand to dismiss the accusation. "But she was so ashamed of what you did she paid me to keep quiet. Do you know that? When I turned seventeen and my mother kicked me out, I went looking for you. I wanted to make you pay. To make you see what you'd done to me. But your granny wanted you to keep having your perfect fairy tale life. She offered me money in exchange for silence, and I took it. All while I tried to come up with a way to make you pay for what you'd done."

"She never told me."

"Of course she didn't. Self-centered brat. How could she have? You were never around! A few years later, I knew that what I had wasn't enough. Then, I met Alec here. Excellent thief, by the way. He stole my wallet along with my heart." She licks the side of his face, and my stomach rolls again.

How did she hide so much madness?

"I'm sorry, Andie. I'm really sorry," Alec whimpers.

"Shut. Up. Alec." She slaps the back of his head then goes back to her seat. "Anyway. Alec was merely my way in. We were supposed to do this together, and he betrayed me."

"Do what together?" Fear claws at my throat. How am I

supposed to get out of this? Who knows I'm missing? If Elijah and Jaxson are both—

I can't even think the words.

God, please.

"We were going to make you pay for what you did. For everything you put me through. I destroyed your precious grandmother's house like you destroyed my life. I killed your mother the way you killed my father. And now, it's your turn."

"Why wait so long?" I ask quickly. *Keep her talking. Buy time. God, please. Help me survive this. Please give me strength.*

"The money was good," she replies. "Until your grandmother went and died." Diana rolls her eyes. "After that, I knew there was nothing left for my silence. It was time to act. And I have enjoyed every minute of watching you crack! Strong, resilient, stoic Andie Montgomery breaking at the seams. Elijah was just icing on the cake. Gorgeous man, Andie. Nothing like that Michael though. Now *there* is a man. It really is a shame they got involved with you."

"Did you hurt them?" I'm almost afraid to know the answer. Terrified that, if I learn she killed him back at the scene of the accident, I'll have no fight left in me.

"I thought about it. After all the trouble he caused me, I genuinely considered killing him where he lay. But I couldn't risk it. There wasn't time. No worries though, I sent him a present, and he should be getting it—" She checks her watch. "Any minute now."

I go lightheaded. "What did you do?"

"Enough." She claps her hands together and laughs. "Now, before I kill you, I want to enjoy this one final dinner. We are family after all. Stepsisters and all that."

Dread coils in my belly like a snake about to strike.

I struggle against the ropes holding me, fear burning me up for whatever plans she has for Elijah. So I turn to the only One who can bring us through this. *Dear God, please, please, please let him survive. Please don't take him from me.*

CHAPTER 29

Elijah

"Don't get mad, but I went through Edna's accounts."

I look up at Jaxson. "What?"

"Edna's bank accounts. I have connections," he replies when I don't immediately respond. After setting his laptop down on my desk, he gestures to the screen, specifically to a two-thousand-dollar payment sent last month.

"What is this?"

"These payments happen every month, on the first day, and are sent into a bank account under the name Alec Malik."

"Alec. The investor who works for Andie's father."

Jaxson nods. "I've already reached out to Jack Gannon about it. He claims that he had no idea and has opened his office so that NYPD can get into Alec's desk. I have a buddy out there who is taking lead."

"We knew that Edna was in contact with Andie's father," Michael says. "But why would she be paying money to his assistant?"

"Edna wrote everything down." I jump up and grab the wooden box full of Edna's letters to Andie. Could it be so simple? Could the answer have been inside here this entire time? I immediately go to the back, the final letter she wrote, and scan the words.

Dearest Andie,

Today was a hard day. I'm feeling weaker. More worn down than I have in years. I'm afraid to call you though because the last thing I want to do is put pressure on you. You've already struggled so much, child.

So much more than anyone should ever struggle.

I want you to know how sorry I am that I failed to see the signs before you left. I am so sorry that I didn't step in sooner. That I didn't rescue you from your parents well before the divorce.

You should know your father has been in contact with me for quite some time now. I know he doesn't deserve it, but you should truly give him the chance to explain himself. I hate that you'll have no one else when I'm gone.

Hate that you'll be alone.

Please don't be alone.

You don't have to share any of the other letters with Elijah if you don't want to. But please, please, show him this one. Let him know how much he meant to me. How grateful I was to have someone watching out for me. In a lot of ways, he's stubborn just like you. Afraid of showing any kind of weakness because it opens the heart to pain. But love is worth that heartache, child.

I thank God every single day for the time I had with you. And please forgive me for the secrets I kept from you. I promise to tell you everything in the next few letters, I just— I needed you to read this one first.

And please watch out for Elijah. He doesn't know it, but he needs someone too.

Unable to continue, I stop reading, fold the letter, then tip the box and dump them all onto the floor.

"Whoa, what are you doing?"

"There has to be something here," I tell Lance. "Something that will put all of this together for us. Pick up a letter," I tell them, silently apologizing to Andie for the invasion of privacy. But her life is worth more. I set the box aside. "Start reading, I—"

There's a difference in pattern between the bottom of the box and the sides. Reaching forward, I run my fingers over it. The wood isn't nearly as smooth as the rest of the carefully crafted container.

Using my index finger, I push down on one corner, and it pops open.

"Edna had secrets," Lance comments as I remove the bottom and stare down at a handful of papers. I withdraw the thin, white envelope first then lift an old newspaper clipping from the bottom.

A photograph of Andie's stepfather stares back at me along with the title LOCAL MAN FOUND DEAD. Could it be that this is all tied back to him somehow? Lance reaches in and pulls out the stack of papers beneath, splitting them into three piles and handing one to Michael, the other to Jaxson, and keeping one for himself, while I open the white envelope in my hand.

A bright pink sticky note is stuck to the top of images printed from the internet.

Your granddaughter killed my father.
I will make her pay.
They will all know that she is a killer.
She will lose everything.

Pictures of Andie at events, photographs of her walking on the side of the street.

"Elijah," Lance says.

I look up at him, my mind still trying to wrap around the fact that whoever is targeting Andie believes that Troy was their father. But he'd had no children. I looked into it. "What is it?"

"Diana Pallum's birth certificate," he says as he holds it out.

I take it from him. The father space was empty until someone wrote "Troy Hanover" into it. His name is in the same handwriting as the sticky note. I note the woman's name written as mother and rush over to my computer.

With adrenaline pulsing through my system, I pull up her information on a database I technically shouldn't be in.

As soon as I have the number she used on her last tax return, I make the call.

On the third ring, a woman answers. "Hello?"

I put it on speaker and point to Jaxson since he's the only one with any real authority outside of this room. "Is this Mrs. Karen Pallum?"

"It is," she replies. "What is this in regards to? I have a client coming in."

"This is Detective Jaxson Payne with the Los Angeles Police Department."

The woman mutters a string of curses. "It's Diana, isn't it? Where was she found?" There's a hint of emotion in her voice.

"She's not dead," he tells her. "But we think she's involved in a kidnapping. Can you tell me anywhere she might have gone? Somewhere she could hide?"

"Not anywhere near LA," she replies.

"Where?" Jaxson asks.

It takes everything in me not to take over the phone call, so I stand and pace.

"As soon as she found out about her loser father, she became obsessed with some small town in Maine."

Jaxson's gaze meets mine. "Hope Springs?"

"Yes. He moved there when he met some trollop. Ended up dead for his troubles. Good riddance is what I told Diana, but she never saw it as that."

"You believe she's in Hope Springs?" Jaxson asks.

"That would be my guess. He left her a few acres out there. Lovely, right? He abandoned us for greener pastures before Diana was even born then had the audacity to leave her useless property. Just one more thing to take care of."

"Do you know where it is?"

"No. I never cared to know. Diana found it though. Or I think she did. She hasn't been in contact with me for years now. Not since I told her she needed to let it go and get help. She's been obsessed with this fashion designer out of New York."

"Andie Montgomery?" I ask, unable to keep my mouth shut any longer.

The woman hesitates. "Yes. That's her. If you find Diana, she needs help. Don't be like the others who have arrested her. Please. They just keep letting her go, but she needs real help."

"We will do our best. Thank you, Mrs. Pallum." He ends the call.

"I've got the property," Michael says as he gestures to his computer screen. "It's on the outskirts of town. About a seven-minute drive."

"Let's go." I grab my pistol and secure it at my back then slip my knife into the waistband of my jeans.

"I'll call the sheriff on the way," Jaxson says as he withdraws his cell and heads for the front door.

Lance hits the unlock on his truck.

Boom.

CHAPTER 30
Andie

"Please. Do whatever you have planned for me, but leave Elijah alone. He didn't do anything. He has no part in this."

"He got in my way, Andrea. And I don't like it when anyone gets in my way. You nearly died too soon because he just *had* to come with you to New York." She toys with a knife, picking the dirt out from beneath her fingernails. She may not have been working for me long, but I never would have thought her capable of something like this.

Of such madness.

"Please, Diana. Don't hurt him."

"Oh, honey," she says, pouting. "It's already been done. But hey! Don't you worry. Because if you believe in such things, you'll be seeing him again...very, very soon." In a blur of movement, she brings her blade up and stabs it into Alec's arm.

He screams, a twisted sound of agony.

"No!" I yell.

"You would argue for his life?" She throws her head back and laughs. "No need. He's not going to die. He's just in trouble." She yanks the blade free then grips his chin. "Aren't you? Bad boy."

Diana comes over to me and shoves my chair back. The rope tightens on my throat and keeps me upright. "I've thought of this moment for so long. So many years spent dreaming of this right here. Of watching the life fade from your eyes." She leans in closer. "I cannot wait to see it."

I struggle to breathe, but even as I want to fight, I know that any movement will only make this quicker. If the chair falls—

The front door splinters.

Elijah rushes in, rifle raised.

Diana screams and kicks my chair out from under me.

The rope tightens, constricting until I can't breathe. I fight, thrashing. Elijah rips his knife free and slices through the strands then catches me before I would have hit the floor. He rips the rope over my head, and I suck in a pained breath as he cuts the ropes binding me to the chair.

"Andie. Thank God." He holds me against his chest, and I wrap both arms around his neck. Tears stream down my cheeks as I cling to him.

"You came for me."

He pulls me back, cupping my face. "Did you ever have any doubt?"

"No," I cry.

He slams his mouth to mine in a blood-searing kiss then tightens his arms around me.

Alec whimpers as Jaxson cuts him free. "She stabbed me," he cries. "I need medical help!"

"You're going to get all the help you need," the detective says. "Then you'll have some questions to answer."

"She needs to die! She has to die! Like he died!" Diana screams. She's handcuffed and sitting on the floor, glaring at me.

"Get up." Lance tugs her to her feet and takes her out the front door.

"This isn't over!" she screams back at me.

"It is," Elijah assures me.

"She's Troy's daughter," I say as I lean against his chest, using the beat of his heart to ease my fear.

"I know," he says.

Sirens scream in the distance, so Elijah helps me to my feet then lifts me. I let him carry me, adrenaline waning. I begin to shake as it dissipates. And as the paramedics drive down the overgrown driveway of a house I fled a long, long time ago, I turn my face to the sky.

Thank you, God. Thank you for not leaving me even when I turned away from You.

———

"You're going to be just fine," Doc says as he steps away from the hospital bed. We're in the emergency room, getting looked over, and even though he's not the one on call, he'd come in the moment Lance called him. After spending so much time in a VA hospital, getting poked and prodded by strangers, I'm not fond of doctors. But I trust Doc. "You're lucky." He smiles at me then Elijah before leaving the room.

Elijah hasn't left my side since he found me, and as soon as Doc is gone, he steps closer.

"What happened to your head?" I ask, noting the stitches in his hairline.

"The accident," he replies then withdraws a folded piece of paper from his back pocket.

"What's that?"

"I dumped out your gran's letters, so they're all out of order."

I arch a brow.

"It's a good thing we did. Otherwise, we wouldn't have figured out the connection as quickly."

"I'm not mad," I assure him with a soft laugh.

"But I did read this one first. It was the last letter she wrote you. And I—I want you to read it." He hands it to me.

"Right now?"

"Yes. Please."

"Okay," I say softly then unfold the letter and run my finger over her familiar writing.

Dearest Andie,

Today was a hard day. I'm feeling weaker. More worn down than I have in years. I'm afraid to call you though because the last thing I want to do is put pressure on you. You've already struggled so much, child.

So much more than anyone should ever struggle.

Tears blur my vision, so I quickly wipe them away.

I want you to know how sorry I am that I failed to see the signs before you left. I am so sorry that I didn't step in sooner. That I didn't rescue you from your parents well before the divorce.

You should know your father has been in contact with me for quite some time now. I know he doesn't deserve it, but you should truly give him the chance to explain himself. I hate that you'll have no one else when I'm gone.

Hate that you'll be alone.

Please don't be alone.

You don't have to share any of the other letters with Elijah if you don't want to. But please, please, show him this one. Let him

know how much he meant to me. How grateful
I was to have someone watching out for me.
In a lot of ways, he's stubborn just like you.
Afraid of showing any kind of weakness
because it opens the heart to pain. But love is
worth that heartache, child.

I thank God every single day for the time
I had with you. And please forgive me for
the secrets I kept from you. I promise to tell
you everything in the next few letters, I just—
I needed you to read this one first.

And please watch out for Elijah. He
doesn't know it, but he needs someone too.

You both do.

All my love,

Gran

I look up at him through tears.

"I don't need someone," he says softly. "I *need* you.
I've spent my entire life running from relationships because
I was terrified of my scars. Of facing my past and opening
up. Vulnerability terrifies me, Andie. But not nearly as
much as the thought of losing you."

He takes my free hand in his. "God brought Edna into
my life at a time when I needed a friend. And when I
thought I'd lost someone who had become one of the most

important people in my life, He brought you to me. I love you, Andie Montgomery. With my entire heart and every piece of my soul."

I choke on a sob then toss the letter aside and lunge up. My muscles ache with the movement, but I ignore the pain as I throw my arms around his neck and take his mouth. I pour everything I'm feeling into this kiss.

The pain of what I lost.

The joy in what I found.

The love I never saw coming.

"I love you too, Elijah," I whisper. "More than I ever thought I could love anyone. You've reminded me that I am more than my past. I will never stop thanking God for bringing you into my life."

"Or your gran for putting us on the deed to her house."

Laughing, I wipe my eyes. "She was determined to have her way, wasn't she?"

His expression turns serious. "I am going to show you how much I love you, Andie. Every single day, I will show you that you are so much more than I deserve."

I cup his face. "I feel the same about you, Mr. Breeth."

CHAPTER 31
Elijah

With Andie at my side, I walk up onto the porch of Edna's house. After Rebecca's funeral, Andie and I dove headfirst into putting everything back together.

So here we stand, hand in hand, in front of the door. Four months of hard work have finally put it back together, though so many of Edna's things were broken I know it will never look the same. In her other hand, Andie holds a bouquet of wildflowers she cut from Mrs. McGinley's garden.

The librarian and Edna's oldest friend insisted that we use her garden instead of buying the first bouquet from the store. Soon, I hope to have Edna's garden restored to its original glory. But that's a project for another day.

Slipping the key into the lock, I unlock the door and push it open.

"Surprise!"

The lights come on and Andie jumps back. I laugh, holding her in place. She stares straight ahead, wide-eyed, at everyone who's come together to bring her a proper welcome home.

This time, it's going to stick.

She's still designing, though she insisted on moving her office here to Hope Springs even though I would have followed her to the ends of the earth if that's what it took to stay at her side.

There's nowhere else I will ever be.

Her investors all remained, well—invested—in her work once Diana and Alec confessed to slipping a security camera into Andie's office and stealing her designs. Thankfully, they won't be seeing anything but the inside of a jail cell for a long, long time.

"You guys!" she exclaims as she steps into the house. Lilly and Alex are in the kitchen, Lance, Eliza, Michael, and Jaxson off to the side of the living room, all of them grinning widely.

Pastor Redding is the first to come forward and offer Andie a hug, his wife second. "We're so glad you're staying," the woman says with a smile.

"Me too," Andie replies. She looks around the room, her gaze finding her father. While things are still—and probably always will be—rocky between them, she's offered him the chance to be in her life in a less behind-the-scenes capacity.

There's still so much pain, but I know getting to know him again has made her happy.

She looks up at me. "You planned this."

"It was a group effort."

"Those are beautiful!" Mrs. McGinley rushes forward and takes the flowers. "Good choices, dear. You have an eye like your gran. I'll get them in some water." But she doesn't move.

I swallow hard, knowing it's my turn to put my heart on my sleeve. Clearing my throat, I turn Andie to look at me.

"I love you," I tell her.

"I love you too," she replies with a smile.

Reaching toward a table near the door, I grab a white box encircled with a green ribbon the same shade as her eyes. "This is for you. A welcome home gift."

"You didn't need to get me anything," Andie says with a laugh as she tugs on the ribbon. She lifts the lid and grins as she withdraws a teddy bear with a *Get Well Soon* t-shirt. It matches the one she got me when I was in the hospital.

And then her gaze lands on the small velvet box beneath the stuffed animal. "Elijah," she whispers.

I drop to one knee. "I always brought your gran vases," I tell her. "She loved them, and they were the only gift I was allowed to bring into her house. I figured teddy bears could be our thing."

"Here, I'll hold that," Eliza offers as she steps up and takes the gift box and bear from Andie's hands.

Andie opens the velvet box and stares down at the ring inside. "Elijah, it's beautiful."

"I want to spend every single moment of my life with you, Andie Montgomery. I want to love you. Cherish you. I want a family with you. And I want to grow old with you. Wherever this life takes us."

She stares down at me with tears in her eyes.

"Will you marry me?" I ask.

"I guess you really do like me then," she chokes out on a laugh.

The first time we met in person, she accused me of not liking her, and I'd told her that I didn't know her. I thought I'd made my mind up then, but I'd been so wrong about her. I'd wanted nothing to do with her, and I can't imagine my life without her now.

"I love you," I reply. "But I still need you to answer the question."

"Yes! Absolutely yes!" She throws her arms around my neck, and I stand, lifting her and spinning in a circle as everyone who matters to us cheers. After a quick kiss, I pull back just enough to slip the ring onto her finger.

"Here's to forever," I tell her.

"Forever and a day," she replies.

I ABSOLUTELY ADORE ENEMIES TO LOVERS AND I LOVE how both Elijah and Andie were so hesitant to take that step that brought them closer, but when they finally did it was beautiful! Please consider leaving a review!

Keep reading for a bonus epilogue, AND the first two chapters of the next book, SECOND CHANCE SEREN-ITY, featuring Michael Anderson and the woman he left behind, Reyna Acker. Pre-order it today.

If you are interested in bonus content, deleted scenes, sneak peeks prior to the release, and want to get your hand on a free novella then join my newsletter! Become a subscriber on my website.

CHAPTER 32
BONUS Epilogue

There really isn't anything that can prepare you for war.

For the stench of sweat and blood as you fight your way through a battlefield.

For the fear when you're pinned down by the enemy, waiting for reinforcements to arrive.

For the doubt that plagues you in those moments. The intrusive thoughts that tell you you're better off dead.

Or the knowledge that, even when you leave the war, you'll never forget the battle.

After a deep breath, I take a drink of my coffee. I allowed the knowledge of what I faced when I'd been in the service run my life for the first year I'd been out. Then I focused entirely on building my relationship with God and forgiving myself for the things I'd done both overseas and back home.

Unfortunately, even though I truly believe He has forgiven me, not everyone has.

Reyna stands across from me, cutting streamers for the town's End of Summer celebration—a potluck and dance hosted in the school gym for anyone and everyone in Hope Springs.

As usual, she doesn't spare me a glance as she smiles and chats happily with the high school students and parents helping with the decorations. Just being close to her soothes the ache I've felt since the day I left her behind.

A day I've regretted more than anything else I've ever done.

Johnny, the town librarian's grandson, makes his way over with a ladder and sets it up beside her. She says something that makes the woman beside her laugh, and I feel cold inside.

She climbs up onto the first few rungs of the ladder, and nerves twist in my gut. Abandoning the sign I was painting, I walk toward her.

"Reyna, I can do that," I say.

"No." She doesn't even bother trying to hide her annoyance that I'm here in the first place. Not that it would do any good—everyone in town knows what I did to her. How I promised her forever then ran the second I let fear take the reins.

"Please."

"I don't need you, Mr. Anderson," she snaps, glaring down at me with dark eyes that haunt my every waking moment. "Let me see that, please, Johnny." She stretches down, and the high school football star stretches up to hand her a corner of the banner. Reyna sways a bit on the ladder, so I step closer.

"Come on, Reyna. I'm taller. Let me do it."

"I don't need you," she says again, and the words sear into my soul.

She doesn't need me. Something she made completely clear the first day I returned to town when I'd gone to apologize.

Reyna rises on her tiptoes, holding the banner up with one hand. She stretches up with the other and staples it to the beam above her. As she starts to come down, though, a student on the other side of the gym throws a football.

"Johnny, catch!"

Johnny's first instinct is to turn, and he jerks the ladder.

Reyna screams.

I lunge forward and catch her in my arms. She hits me with a thud, eyes closed, breathing heavy, stapler clutched to her chest. My heart is hammering, the understanding of what could have just happened barreling through my mind.

She opens her eyes and stares up at me, a million unsaid things sizzling between us. I open my mouth to apologize yet again but think better of it. She's made it clear that it will do no good.

But knowing that doesn't keep me from letting my gaze travel over her beautiful face. The dusting of freckles along her nose, the full lips I dream of tasting.

"As I said, I'm taller."

Her gaze flashes murderously. "Put. Me. Down."

"Fine." I set her down, hating the moment she's out of my arms. It felt so good to be touching her again even if it was only for a moment. "But I'll do the other side." Without waiting for her to agree, I pluck the stapler from her hands, move the ladder, then climb up and fasten the other side of the banner.

As soon as it's done, I climb down and hand it back to her.

She takes it angrily. "I don't need you," she repeats.

"Maybe not." *But I need you.* My cell rings, so I reach into my pocket and check the read out. *Jaxson.* The former LAPD detective moved out here to work with us at the firm after helping us on more than one occasion.

"What's up?" I ask, pressing it to my ear.

"We got a job. Sunny Patterson."

"The actress?"

"One and the same," he replies. "She's heading to a red-carpet premiere in L.A. and wants some additional protection after receiving some threats over her new movie. You'll be running lead with her established team."

"Fantastic." I look over at Reyna, who has already moved on to doing something else.

"You good to take it? You'd need to leave today."

For a brief moment, Reyna looks up at me then redirects her attention just as quickly. Will she ever look at me without hatred in her eyes?

"Yeah, I'll take it. God must have known I could use the distraction. Be at the office in an hour."

———————

THE STORY CONTINUES IN SECOND CHANCE SERENITY!

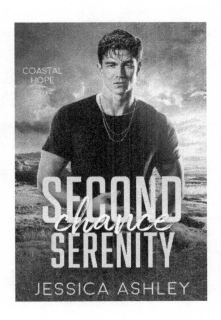

A WOMAN WHO CAN'T LET GO. THE WOUNDED VETERAN who broke her heart.

The day Michael Anderson left town to join the military is the day Reyna's world came crashing down around her. They'd been high school sweethearts destined to walk down the aisle...until they weren't.

Now, years later, he's back and desperate for a second chance.

When someone tries to abduct her, Michael offers her his protection. But she worries it comes at a cost she can't pay...her still broken heart.

Former Army Ranger Michael Anderson is good at what he does. A bodyguard for Knight Security, he's highly sought after. So when someone tries to kidnap the woman he still loves, Michael knows there is no one more qualified to protect her.

Unfortunately, Reyna's trust in him was broken a long time ago. And if he's going to earn it back, he has to do the second hardest thing he's ever done...walk away and allow another member of his team to take the lead.

But after tragedy strikes, Michael and Reyna are pushed together once more, and this time he plans to make her see that he's no longer the teen who walked away...but a man ready to risk it all.

CHAPTER 33
Second Chance Serenity

MICHAEL

The thrill of the chase is one of my favorite parts of this job.

Boots hammering against the pavement, I sprint through a back alley in downtown L.A. My body is coated in a thin layer of sweat thanks to the humidity clinging to the air, and my muscles are warm. I pay little attention to the trash littering the ground, or the stench of dirty, wet pavement as I run.

The guy I'm after, a would-be stalker who stole some photographs my client would rather not get out, glances over his shoulder. His beady eyes widen and he pumps his arms harder, as though that is going to speed him up. Truth is, I could have caught him nearly as soon as I started chasing him, but he deserves to worry awhile. And from the looks of it, that's exactly what he's doing.

His face is beat red, his expression one of fear as he glances back again. *Good.* I grin. A man who would target a woman who'd just had a baby, simply so he could make some spare change off "never before seen photographs" should be afraid of what's going to happen when I catch him.

I may be a man of God, willing to let justice be served by appropriate channels, but he doesn't have to know that.

The man trips, his foot catching on a piece of broken pavement, and he tumbles forward, face sliding against the pavement. He cries out in pain, and tries to roll over, but I'm faster as I slide to his side, then slam my knee down into the middle of his back. With him pinned to the ground, I search his pockets, finding the phone he'd used within seconds.

"I'm sorry, man! I didn't do anything!" he yells as I rip the cell free from his possession.

"I'm confused," I reply. "Are you sorry or did you not do anything?" I ask as I quickly check his phone for the photographs. As soon as I've double checked he didn't delete them, I shove the phone into my pocket and withdraw zip ties from my back pocket.

His wrists bound, I haul him up so he's sitting, then pull out my own phone to make a call to the officer one of my partners, Jaxson, told me to contact.

"Diaz." He sounds distracted, but answers on the third ring.

"It's Michael Anderson. I've got some scum for you to pick up."

Interest perked, his tone changes. "Send your location. I'll get uniforms over there."

"Great. Thanks." I end the call and share my location with the officer. As soon as that's done, I take a deep breath and stretch, rolling my neck and enjoying every pop from the aches.

I survey the man sitting on his back. He's short, probably at least a foot below my six-foot-six inches, and his face is red and bloodied thanks to the pavement rash. All in all, dude looks rough. "Long day?" I ask, reaching into my pocket and popping a piece of gum into my mouth. Chewing gum has become a habit of mine ever since I got back from overseas. Being deployed in war zones, shot at, blown up, and nearly killed a time or two has left me with more than just physical scars. And for some reason, the monotony of simply chewing gum helps lower my anxiety.

Not that I'm having any right now. No, right now I'm dealing with the desire to scare this guy so badly he'll never consider doing this ever again. "Long day?" I ask, leaning against the wall and firing off a text to my client, letting her know the images are soon to be in the hands of police.

He glares up at me. "They were just pics, man."

"They were an invasion of privacy," I tell him. "Surely you can understand someone's desire for discretion after they just had a baby."

"Someone's going to get them, might as well be me. They won't get me on anything."

"Maybe not on the pictures," I admit. "Those will likely be a slap on the wrist." I snap my fingers, then push off the wall. "Except for the fact that my team got footage of you trying to rip the baby from her arms when she wouldn't let you photograph him. That makes it attempted kidnapping."

His eyes go so wide it's nearly comical. "I was going to give him back! I just wanted a picture!"

"Take it up with your lawyers. But I can guarantee they'll be no match for hers. Deep pockets and all." Sirens echo down the street moments before red and blue lights bathe us in color. "Let's go." I haul him up to his feet, then march him forward as two uniformed officers climb out of the squad car.

"Michael Anderson?" the one closest to me asks.

"That's me." I open my jacket so he can see the Knight Security badge strapped just inside my leather jacket. "The images on his cell phone are of a sensitive nature, so I'll be delivering them myself. But I'd appreciate it if you could get this guy booked for attempted kidnapping." I hand the target over to the police, then start back up the street to get my bike.

"You heading to the station?" one of the officers call out.

I wave my hand in response, not looking back at them as I climb onto my rented bike, fire up the engine, and take off down the street.

———

"YOU'RE SURE THE PICTURES ARE SAFE?" SUNNY questions as she cradles her newborn son against her chest. As one of the most popular—and private—actresses in show business these days, having the birth of her son protected was enough to make the call to Lance and hire me.

It's not the first time I've worked for her, and over the last year since she'd called and had me work a red-carpet premier, I've grown close to both her and her producer husband Geoff. He stands behind her now, his hand on her shoulder. They're nearly complete opposites. As her name would suggest, Sunny has a bright smile and platinum hair that shines beneath the rays of sunshine sneaking in through the windows.

Her husband is nearly as tall as I am, and his hair is nearly black, his eyes a dark brown. He was a stunt man in his earlier years, and ended up losing his right arm in the process.

"The pictures will never see the light of day," I tell them both. I saw to it that they were permanently deleted as soon as the Captain had written up his report. The phone didn't leave my hands from the moment I caught him until the photos were removed."

"You don't believe the man who took them sent them off to anyone before?" Geoff questions.

"He didn't have time," I reply with a satisfied smile. "He was on the run the moment he snapped them, and the phone was in his pocket until I dropped him to the ground."

Sunny smiles up at her husband, relief on her face. "Close call."

"Yes, it was," he replies, then leans down to kiss her on the top of her head. "What can we do to repay you?"

"Pay your invoice," I reply.

Sunny laughs. "Obviously. But there has to be something else."

"We've given your name to all of our closest friends," Geoff says. "You are highly recommended in our circle."

Pride warms my chest. When I'd been medically retired from the military after suffering injuries that wouldn't allow me to remain in the service, I'd thought my time of helping others and fighting the good fight was over.

But then Lance opened his security firm, and my new destiny was revealed. One that allowed me to return to my hometown, while also seeing the world and helping as God leads me to do.

"I appreciate that." I reach forward and shake his hand. "Let me know if you need anything else. You can always give me a call."

"We will," Sunny replies.

I offer Sunny a wave, then head toward the front door of their private house. Geoff walks behind me, following me out. As we reach the door, I turn to face him. "It was good to see you again, Geoff."

"You, too, Michael. And listen, let me know if you ever want to take me up on that stunt work. I think you'd be good at it."

"I'd be great at it," I reply with a grin. "But it's not for me. My life is in Hope Springs."

"Life?" He arches a brow. "I didn't take you for a family man."

"Not yet," I reply with a laugh. "But maybe someday. See you around." I step out into the bright Los Angelos sunshine. My bike sits at the front of their circular drive, and since my flight isn't for another five hours, I opt for a ride along the coast before joining the craziness of the airport.

But before I climb on, I pull my cell out and tap on Lance's contact.

"Knight," he answers.

"I'm going to head to the airport," I tell him.

"Everything go okay?"

"Smooth as butter," I reply.

Lance chuckles. "Good to know."

"How are things back home?" I ask.

"She's fine," he tells me. I'm not at all surprised that he

can read between the lines. Lance Knight was my Officer In Charge when I'd been in the service, and we've been close friends since the day we nearly died together, alongside our other partner, Elijah. He knows me better than I know myself most times, and Reyna Acker—the woman whose heart I broke when I'd been a teenager—is always on my mind.

"Good. Well, I'll get my report to you as soon as I get back to the office."

"Your plane lands late tonight?"

"Ten-fifteen," I reply. "So it'll be tomorrow before I get to it."

"Not a problem. Looking forward to having you back in town."

I end the call and climb onto the bike. After firing up the engine, I leave their estate through a massive iron gate, and hit the highway.

Wind whips past me as I drive. Warm air that kisses my skin. As she usually does, Reyna pops into my head. The girl I'd left behind when I joined the military. I'd promised her a future. A ring. Kids. And then I left without so much as a simple goodbye.

Now I can't get her to give me the time of day.

Not that I blame her. I'd been focused on myself and wanting a life other than the one my father had set out for me, and she'd been planning for a future that would never come to pass.

Forgiveness. I'd told Geoff a family could be on the

horizon for me someday, but the truth is I know it'll never happen. A family for me doesn't exist without Reyna. But I've been home for almost five years now, and she still won't give me the time of day.

Does that mean I'll stop trying? Absolutely not.

Even if it means watching her marry someone else.

CHAPTER 34
Second Chance Serenity

REYNA

"So anyways, that's the gist of what I do. How about you?"

I smile at the handsome man across from me, appreciating that this entire time we've been out to eat, he's been attentive, kind, and charming...so why can't I feel *anything* beyond base attraction? Why can't my stomach fill with butterflies, or my legs go weak?

"I'm a principal at the school," I tell him. "We're a K-12, so I oversee kids as young as five and as old as eighteen."

"Sounds exciting."

"It's never dull, that's for sure." I take a bite of the chocolate cake in front of me. Years of dating. Of searching for anything that even mildly resembles the spark I feel for

—*No, Reyna.* I shove thoughts of Michael Anderson out of my head.

Liam Hollander is handsome, stable, looking for a partner, and would probably never leave me the month before we're going to get married so he can go off and start a new life.

"You grew up in Hope Springs, right? Do you have any family here?"

"My parents," I tell him with a smile. "My brother lives in Boston with his wife and kids. He's a prosecutor for the city."

"Nice. Do you see him often?"

"Once a month," I reply. "We get together for dinner. Alternating who makes the weekend trip. Sometimes they come here, other times we go there."

"Your brother is older?"

I nod. "Three years. How about you? Do you have any siblings?"

He shakes his head. "Only child. My parents both live in New Jersey. I see them once every few months."

"What brought you to Hope Springs?" He moved here only a few months ago, and runs a remote finance management company from his house. It had been the buzz of town for a while, and Mrs. McGinley actually arranged a meeting for the both of us, without us realizing it until we both suddenly *had* to get to the library to pick up a book she'd ordered for us.

The woman is a lovable menace.

"I wanted a fresh start. I'd lived in Jersey my entire childhood, then spent some time in Philly. After that, I knew I wanted a small town, and after my mom shoved a book in my hand and told me the author was from here, I decided to come visit. I've been wanting to write one, myself."

"Who is the author?"

"Eliza Knight. Do you know her?"

Why does it make my stomach churn? I adore Eliza. We attend a girls dinner once a month together. But since she's married to Michael's boss, and close friends with him, that makes our relationship...well...complicated. "She's really sweet. Married to a guy who runs a security company in town."

"Yes! I've been trying to come up with a way to introduce myself, just to get my copy of her book signed and pick her brain over the route she took with her publishing journey, but I'm not entirely sure how to do it without coming across as creepy."

I smile, because it's honestly so ridiculously innocent, that it makes my heart melt just a bit for him. Michael wouldn't have hesitated to introduce himself. The man is a bull in a china shop, never fearing anything. "I would be happy to introduce the two of you."

"Really?" His expression lights up like a kid on Christmas morning.

"Sure thing. She's doing a reading at the—"

"Library tomorrow," he says with a nod. "I was planning to attend. I'm sorry, this is weird isn't it? It's weird. I'm a big book nerd and my mom loves her stuff so—"

I reach over the table without thinking and close my hand over his.

He smiles warmly, attraction burning in his gaze. Man, I wish I felt the same. "Not weird," I tell him. "It's kind. And since I was planning to attend the reading, too, I will happily introduce you afterward."

"That would be great. So great. Now that you know I'm a big reader, tell me about your hobbies. What do you do when you're not at school?" Liam asks.

"I like to hike," I tell him. "Bake sourdough, and volunteer whenever I can."

"Sourdough? That sounds delicious."

"It is. There's so much you can do with it. Dessert bread, Italian loaves, bagels, sandwiches," I reply, realizing suddenly that I'm more passionate about baking bread than I am about this date. And that realization makes me feel terrible. He's being sweet and I can't stop comparing him to the man who left me over a decade ago.

"I'd love to try some sometime."

"Sure." I smile, then check the time. "I really should be going, though, I have budget reports to finalize before tomorrow."

"Oh, of course. I'm sorry." He reaches into his pocket and sets some bills on top of the check, then stands and offers me his hand.

I slide mine into his, hoping for a zing. A zap. A

connection of any kind—but get none. *God, why can't I find someone—anyone—else?*

"Are you okay?" he asks, brow furrowing.

"Yes. Sorry. Mind on work. It happens this time of year." School starts in just over a month, and I've had to hire three new teachers, while also managing to squeeze in a new arts program for our middle grades. The budget will be stretched to the max, but with some strategically placed fundraisers, we should squeeze by just fine.

"No problem." He walks me out of the small, Italian restaurant that sits on the water near the edge of town, then leans in to kiss my cheek. "Can I call you tomorrow?"

"Of course. I look forward to it."

After saying my goodbyes, I climb into the car and lean my head on the steering wheel. Liam didn't grow up here, which means that he doesn't have any idea who Michael is. Which means, he is practically the last available man in Hope Springs willing to give a relationship with me a try.

The other few that are left grew up with Michael, and don't want to do anything that would risk taking his wrath. Pathetic really. Though, I suppose since Michael was a prodigy boxer and star quarterback, I can understand on some level.

Even if it infuriates me.

Michael. Ugh. Ruining my life without even trying. He's always around. At the school, helping decorate for functions. Volunteering as an assistant football coach during the season. Giving boxing tutorials as extra-curricular after school events.

Michael.

Michael.

Michael.

I swallow hard and lean back in my seat, taking a deep, steadying breath. Well, I guess that's it. I'm just going to have to settle for a minimal connection or die alone. Who knows, maybe not having a blood-searing, soul-deep romance will be better. After all, the last thing I want is to give someone else the power to break me the same way Michael did...right?

———

BY THE TIME DAWN ROLLS AROUND, I'VE MANAGED TO finalize all of my budget reports, set up our first meeting of the school year, and finish planning the annual fundraising ball for the women and children's shelter in Boston.

The sun rises above the water, casting the ocean in glorious shades of orange and gold. Body slick with a thin layer of sweat from the four miles I've run this morning, I stand on the beach, overlooking God's masterpiece as he paints the early morning.

I'm always filled with such hope when dawn rolls around. Like today, anything is possible. Today, I can let go of the ghosts of my past—at least momentarily—and focus only on the dawn of a new day.

"Morning."

His voice washes over me like acid rain. I turn and face Michael Anderson, a former Army Ranger and the man who broke my heart when we'd been eighteen. He stands a few feet away from me, wearing shorts, and a loose tank top.

He's barefoot, as he always is whenever he runs, and his dark obsidian hair is curly thanks to the humidity and sweat from exercise. Why does he have to be so beautiful?

"Morning." My response is curt, and I don't wait around for him to try and talk to me more as I turn and head back up the beach. I need to shower, get to the hospital for my volunteer hours, then get home in time to start baking for the first school board meeting of the year.

Unfortunately, Michael falls into step beside me. "Sleep well?"

"Fine."

"Busy day?"

"Yup." As always, I keep my responses short, but as usual, Michael doesn't seem to care.

"Me, too. Just got back into town and I've got some paperwork to catch up on."

"Good for you."

"Reyna—"

"What do you want, Michael? I'm busy." Stopping, I turn to face him and cross both arms. It hurts to look at him, like staring into the sun. Because he was that for me for so long. My light. My everything. And he'd thrown it all away without a second glance.

"I just—" He runs a hand over the back of his hair. "I miss talking to you."

"Then you should have thought about that before you left town."

"Are you ever going to not hate me?"

"I don't hate you, Michael. I just want nothing to do with you. Have a good day." I turn away from him and start running down the beach, hoping that my past stays exactly where it belongs—behind me.

———

Pre-order SECOND CHANCE SERENITY today!
You can pre-order it here.

Did you know I have a Facebook group? Come hang out in the Coastal Hope Book Corner for special previews, updates, and sneak peeks! Tap here to check it out!

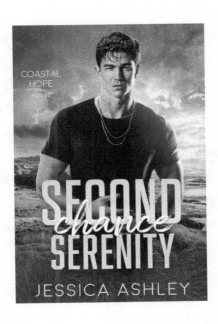

A woman who can't let go. The wounded veteran who broke her heart.

The day Michael Anderson left town to join the military, is the day Reyna's world came crashing down around her. They'd been high school sweethearts destined to walk down the aisle...until they weren't.

Now, years later, he's back and desperate for a second chance.

When someone tries to abduct her, Michael offers her his protection. But she worries it comes at a cost she can't pay...her still broken heart.

Former Army Ranger Michael Anderson is good at what he does. A bodyguard for Knight Security, he's highly sought after. So when someone tries to kidnap the woman he still loves, Michael knows there is no one more qualified to protect her.

Unfortunately, Reyna's trust in him was broken a long time ago. And if he's going to earn it back, he has to do the second hardest thing he's ever done…walk away and allow another member of his team to take the lead.

But after tragedy strikes, Michael and Reyna are pushed together once more, and this time he plans to make her see that he's no longer the teen who walked away…but a man ready to risk it all.

Scan the code below with your phone's camera to download your copy of Second Chance Serenity! Or, go to https://geni.us/SecondChanceSerenity.

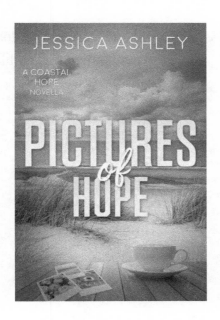

JESSICA ASHLEY

A COASTAL
HOPE
NOVELLA

PICTURES
of
HOPE

Get your hands on Alex and Lilly's story for free today!

As a travel photographer, my life has been one adventure after the next.

Every location I visit a far cry from the small town I grew up in.

A place I'd been desperate to escape after my ex broke off our engagement and joined the military.

However, home has a way of calling you back.

Three years after my mother's death, I find myself returning to Hope Springs.

But I'm not the only one who came home.

The man who practically left me at the alter is here, too.

And he's determined to heal what he shattered all those years ago: me.

Scan this with your phone's camera to download your freebie! Or, go to www.authorjessicaashley.com/free-novella

About the Author

Jessica Ashley started her career writing spicy romance novels, and had written over sixty before deciding she wanted to use her love of storytelling to help bring people closer to God.

Now, she writes inspirational romance and hopes that each book will draw people closer to seeking His word.

She is an Army veteran, who resides in Texas with her husband and their three children (whom she homeschools).

You can find out more about her and her books by scanning the QR code with your phone's camera, visiting her website: www.authorjessicaashley.com or by joining her Facebook group, Coastal Hope Book Corner.

Also by Jessica Ashley

Coastal Hope Series

Pages of Promise: Lance Knight

Searching for Peace: Elijah Pierce

Second Chance Serenity: Michael Anderson

More coming soon...